The Children's Hours

The Children's Hours

Stories About Childhood

Edited by Richard Zimler and Raša Sekulović

ARCADIA BOOKS

Arcadia Books Ltd
15–16 Nassau Street
London W1W 7AB

www.arcadiabooks.co.uk

Contents

Introduction and Acknowledgments

Richard Zimler

In 2003, I received a kind and intelligent email from a journalist, translator and children's rights advocate from Belgrade who had just read the Serbian edition of one of my novels. His name was Raša Sekulović, and he and I stayed in touch over the next couple of years. In the summer of 2005, we happened to be in New York at the same time, and Raša took the train out to my mother's house on Long Island so we could finally meet. We ate lunch with my mom, and then the three of us spent another couple of hours sitting around the kitchen table, chatting about books, politics and what life was like in Serbia. Later that afternoon, while I was taking Raša on a tour of the colonial towns and manor houses nearby, he challenged me to come up with a project that would mix his two passions: literature and children's rights.

On the drive home, I had the idea for the anthology of short stories about children and adolescents for which all the authors' royalties would go to Save the Children, the charitable organization for which Raša was then working. He thought it was a great idea, so I wrote up a book proposal once I returned to Portugal, where I live, and sent it to my old friends at Arcadia Books in London, Gary Pulsifer and Daniela de Groote. Happily, Gary and Daniela soon gave the project their blessing.

I was worried that getting top fiction writers to help us might prove a problem, since most of them are swamped with requests for assistance, but the response to our call for short stories was positive right from the start. I first sent emails to writer friends and acquaintances like David Almond, Ali Smith, Melvin Burgess and Nicholas Shakespeare, and once I had them on board it proved reasonably easy to convince others. Raša contacted a dozen or so authors he'd either interviewed for the Serbian press or translated, and a number of them also agreed to give us work. A few writers – most notably André Brink, Karina Magdalena Szczurek and Nadine Gordimer – expressed so much enthusiasm for the project that their kind words boosted me up and over the occasional hurdle.

Nearly all the twenty-six stories in *The Children's Hours* are either new or available only in out-of-print anthologies or in back issues of small literary magazines. In keeping with my original idea, all authors' royalties will go directly to Save the Children, and neither Raša nor I has received any remuneration for our work.

I first want to express my gratitude to my editing partner, Raša. He has recently embarked on a new children's rights project in Thailand, and I wish him much happiness and success in his new job. I'm also very grateful to Gary, Daniela and everyone else at Arcadia Books for doing such a wonderful publishing job – grateful, too, to our book distributors all over the English-speaking world.

I owe a huge *thank you* to all the writers for giving their talents and time to this project. It's a special thrill to have some of my favourite authors united in this effort.

Thanks, as well, to four people who helped me get in touch with writers for whom I had no reliable addresses: Australian journalist Ben Naparstek, bookshop owner Odile Hellier (of the *Village Voice* in Paris), freelance editor Joanne Gruber and literary agent Anna Jarota.

Personal thanks, too, to Alex and my mother.

I hope that readers will find the stories in *The Children's Hours* as moving, disturbing, surprising and mysterious as I did, and that together we can raise a significant amount of funding to fight for the health, education and protection of young people everywhere.

The Fragile and Precious Hours of Children

Raša Sekulović

For centuries, the concept of childhood as the happiest, most care-free period of our lives has been a standard fairy tale promoted throughout the world. The reality is far grimmer and more alarming: official statistics show that more than one million children will be trafficked across international borders over the next year, but the real figure is likely to be much higher. Many of these children will be forced into prostitution, mining, and other forms of hazardous labour. Street children fight for survival on a daily basis on the alleyways and boulevards of São Paulo, Mumbai, Lagos and other huge, globalized cities, exploited by criminals and sometimes hunted by the police. One out of every ten schoolchildren faces violence at school, and many of them are exposed to physical and humiliating punishment in their own homes – some of it so traumatic that suicide seems the only way out.

In England, 27,900 children were put on the Child Protection Register in 2007 as having been abused. Nearly 800,000 children go missing in the United States each year.

Throughout the world, children find themselves in the snares of adult-generated conflicts: wars, coups, military incursions and ethnic cleansings, for example. These conflicts are promoted by men and women who, by some strange and mysterious process of forgetfulness, fail to recognize that they were once themselves protagonists on the stage of childhood. They, too, at sometime in their lives, probably felt themselves cornered by injustice and lack of opportunity.

Despite the near-universal recognition of children as full human beings endowed with indivisible, universal rights, they remain grossly exposed to the kind of abuse and corrosive degradation that destroys potential and creates societies that accept the unacceptable:

that it is okay for children to be beaten, starved, humiliated, taunted and tortured.

Violence has many different faces, and it can take place anywhere children spend their time – in the home, in the street, in schools and in residential care facilities. But no matter what the abuse and where it takes place, the root causes are often the same – poverty, social exclusion and discrimination, to name but a few.

Even so, violence against children has remained until now a largely vague and unexplored area of research and investigation. Somewhere between theory and practice something has been missing.

To rectify this situation, the United Nations launched its Global Study of Violence Against Children in October of 2006. By now, it has produced a clear picture of exactly what happens to children in five different settings: the school, the home, the workplace, institutions and the community. To produce its study, the UN brought together experts in a wide range of fields, as well as children themselves. They looked at what has gone wrong and endeavoured to find ways to turn things around.

The UN's groundbreaking study – as well as the ongoing work of children's rights organizations like Save the Children – can be seen as a call to action and a chance to break through the silence surrounding the abuse of children. It can also be seen as an effort to mobilize and motivate all of us who are concerned about the welfare of young people, and to establish a political agenda that will change how children live – to create a world where violence against them is universally prohibited and prosecuted.

Towards this end, writers have an important and powerful role to play, since they can contribute their own most important resource to the struggle for children's rights: the written word. Writers can both raise awareness of the issues involved and inspire individual and public action. With their stories, they can remind us how fragile and precious every child's life is – and every hour that is a part of that life...

Making Poison

Margaret Atwood

When I was five my brother and I made poison. We were living in a city then, but we probably would have made the poison anyway. We kept it in a paint can under somebody else's house and we put all the poisonous things into it that we could think of: toadstools, dead mice, mountain ash berries which may not have been poisonous but looked it, piss which we saved up in order to add it to the paint can. By the time the can was full everything in it was very poisonous.

The problem was that once having made the poison we couldn't just leave it there. We had to do something with it. We didn't want to put it into someone's food, but we wanted an object, a completion. There was no one we hated enough, that was the difficulty.

I can't remember what we did with the poison in the end. Did we leave it under the corner of the house, which was made of wood and brownish yellow? Did we throw it at someone, some innocuous child? We wouldn't have dared an adult. Is this a true image I have, a small face streaming with tears and red berries, the sudden knowledge that the poison was really poisonous after all? Or did we throw it out, do I remember those red berries floating down the gutter, into a culvert, am I innocent?

Why did we make the poison in the first place? I can remember the glee with which we stirred and added, the sense of magic and accomplishment. Making poison is as much fun as making a cake. People like to make poison. If you don't understand this you will never understand anything.

Invierno

Junot Díaz

From the top of Westminster, our main strip, you could see the sliver of ocean cresting the horizon to the east. My father had been shown that sight – the management showed everyone – but as he drove us in from JFK he didn't stop to point it out. The ocean might have made us feel better, considering what else there was to see. London Terrace itself was a mess; half the buildings still needed their wiring and in the evening light these structures sprawled about the landscape like ships of brick that had run aground. Mud followed gravel everywhere and the grass, planted late in fall, poked out of the snow in dead tufts.

Each building has its own laundry room, Papi said. Mami looked vaguely out of the snout of her parka and nodded. That's wonderful, she said. I was watching the snow sift over itself and my brother was cracking his knuckles. This was our first day in the States. The world was frozen solid.

Our apartment seemed huge to us. Rafa and I had a room to ourselves, and the kitchen, with its refrigerator and stove, was about the size of our house on Summer Welles. We didn't stop shivering until Papi set the apartment temperature to about eighty. Beads of water gathered on the windows like bees and we had to wipe the glass to see outside. Rafa and I were stylish in our new clothes and we wanted out, but Papi told us to take off our boots and our parkas. He sat us down in front of the television, his arms lean and surprisingly hairy right up to the short-cut sleeves. He had just shown us how to flush the toilets, run the sinks, and start the shower.

This isn't a slum, Papi began. I want you to treat everything around you with respect. I don't want you throwing any of your garbage on the floor or on the street. I don't want you going to the bathroom in the bushes.

4

Rafa nudged me. In Santo Domingo I'd pissed everywhere, and the first time Papi had seen me in action, whizzing on a street corner, on the night of his triumphant return, he had said, What are you doing?

Decent people live around here and that's how we're going to live. You're Americans now. He had his Chivas Regal bottle on his knee.

After waiting a few seconds to show that yes, I'd digested everything he'd said, I asked, Can we go out now?

Why don't you help me unpack? Mami suggested. Her hands were very still; usually they were fussing with a piece of paper, a sleeve, or each other.

We'll be out for just a little while, I said. I got up and pulled on my boots. Had I known my father even a little I might not have turned my back on him. But I didn't know him; he'd spent the last five years in the States working, and we'd spent the last five years in Santo Domingo waiting. He grabbed my ear and wrenched me back onto the couch. He did not look happy.

You'll go out when I tell you you're ready. I don't want either of you getting lost or getting hurt out there. You don't know this place.

I looked over at Rafa, who sat quietly in front of the TV. Back on the island, the two of us had taken *guaguas* clear across the capital by ourselves. I looked up at Papi, his narrow face still unfamiliar. Don't you eye me, he said.

Mami stood up. You kids might as well give me a hand.

I didn't move. On the TV the newscasters were making small, flat noises at each other.

Since we weren't allowed out of the house – it's too cold, Papi said – we mostly sat in front of the TV or stared out at the snow those first days. Mami cleaned everything about ten times and made us some damn elaborate lunches.

Pretty early on Mami decided that watching TV was beneficial; you could learn English from it. She saw our young minds as bright, spiky sunflowers in need of light, and arranged us as close to the TV as possible to maximize our exposure. We watched the news, sitcoms, cartoons, *Tarzan*, *Flash Gordon*, *Jonny Quest*, *Herculoids*, *Sesame Street* – eight, nine hours of TV a day, but it was *Sesame Street* that gave us our best lessons. Each word my brother and I learned we passed between ourselves, repeating over and over, and when Mami asked us how to say it, we shook our heads and said, Don't worry about it.

Just tell me, she said, and when we pronounced the words slowly, forming huge, lazy soap bubbles of sound, she never could duplicate them. Her lips seemed to tug apart even the simplest constructions. That sounds horrible, I said.

What do you know about English? she asked.

At dinner she'd try her English out on Papi, but he just poked at his *pernil*, which was not my mother's best dish.

I can't understand a word you're saying, he said one night. Mami had cooked rice with squid. It's best if I take care of the English.

How do you expect me to learn?

You don't have to learn, he said. Besides, the average woman can't learn English.

Oh?

It's a difficult language to master, he said, first in Spanish and then in English.

Mami didn't say another word. In the morning, as soon as Papi was out of the apartment, Mami turned on the TV and put us in front of it. The apartment was always cold in the morning and leaving our beds was a serious torment.

It's too early, we said.

It's like school, she suggested.

No, it's not, we said. We were used to going to school at noon.

You two complain too much, She would stand behind us and when I turned around she would be mouthing the words we were learning, trying to make sense of them.

Even Papi's early-morning noises were strange to me. I lay in bed, listening to him stumbling around in the bathroom, like he was drunk or something. I didn't know what he did for Reynolds Aluminium, but he had a lot of uniforms in his closet, all filthy with machine oil.

I had expected a different father, one about seven feet tall with enough money to buy our entire *barrio*, but this one was average height, with an average face. He'd come to our house in Santo Domingo in a busted-up taxi and the gifts he brought us were small things – toy guns and tops – that we were too old for, that we broke right away. Even though he hugged us and took us out for dinner at the Malecón – our first meat in years – I didn't know what to make of him. A father is a hard thing to get to know.

Those first weeks in the States, Papi spent a great deal of his home time downstairs with his books or in front of the TV. He said little to us that wasn't disciplinary, which didn't surprise us. We'd seen other dads in action, understood that part of the drill.

What he got on to me about the most was my shoelaces. Papi had a thing with shoelaces. I didn't know how to tie them properly, and when I put together a rather formidable knot, Papi would bend down and pull it apart with one tug. At least you have a future as a magician, Rafa said, but this was serious. Rafa showed me how, and I said, Fine, and had no problems in front of him, but when Papi was breathing down my neck, his hand on a belt, I couldn't perform; I looked at my father like my laces were live wires he wanted me to touch together.

I met some dumb men in the Guardia, Papi said, but every single one of them could tie his motherfucking shoes. He looked over at Mami. Why can't he?

These were not the sort of questions that had answers. She looked down, studied the veins that threaded the backs of her hands. For a second Papi's watery turtle-eyes met mine. Don't you look at me, he said.

Even on the days I managed a halfway decent retard knot, as Rafa called them, Papi still had my hair to go on about. While Rafa's hair was straight and dark and glided through a comb like a Caribbean grandparent's dream, my hair still had enough of the African to condemn me to endless combings and out-of-this-world haircuts. My mother cut our hair every month, but this time when she put me in the chair my father told her not to bother.

Only one thing will take care of that, he said. Yunior, go get dressed.

Rafa followed me into my bedroom and watched while I buttoned my shirt. His mouth was tight. I started to feel anxious. What's your problem? I said.

Nothing.

Then stop watching me. When I got to my shoes, he tied them for me. At the door my father looked down and said, You're getting better.

I knew where the van was parked but I went the other way just to catch a glimpse of the neighbourhood. Papi didn't notice my defection until I had rounded the corner, and when he growled my name I hurried back, but I had already seen the fields and the children on the snow.

I sat in the front seat. He popped a tape of Jonny Ventura into the player and took us out smoothly to Route 9. The snow lay in dirty piles on the side of the road. There can't be anything worse than old snow, he said. It's nice while it falls but once it gets to the ground it just causes trouble.

Are there accidents?

Not with me driving.

The cattails on the banks of the Raritan were stiff and the colour of sand, and when we crossed the river, Papi said, I work in the next town.

We were in Perth Amboy for the services of a real talent, a Puerto Rican barber named Rubio who knew just what to do with the *pelo malo*. He put two or three creams on my head and had me sit with the foam a while; after his wife rinsed me off he studied my head in the mirror, tugged at my hair, rubbed an oil into it, and finally sighed.

It's better to shave it all off, Papi said.

I have some other things that might work.

Papi looked at his watch. Shave it.

All right, Rubio said. I watched the clippers plough through my hair, watched my scalp appear, tender and defenceless. One of the old men in the waiting area snorted and held his paper higher. When he was finished Rubio massaged talcum powder on my neck. Now you look *guapo*, he said. He handed me a stick of gum, which would go right to my brother.

Well? Papi asked. I nodded. As soon as we were outside the cold clamped down on my head like a slab of wet dirt.

We drove back in silence. An oil tanker was pulling into port on the Raritan and I wondered how easy it would be for me to slip aboard and disappear.

Do you like negras? my father asked.

I turned my head to look at the women we had just passed. I turned back and realized he was waiting for an answer, that he wanted to know, and while I wanted to blurt that I didn't like girls in any denomination, I said instead, Oh yes, and he smiled.

They're beautiful, he said, and lit a cigarette. They'll take care of you better than anyone.

Rafa laughed when he saw me. You look like a big thumb.

Dios mío, Mami said, turning me around.

It looks good, Papi said.

And the cold's going to make him sick.

Papi put his cold palm on my head. He likes it fine, he said.

Papi worked a long fifty-hour week and on his days off he expected quiet, but my brother and I had too much energy to be quiet; we didn't think anything of using our sofas for trampolines at nine in the morning, when Papi was asleep. In our old *barrio* we were accustomed to folks shocking the streets with merengue twenty-four hours a day. Our upstairs neighbours, who themselves fought like trolls over everything, would stomp down on us. Will you two please shut up? and then Papi would come out of his room, his shorts unbuttoned and say, What did I tell you? How many times have I told you to keep it quiet? He was free with his smacks and we spent whole afternoons on Punishment Row – our bedroom – where we had to lie on our beds and not get off, because if he burst in and caught us at the window, staring out at the beautiful snow, he would pull our ears and smack us, and then we would have to kneel in the corner for a few hours. If we messed that up, joking around or cheating, he would force us to kneel down on the cutting side of a coconut grater, and only when we were bleeding and whimpering would he let us up.

Now you'll be quiet, he'd say, satisfied, and we'd lay in bed, our knees burning with iodine, and wait for him to go to work so we could put our hands against the cold glass.

We watched the neighbourhood children building snowmen and igloos, having snowball fights. I told my brother about the field I'd seen, vast in my memory, but he just shrugged. A brother and sister lived across in apartment four, and when they were out we would wave to them. They waved to us and motioned for us to come out but we shook our heads, We can't.

The brother shrugged, and tugged his sister out to where the other children were, with their shovels and their long, snow-encrusted scarves. She seemed to like Rafa, and waved to him as she walked off. He didn't wave back.

North American girls are supposed to be beautiful, he said.

Have you seen any?

What do you call her? He reached down for a tissue and sneezed out a double-barrel of snot. All of us had headaches and colds and coughs; even with the heat cranked up, winter was kicking our asses. I had to wear a Christmas hat round the house to keep my shaven head warm; I looked like an unhappy tropical elf.

I wiped my nose. If this is the United States, mail me home.

Don't worry, Mami says. We're probably going home.

How does she know?

Her and Papi have been talking about it. She thinks it would be better if we went back. Rafa ran a finger glumly on the window; he didn't want to go; he liked the TV and the toilet and already saw himself with the girl in apartment four.

I don't know about that, I said. Papi doesn't look like he's going anywhere.

What do you know? You're just a little *mojón*.

I know more than you, I said. Papi had never once mentioned going back to the Island. I waited to get him in a good mood, after he had watched *Abbott and Costello*, and asked him if he thought we would be going back soon.

For what?

A visit.

Maybe, he grunted. Maybe not. Don't plan on it.

❧

By the third week I was worried we weren't going to make it. Mami, who had been our authority on the Island, was dwindling. She cooked our food and then sat there, waiting to wash the dishes. She had no friends, no neighbours to visit. You should talk to me, she said, but we told her to wait for Papi to get home. He'll talk to you, I guaranteed. Rafa's temper, which was sometimes a problem, got worse. I would tug at his hair, an old game of ours, and he would explode. We fought and fought and fought and after my mother pried us apart, instead of making up like the old days, we sat scowling on opposite sides of our room and planned each other's demise. I'm going to burn you alive, he promised. You should number your limbs, *cabrón*, I told him, so they'll know how to put you back together for the funeral. We squirted acid at each other with our eyes, like reptiles. Our boredom made everything worse.

One day I saw the brother and sister from apartment four gearing up to go play, and instead of waving I pulled on my parka. Rafa was sitting on the couch, flipping between a Chinese cooking show and an all-star Little League game. I'm going out, I told him.

Sure you are, he said, but when I pushed open the front door, he said, Hey!

The air outside was very cold and I nearly fell down our steps. No one in the neighbourhood was the shovelling type. Throwing my scarf over my mouth, I stumbled across the uneven crust of snow. I caught up to the brother and sister on the side of our building.

Wait up! I yelled. I want to play with you.

The brother watched me with a half grin, not understanding a word I'd said, his arms scrunched nervously at his side. His hair was a frightening no-colour. His sister had the greenest eyes and her freckled face was cowled in a hood of pink fur. We had on the same brand of mittens, bought cheap from Two Guys. I stopped and we faced each other, our white breath nearly reaching across the distance between us. The world was ice and the ice burned with sunlight. This was my first real encounter with North Americans and I felt loose and capable on that plain of ice. I motioned with my mittens and smiled. The sister turned to her brother and laughed.

He said something to her and then she ran to where the other children were, the peals of her laughter trailing over her shoulder like the spumes of her hot breath.

I've been meaning to come out, I said. But my father won't let us right now. He thinks we're too young, but look, I'm older than your sister, and my brother looks older than you.

The brother pointed at himself. Eric, he said.

My name's Joaquín, I said.

Juan, he said.

No, Joaquín, I repeated. Don't they teach you guys how to speak?

His grin never faded. Turning, he walked over to the approaching group of children. I knew that Rafa was watching me from the window and fought the urge to turn around and wave. The gringo children watched me from a distance and then walked away. Wait, I said, but then an Oldsmobile pulled into the next lot, its tires muddy and thick with snow. I couldn't follow them. The sister looked back once. A lick of her hair peeking out of her hood. After they had gone, I stood in the snow until my feet were cold. I was too afraid of getting my ass beat to go any farther.

Was it fun? Rafa was sprawled in front of the TV.

Hijo de la gran puta, I said, sitting down.

You look frozen.

I didn't answer him. We watched TV until a snowball struck the glass patio door and both of us jumped.

What was that? Mami wanted to know from her room.

Two more snowballs exploded on the glass. I peeked behind the curtain and saw the brother and the sister hiding behind a snow-buried Dodge.

Nothing, Señora, Rafa said. It's just the snow.

What, is it learning how to dance out there?

It's just falling, Rafa said.

We both stood behind the curtain, and watched the brother throw fast and hard, like a pitcher.

Each day the trucks would roll into our neighbourhood with the garbage. The landfill stood two miles out, but the mechanics of the winter air conducted its sound and smells to us undiluted. When we opened a window we could hear the bulldozers spreading the garbage out in thick, putrid layers across the top of the landfill. We could see the gulls attending the mound, thousands of them, wheeling.

Do you think kids play out there? I asked Rafa. We were standing on the porch, brave; at any moment Papi could pull into the parking lot and see us.

Of course they do. Wouldn't you?

I licked my lips. They must find a lot of crap out there.

Plenty, Rafa said.

That night I dreamed of home, that we'd never left. I woke up, my throat aching, hot with fever. I washed my face in the sink, then sat next to our window, my brother snoring, and watched the pebbles of ice falling and freezing into a shell over the cars and the snow and the pavement. Learning to sleep in new places was an ability you were supposed to lose as you grew older, but I never had it. The building was only now settling into itself; the tight magic of the just-hammered-in nail was finally relaxing. I heard someone walking around in the living room and when I went out I found my mother standing in front of the patio door.

You can't sleep? she asked, her face smooth and perfect in the glare of the halogens.

I shook my head.

We've always been alike that way, she said. That won't make your life any easier.

I put my arms around her waist. That morning alone we'd seen three moving trucks from our patio door. I'm going to pray for Dominicans, she had said, her face against the glass, but what we would end up getting were Puerto Ricans.

She must have put me to bed because the next day I woke up next to Rafa. He was snoring. Papi was in the next room snoring as well, and something inside of me told me that I wasn't a quiet sleeper.

At the end of the month the bulldozers capped the landfill with a head of soft, blond dirt, and the evicted gulls flocked over the development, shitting and fussing, until the first of the new garbage was brought in.

❧

My brother was bucking to be Number One Son; in all other things he was generally unchanged, but when it came to my father he listened with a scrupulousness he had never afforded our mother. Papi said he wanted us inside, Rafa stayed inside. I was less attentive; I played in the snow for short stretches, though never out of sight of the apartment. You're going to get caught, Rafa forecasted. I could tell that my boldness made him miserable; from our windows he watched me packing snow and throwing myself into drifts. I stayed away from the gringos. When I saw the brother and sister from apartment four, I stopped farting around and watched for a sneak attack. Eric waved and his sister waved; I didn't wave back. Once he came over and showed me the baseball he must have just gotten. Roberto Clemente, he said, but I went on with building my fort. His sister grew flushed and said something loud and rude and then Eric sighed. Neither of them were handsome children.

One day the sister was out by herself and I followed her to the field. Huge concrete pipes sprawled here and there on the snow. She ducked into one of these and I followed her, crawling on my knees.

She sat in the pipe, cross-legged and grinning. She took her hands out of her mittens and rubbed them together. We were out of the wind and I followed her example. She poked a finger at me.

Joaquín, I said. All my friends call me Yunior.

Joaquín Yunior, she said. Elaine, Elaine Pitt.

Elaine.

Joaquín.

It's really cold, I said, my teeth chattering.

She said something and then felt the ends of my fingers. Cold, she said.

I knew that word already. I nodded. *Frío*. She showed me how to put my fingers in my armpits.

Warm, she said.

Yes, I said. Very warm.

❧

At night, Mami and Papi talked. He sat on his side of the table and she leaned close, asking him, Do you ever plan on taking these children out? You can't keep them sealed up like this; they aren't dead yet.

They'll be going to school soon, he said, sucking on his pipe. And as soon as winter lets up I want to show you the ocean. You can see it around here, you know, but it's better to see it up close.

How much longer does winter last?

Not long, he promised. You'll see. In a few months none of you will remember this and by then I won't have to work too much. We'll be able to travel in spring and see everything.

I hope so, Mami said.

My mother was not a woman easily cowed, but in the States she let my father roll over her. If he said he had to be at work for two days straight, she said okay and cooked enough *moro* to last him. She was depressed and sad and missed her father and her friends. Everyone had warned her that the U.S. was a difficult place where even the devil got his ass beat, but no one had told her that she would have to spend the rest of her natural life snowbound with her children. She wrote letter after letter home, begging her sisters to come as soon as possible. I need the company, she explained. This neighbourhood is empty and friendless. And she begged Papi to bring his friends over. She wanted to talk about unimportant matters, and see a brown face who didn't call her mother or wife.

None of you are ready for guests, Papi said. Look at this house. Look at your children. *Me dan vergüenza* to see them slouching around like that.

You can't complain about this apartment. All I do is clean it.

What about your sons?

My mother looked over at me and then Rafa. I put one shoe over the other. After that, she had Rafa keep after me about my shoelaces. When we heard the van arriving in the parking lot, Mami called us over for a quick inspection. Hair, teeth, hands, feet. If anything was wrong she'd hide us in the bathroom until it was fixed. Her dinners grew elaborate. She even changed the TV for Papi without calling him a *zángano*.

Okay, he said finally. Maybe it can work.

It doesn't have to be that big a production, Mami said.

Two Fridays in a row he brought a friend over for dinner and Mami put on her best polyester jumpsuit and got us spiffy in our red pants, thick white belts, and amaranth-blue Chams shirts. Seeing her asthmatic with excitement made us hopeful that our world was about to be transformed, but these were awkward dinners. The men were bachelors and divided their time between talking to Papi and eyeing Mami's ass. Papi seemed to enjoy their company but Mami spent her time on her feet, hustling food to the table, opening beers, and changing the channel. She started out each night natural and unreserved, with a face that scowled as easily as it grinned, but as the men loosened their belts and aired out their toes and talked their talk, she withdrew; her expressions narrowed until all that remained was a tight, guarded smile that seemed to drift across the room the way a splash of sunlight glides across a wall. We kids were ignored for the most part, except once, when the first man, Miguel, asked, Can you two box as well as your father?

They're fine fighters, Papi said.

Your father is very fast. Has good hand speed. Miguel shook his head, laughing. I saw him finish this one *tipo*. He put *fulano* on his ass.

That *was* funny, Papi agreed. Miguel had brought a bottle of Bermúdez rum; he and Papi were drunk.

It's time you go to your room, Mami said, touching my shoulder.

Why? I asked. All we do is sit there.

That's how I feel about my home, Miguel said.

Mami's glare cut me in half. Such a fresh mouth, she said, shoving us toward our room. We sat, as predicted, and listened.

On both visits, the men ate their fill, congratulated Mami on her cooking, Papi on his sons, and then stayed about an hour for propriety's sake. Cigarettes, dominoes, gossip, and then the inevitable, Well, I have to get going. We have work tomorrow. You know how that is.

Of course I do. What else do we Dominicans know?

Afterward, Mami cleaned the pans quietly in the kitchen, scraping at the roasted pig flesh, while Papi sat out on our front porch in his short sleeves; he seemed to have grown impervious to the cold these last five years. When he came inside, he showered and pulled on his overalls. I have to work tonight, he said.

Mami stopped scratching at the pans with a spoon. You should find yourself a more regular job.

Papi smiled. Maybe I will.

As soon as he left, Mami ripped the needle from the album and interrupted Felix de Rosario. We heard her in the closet, pulling on her coat and her boots.

Do you think she's leaving us? I asked.

Rafa wrinkled his brow. It's a possibility, he said. What would you do if you were her?

I'd already be in Santo Domingo.

When we heard the front door open, we let ourselves out of our room and found the apartment empty.

We better go after her, I said.

Rafa stopped at the door. Let's give her a minute, he said.

What's wrong with you? She's probably face down in the snow.

We'll wait two minutes, he said.

Shall I count?

Don't be a wiseguy.

One, I said loudly. He pressed his face against the glass patio door. We were about to hit the door when she returned, panting, an envelope of cold around her.

Where did you get to? I asked.

I went for a walk. She dropped her coat at the door; her face was red from the cold and she was breathing deeply, as if she'd sprinted the last thirty steps.

Where?

Just around the corner.

Why the hell did you do that?

She started to cry, and when Rafa put his hand on her waist, she slapped it away. We went back to our room.

I think she's losing it, I said.

She's just lonely, Rafa said.

&

The night before the snowstorm I heard the wind at our window. I woke up the next morning, freezing. Mami was fiddling with the thermostat; we could hear the gurgle of water in the pipes but the apartment didn't get much warmer.

Just go play, Mami said. That will keep your mind off it.

Is it broken?

I don't know. She looked at the knob dubiously. Maybe it's slow this morning.

None of the gringos were outside playing. We sat by the window and waited for them. In the afternoon my father called from work; I could hear the forklifts when I answered.

Rafa?

No, it's me.

Get your mother.

How are you doing?

Get your mother.

We got a big storm on the way, he explained to her – even from where I was standing I could hear his voice. There's no way I can get out to see you. It's gonna be bad. Maybe I'll get there tomorrow.

What should I do?

Just keep indoors. And fill the tub with water.

Where are you sleeping? Mami asked.

At a friend's.

She turned her face from us. Okay, she said. When she got off the phone she sat in front of the TV. She could see I was going to pester her about Papi; she told me, Just watch the TV.

Radio WADO recommended spare blankets, water, flashlights and food. We had none of these things. What happens if we get buried? I asked. Will we die? Will they have to save us in boats?

I don't know, Rafa said. I don't know anything about snow. I was spooking him. He went over to the window and peeked out.

We'll be fine, Mami said. As long as we're warm. She went over and raised the heat again.

But what if we get buried?

You can't have that much snow.

How do you know?

Because twelve inches isn't going to bury anybody, even a pain-in–the-ass like you.

I went out on the porch and watched the first snow begin to fall like finely-sifted ash. If we die, Papi's going to feel bad, I said.

Don't talk about it like that, Rafa said.

Mami turned away and laughed.

Four inches fell in an hour and the snow kept falling.

Mami waited until we were in bed, but I heard the door and woke Rafa. She's at it again, I said.

Outside?

You know it.

He put on his boots grimly. He paused at the door and then looked back at the empty apartment. Let's go, he said.

She was standing on the edge of the parking lot, ready to cross Westminster. The apartment lamps glowed on the frozen ground and our breath was white in the night air. The snow was gusting.

Go home, she said.

We didn't move.

Did you at least lock the front door? she asked.

Rafa shook his head.

It's too cold for thieves anyway, I said.

Mami smiled and nearly slipped on the sidewalk. I'm not good at walking on this *vaina*.

I'm real good, I said. Just hold onto me.

We crossed Westminster. The cars were moving very slowly and the wind was loud and full of snow.

This isn't too bad, I said. These people should see a hurricane.

Where should we go? Rafa asked. He was blinking a lot to keep the snow out of his eyes.

Go straight, Mami said. That way we don't get lost.

We should mark the ice.

She put her hands around us both. It's easier if we go straight.

We went down to the edge of the apartments and looked out over the landfill, a misshapen, shadowy mound that abutted the Raritan. Rubbish fires burned all over it like sores and the dumptrucks and bulldozers slept quietly and reverently at its base. It smelled like something the river had tossed out from its floor, something moist and heaving. We found the basketball courts next and the pool, empty of water, and Parkridge, the next neighbourhood over, which was full and had many, many children. We even saw the ocean, up there at the top of Westminster, like the blade of a long, curved knife. Mami was crying but we pretended not to notice. We threw snowballs at the sliding cars and once I removed my cap just to feel the snowflakes scatter across my cold, hard scalp.

The Miami Dolphins

Patricia Volk

'Left *after* the Coppertone sign,' Ma says. 'We almost missed our turn!'

Suddenly we're on a dirt road, bouncing along. Two hours we're in the car looking for my birthday present.

'*Now* right,' Ma says.

Wild trees line one side. On the other, chain link wraps around the kind of electrical plant that would be at home in *Bride of Franken-stein*. I see a sign. Dad screeches into Betty's Home of the Dolphins.

'Are you the Glassman's?' A woman in a faded bikini leans into the car window. 'Where the hell have you been?'

I look around. There are His and Hers Port-O-Sans, a blue-grey shanty with a hand-lettered OFFICE sign above the doorway, and in the water, concrete pens, the kind you'd see in a fish hatchery, only bigger.

'What's the story?' I say.

They turn in the front seat, look at me and start singing 'Happy Birthday to You.' While they're singing, they point to the pens. 'The Miami Dolphins,' they say. 'You're going to swim with the Miami Dolphins.'

I get out of the car and walk over to the water. I look down. Nothing's there. The water looks black.

'I'm Betty.' The woman pats her sternum. 'You people almost missed orientation.'

Betty has sun-bleached hair and leathery skin. Her body looks like a lifetime of hard work. I take her to be in her fifties even though she could be thirty or seventy. She motions for us to sit at a picnic table with an elderly couple, a skinny boy, and a fat girl. The old man keeps slapping his legs as if bugs are around only they aren't. The little girl is wearing a bathing suit with pieces cut out of the sides and her fat overlaps the holes. The boy wears madras Bermudas with suspenders and Ray-Bans, a cool dude. The girl looks scared. The boy looks angry. The grandfather looks annoyed. The grandmother looks like she's ready to take notes. She's leaning forward. You can tell she loved school.

'Swimming with the dolphins is therapeutic,' Betty begins. 'Autistic kids come here to swim. Psychologists send their patients to Betty's Home of the Dolphins all the time.'

'I never knew that,' the grandma says. 'Why is that?'

'For the autistic,' Betty explains, 'they're hoping to trigger an emotional response. For groups, they're looking for a shared experience to compare reactions.' Betty looks around to see if there are any more questions. 'The cetacean group,' she continues, 'includes whales, dolphins, and porpoises.'

The grandma raises her hand. 'Are these dolphins Flipper?'

Betty nods and tells us these are *Tursiops truncatus*, Atlantic bottle-nosed dolphins.

I scan the pens looking for one.

'Carl,' the grandma taps the grandpa's hand. 'Didn't we have these for dinner last night?'

'The dolphin you eat is a fish not a mammal,' Betty explains. Then she tells us how dolphins echolocate from their foreheads to their lower jaws.

'I love this,' I mouth to my parents, who have been watching for a reaction. 'Thank you.'

My mind flashes briefly to other presents they have given me: a massage that was a series of drill noogies, a one-year membership in The Fad-of-the-Month Club, wall-climbing lessons, an hour with a career counselor, one month of liquid diet.

'Dolphins can tell if you have a pacemaker,' Betty is saying, 'and what your blood pressure is. They can tell if you're pregnant. Or if you have to take a dump.'

I check Ma on 'dump'. She is frowning.

'They can read right through our bodies,' Betty continues. 'They can even pick up foetal heartbeats. They have long wave and short wave and they use it to tell the size of something, its density, and to check out the terrain. They use it to find food too. Dolphins have no sense of smell. But they can taste. And they make love every day. Dolphins are the only animals who have sex for fun besides humans.'

Ma raises her hand. 'What about swans?' she says.

Betty doesn't answer. She's looking at the boy. He's rocking sideways on the picnic bench. He looks like he's about to burst.

'I think it's mean you make the dolphins work,' he says. 'There's no way I'm going.'

'Oh yes, you are,' his grandma says.

Betty starts handing out snorkels, masks, and flippers.

'This is cruelty to animals,' the boy protests. 'Dolphins don't want to take humans for rides. You make them.'

'The dolphins are free to leave any time they want.' Betty points to the canal that leads from the pens to the Atlantic. 'We don't have any gates here. The dolphins can leave anytime they want to. But they don't. The dolphins always come back. Now, do you think they'd do that if they were unhappy?'

'Right,' the boy says, glaring at Betty over his Ray-Bans. 'You feed them, don't you?'

'Of course we do,' Betty says. 'But they're rewarded whether they do their work or not.'

'Jared!' the grandma snaps. 'Do you have to ruin it for everybody?'

'We've already paid for you,' the grandpa says. 'You have to go.'

'Forget it.' The boy parks his elbows on the picnic table. 'I'm not going and you can't make me.'

'I can't refund your money,' Betty says. 'We reserved a place for him.'

'I'll pay for it myself. I have enough. I'll pay you not to go.'

'Well why don't you go in, Carl?' The grandma turns to the grandpa. 'You love to swim.'

The little girl runs over to her grandpa. 'Please, Grandpa,' she says. 'I'm scared. I don't want to go in alone.'

'This lady is going in with you, Tiffany.' The grandma points to me.

'My daughter cannot be legally responsible for her,' Ma says. 'My daughter will not take legal responsibility.'

'I'm not going in,' Tiffany says, and crosses her arms over her chest. The grandpa says, 'Jesus Christ!' then pries off his sandals and starts tugging at his socks. Betty tells us to take off all our rings. 'Their skin is so sensitive,' she says. 'Abrasion from a ring gives them excruciating pain.' She demonstrates how to latch onto a fin. She holds her hands straight out, palms flat. 'Pretend you're doing the breast stroke,' she says. 'Grab it thumb down.' I pretend I'm doing the breast stroke and grab air with my thumbs down.

Ma nudges Dad. Quick he takes a picture.

'You'll each get two rides up front,' Betty says. 'Then you'll have a play time. At the end, you'll each get one more ride. We do that to make sure everybody has *some* time with the dolphins. Sometimes they pick favorites. No one knows why. They'll ignore one person and they won't leave somebody else alone.'

The grandma raises her hand. 'Is it true a dolphin can kill a shark?'

Betty nods as she helps Tiffany with her mask. 'They hammer sharks in the gills with their noses,' she says.

'Who is the natural enemy of the dolphin then?' the grandma asks.

'Man,' says Betty. 'Tuna fishermen. The dolphins get caught in their nets and suffocate. If you ever saw what comes up in a tuna fisherman's net, you'd never eat Chicken of the Sea again. It's enough to break your heart.'

'Are you happy?' Ma asks me.

'This is the best present you've ever given me,' I tell her.

'See?' she nods to Dad.

'Sh-h-h-h,' he says as Betty starts telling us what to expect underwater.

'You'll hear clicks,' she says. 'That's the dolphins checking you out. They love knees. Human knees from the back resemble the dolphins' sexual organs. Sometimes they'll come and put their mouths around your knees. If you don't like it, just swim away. If you feel something coil up your leg, don't be afraid. That means the male likes you a lot. Here at Betty's Home of the Dolphins we call that "The Sea Snake".'

'Jesus,' Dad says under his breath.

'Don't let them do that to you, honey,' Ma says.

The grandpa, Tiffany and I slide down to a small dock in the water. We are wearing our flippers, masks, and snorkels. The three of us look like a catalog picture for what sizes snorkel equipment comes in.

'Smile!' Dad yells down at me. He takes my picture.

Betty stands above us on dry land. She makes a whistling sound with her nose. Suddenly the water moves. Three waves approach the dock we're standing on. These waves get bigger and come close to each other. When they are right at the dock, the waves break and dolphins rise out of them, rearing backward on their tails. They are sleek as chrome. They open their mouths and chirp. It's a loud, flat sound with no range. Two are big, one's little.

'Sparky! Happy! Mike!' Betty introduces us. The dolphins chirp once more then sink into the water.

'Forget it. I'm not going,' Tiffany says.

'Oh yes, you are,' her grandpa says.

Betty tells us that dolphins smile whether they are happy or not. 'Don't reach out to pet them,' she warns us. 'If they want you to pet them, they'll let you know. You wouldn't want to be petted by strangers, would you? Dolphins know who they like.'

Betty tells us to get in the water and swim to the far side of the pen. That's where the dolphins will pick us up. She tells Tiffany to go in first. Tiffany goes in all right but once her head gets wet, she starts thrashing and coughing.

'I can't do it,' she cries. 'I can't do it!'

Betty kneels on the dock and reminds Tiffany how to do it.

'Just bite down and breathe,' she says, adjusting Tiffany's mouthpiece. Betty has a calm animal trainer's way about her. You get the feeling she doesn't mind doing the same thing over and over, reducing it always to its simplest form. She shows the little girl how to spit in her mask to keep the glass clear.

'I can't do this,' the little girl says in a tired, broken way.

'Sure you can,' Betty says and the little girl paddles off.

I go in next. I keep telling myself this has to be okay. You never hear of people being killed by dolphins. This is 2008. Elevators get inspected. Businesses are licensed. Lawyers are waiting in the wings.

The water is warm. 'Got it!' Dad shouts from behind the camera as I swim toward the little girl.

Then her grandfather falls off the dock backward. He's watched too many re-runs of 'Sea Hunt'. You don't go in backward with a snorkel. Even I know that. He surfaces with his mask under his chin. He swims over to where Tiffany and I are lined up.

'Here,' I motion him in front of me. 'You want to be next to Tiffany?'

'Wave!' Dad shouts. I wave, then stick my head in the water. I can't see any dolphins. The water is green with yellow dust all through it. When I surface, the little girl is being towed by Sparky, the littlest dolphin. Her head is in the water. She looks like she knows what she's doing. But when she raises her head, her mask is filled with water and she's crying and choking.

Betty leans down. She talks to the little girl and fixes her mask.

The grandfather turns to me. 'I'm next,' he says. 'God help me.'

I check underwater again to see if I can see the dolphins coming for him. Then I get distracted by a sea anemone doing the hula on the bottom of the pen. When I look back, the little girl and her grandpa are swimming toward me.

I don't know what's going on. I don't know what to expect. I don't know what the dolphin is making of my rapidly beating heart. Maybe it thinks I'm an enemy. Something takes me over that must be a kind of REM sleep for the awake. I'm conscious but it feels like a dream. My eyes are working but I'm not seeing. My ears are okay, but I can't hear. The water breaks beside me. A grey mass is there. It's a warm wet grey. It's hard to believe anything alive could be so perfect. The mass turns. The mass is a head. It looks at me with an eye bigger than a cow's and much, much more intelligent.

'Smile,' Dad shouts. 'Got it!'

I look it straight back in the eye. Now I understand why Shirley MacLaine thinks we were all animals once or vice versa. The dolphin is somehow human. He looks like he can read my mind. It's as if he knows something about me I don't know. In case he is reading my mind, I think nice dolphin thoughts. Pretty dolphin, I think. Smart. You're the best thing in the sea. You're the King of the Sea, I think, then excuse myself for the tunalike reference. I want this dolphin to like me. I want us to be friends. I'm not going to force myself on you, I think. Anything you want is fine with me. You're the boss. How much do you weigh?

'He's waiting for you,' Betty yells, making a megaphone out of her hands.

The dolphin disappears then surfaces again. He wags his fin an inch from my right arm.

I think 'breast stroke' and grab it thumb down. He takes off immediately and we're knifing through the water. I'm swimming the fastest I've ever gone in the water. Much faster. We're leaving a wake. I'm in an element I don't belong in with something that makes me fit. I am swimming like a dolphin, slicing through the water. This dolphin is making me a dolphin. This is the best moment of my life. I always want to remember this. For twenty seconds, I'm a dolphin. He drops me off at the dock and disappears.

The three of us line up in the same order again. We tread water, curling our fingers through a wire fence. The little girl goes, then her grandpa, then me. My plan is to keep my head underwater this time and breathe through the snorkel to make myself even more like a dolphin. But when I do, it's a little less good than it was the first time. Maybe it's because I'm anticipating how great it's going to be. That's what happens with expectations. It's fine. It's wonderful. But it's just fun.

'Free time!' Betty shouts, and we all swim to the middle of the pen. The dolphins have vanished. Maybe they've gone out to sea.

'You were wonderful!' Mom yells. I wave to the camera.

'We got everything!' Dad says.

Just then, all three dolphins surface around the little girl and start nudging her with their noses. She screams through her snorkel then rips it off.

Betty stands on the dock and shouts. 'They're just being friendly! They like you! They want to take you for a ride! Grab one!'

All three wiggle their fin and the little girl takes one. It's Sparky's. The two big dolphins follow Sparky and the little girl like an escort. She keeps coughing and going under, but she doesn't let the dolphin go.

When the dolphins go past us, her grandfather tries to grab a fin.

'Son of a bitch,' comes out of his snorkel. We watch the dolphins court Tiffany.

I swim over to Betty. 'What's the story,' I say.

'Well,' she answers, 'they really like her. They often like the smallest person best.'

The grandfather comes over and complains. 'I'm paying you so I can swim with the dolphins,' he says.

'You know what you can do?' Betty says. 'Try doing something funny underwater. Be a clown. They love that. They'll come if you amuse them.'

So I surface dive and snap my fingers underwater. I pound my stomach and burp into my snorkel. When I resurface, the little girl is still being towed in circles by Sparky, followed by the other two dolphins. She's wailing but she's not letting go. I decide to try humming underwater. I do 'It's Cherry Pink and Apple Blossom White' from the movie *Underwater*. I try to imitate their faint clicking sounds. But no matter what I do, the dolphins won't come. I see some motion underwater and swim toward it. The grandfather is doing the Charleston on the bottom of the pen and hitting himself in the head. When I surface, the little girl is screaming. 'I can't do it!' but she's still holding on. Betty is yelling to her, 'Sparky loves you!'

I try to figure out what the dolphins have against me. Is it the sausage I ate this morning? What makes me undesirable to a dolphin? I could lose a little weight. I've had anxiety lately. Maybe I'm ovulating. I go under again and try to think what a clown would do. I decide to walk into a wall. Just as I get up to the wall of the pen, I feel something wrap around my leg. I panic and pull away. When I turn, nothing is there.

'Free time is over!' Betty shouts. We line up again. The dolphins take us each for a ride and then it's over.

'I got a lot of good shots,' Dad says, handing me a towel.

'I think we should get our money back,' Ma says. 'Those dolphins obviously don't like adults.'

'Don't,' I say. 'This is the best present you ever gave me. I loved it. I swear.'

But no matter what I say, my parents will be disappointed. They will be disappointed because they think I am. The truth is, I am. I would have liked more dolphin rides. I would have liked the dolphins to like me.

As we head for the car, I hear the skinny boy tell his sister, 'I'm going to report you to the ASPCA.'

In the car, we try to make our minds up about dinner. The choice is Crabs R Us, Flynn's Dixie Ribs, or Grilled Anything. I vote for Grilled Anything because I want to see what things can be grilled I never dreamed of. Ma and Dad are not talking in the front seat. I explain to them how much I loved the present, but they will not be consoled. Their daughter has been rejected by dolphins and in the back of their minds, they're wondering why. Is there something wrong with their daughter? Is it something she did? It occurs to me then that even though they've retired to Boca Raton, even though their lives are completely different, nothing has changed. No matter what happens to me, no matter what I do, their joy in me peaked years ago. The best moment they ever had with me has come and gone. It is unduplicatable. It can never happen again. I can never again be a seven-year-old on talent night at Kropnick's Kozy Kabins in the Catskills. I can never again be their tataleh, their bubbaleh, their laban-on-the-keppaleh singing 'She's Too Fat for Me' with a backdrop of mountains on a stage lit by candles in jelly jars. I can never again afford my parents the opportunity of being elbowed by near strangers saying, 'Is she something? Is she delicious? Could you eat her up?'

'No matter what you think, I loved it,' I say.

'I knew she'd hate it,' Dad says to Ma.

'We tried to please her,' Ma shakes her head.

'We tried to do something out of the ordinary and we failed,' Dad says.

'It's enough to break your heart, Dave.'

Writ

Ali Smith

I sit my fourteen-year-old self down opposite me at the table in the lounge so that we can have a conversation, because all she's done so far, the whole time she's been here in my house, is ignore me, stare balefully at a spot just above my head, or look me in the eye then look away from me as if I'm the most boring person on the planet.

I come home from work today and she's here again. I don't ask why, or where she's been since she was last here. I ask her instead to turn down the television. I ask her again to come and sit down at the table.

She sighs. She finally does as I ask. She pulls out a chair clumsily. It is almost as if she's being clumsy on purpose. She sits down, sighs audibly again.

Last week someone, a girl, a woman I hardly know (now when does a girl become a woman? when exactly do we stop being girls?) turned towards me as we walked along a busy street, backed me expertly up against the wall of a builder's restoration of a row of old shops in the middle of London in broad daylight, and kissed me. The kiss, out of nowhere, took me by surprise. When I got home that night my fourteen-year-old self was roaming about in my house knocking into things, wild-eyed, improper and unpredictable as a blunt-nosed foal in a house would be.

It is shocking to see yourself like you haven't been for nearly thirty years. It is also a bit embarrassing, having yourself around, watching your every move as if watching your every move is the last thing that could possibly interest anyone.

What do you reckon to the house, then? I say. Do you like it?

She barely glances round her. She shrugs. My house means nothing to her.

Would you like some coffee? I ask.

She does it again, the insolent look-then-look-away. She makes insolence a thing of beauty. For a moment how good she is at it actually makes me proud and I nod.

You go, girl, I say.

She looks at me as if I'm insane.

Where? she says.

Ha, I say. No, 'you go girl' is a phrase, like, a cliché. It's from music. It means good on you, too right, that kind of thing. It's American. It's borrowed from black culture. It's from later. I mean, you're too young for it.

She makes a tch noise, almost non-existent.

I put the mug of coffee down on the table for her. She picks it up.

Use the coaster, I say.

She is looking at what's in the mug in horror.

No, because I need it to have milk in it, she says and her accent is so where I'm from and so unadulterated that hearing her say more than four words in a row makes my chest hurt inside.

I've no milk, I say. I forgot you took it with milk.

Also it's, like, the too strong kind, she says. It's a bit too strong for me.

She says it quite apologetically.

It's all I've got in, I say.

I like the instant kinds of it, she says. The other kinds taste too much.

Yes, but instants are full of freezing agents, I say. They do all sorts of damage to your synapses –

By the time I've got to the words freezing and agents in this sentence her eyes have gone blank again. She pushes the cup away and puts her head in her hands. I feel suddenly forlorn. I want to say: look, aren't you amazed I ever even managed to buy a house? Doesn't it all look pretty good to you? Doesn't it all look okay? Don't you like how full of books it is? You like books. You don't have to pretend you're not clever to me. I know you are. I'd have loved the idea of a house full of books like this when I was your age.

Was I really going to say that: when I was your age? Would I really have found myself saying that appalling phrase out loud?

There are quite a few things, though, that I do want to say to her.

Concerning our mother for instance, I want to say something like: don't worry, she'll be okay. It's a bad time now, that's all. She doesn't die until you're more than twice the age you are now.

But I can't say that, can I?

I want to say: your exams come out fine all the way down the line. You'll do all right at university. You'll have a really good time. Don't worry that you don't get off with that boy who smells of the linoleum at Crombie Halls of Residence in the first week. You don't have to get off with someone in Fresher's week, it's not necessary, it's not important.

I want to tell her who to trust and who not to trust; who her real good friends are and who's going to fuck her over; who to sleep with, and who definitely not to. Definitely say yes to this person, it's one of the best things that's going to happen to you. And don't be alarmed, I want to say, when you find yourself liking girls as well as boys. It's okay. It's good. It works out very well. Don't even bother yourself worrying about it, not for a single afternoon, not for a single hour in a single afternoon. Don't, by the way, vote Labour in 1997; it's like a vote for the Tories. No, really. And when you're twenty-two and you go for the sales job interview in the middle of Edinburgh and you're backing the Citroen down the road where the Greyfriars Bobby statue is, don't back it so far, just go careful on the clutch, don't panic, because what happens when you panic is you totally collapse the back mudguard against the wall of the pub there and anyway there's no point in you even going for a job like that, I mean you get into the room and they're all wearing their power suits and you're wearing your jeans, so just, you know, know yourself a bit better, that's all I'm saying.

But I look at her sitting there, thin and insolent and complete, and I can't say any of it. It'd be terrible to proffer a friend she hasn't met yet who then turns out not to be a friend, or a left-wing government that turns out not to be. Terrible to tell her, now, about a crushed mudguard one afternoon in 1984. It's somehow terrible even to suggest she'll go to university.

You need to eat more, I say instead.

She puts the end of her hair in her mouth. She takes it out and holds it up and fans it out, examines the wet hair for split ends.

Aw, don't do that, I say, it's disgusting.

She rolls her eyes.

She is spotty round the mouth and in the crevices down the side of her nose, of course she is, with a skin that I now know to call combination dry and greasy. I could tell her how to deal with it. Her middle parting makes her hair look flat and makes her look more cowed that she is. There's a constellation of acne on her forehead beneath it. I could tell her how to deal with that too.

I go and stand at the window and look out. That kiss up against the building site fills the inside of my head again as if someone had opened a lid at the top of my skull, poured in a jug of warm water mixed with flower food, then arranged a bunch of spring flowers in me – cheerfulness, daffodils – using me as the vase. But the light is coming down, February, early dusk, and the common is still patchy with snow. I know now, though I didn't know it when I bought this house, that the common is actually a common burial ground; it's where they buried most of this city's thousands of plague-dead centuries ago. Beneath the feet of the dog-walkers and the people coming back from the supermarket, under the grass and the going snow, under the mound where the paths all come together, are all the final shapes their lives took, all the bare bones. Above them the black of the common, and above it the sky the deep blue it goes just before dark. It's a clear night. The stars'll be out later. It'll be beautiful, all the stars and planets spread in their winter-spring alignments above the common. Are the stars out tonight? I don't know if it's cloudy or bright. Cause I only have eyes. Art Garfunkel, it was. The song coming into my head gives me an idea.

What's number one right now? I say. In the top twenty?

Figaro by The Brotherhood of Man, she says. It's appalling.

They're appalling, I say.

It's music for, like, infants, she says.

And that song Angelo, I say.

I hate that song, she says. It's crap.

It's such a steal from the Abba song, Fernando, I say. You just have to think about it and it's so obvious.

Yeah, she says. It is. It's like really a steal. They just took the idea Abba had and they wrote it into a so much less good song.

Her voice, for the first time since she's been here, sounds almost enthusiastic. I don't turn round. I rack my brains to remember something I know she'll like.

I sing: Hey you with the pretty face. Welcome to the human race.

I really really like the way the piano they use in Mr Blue Sky has an electronic voice and you think it might even be the voice the sky has, if the sky had a voice, she says. I actually really really like that whole idea of an electric light orchestra because of the idea of, like, light-orchestral kind of thing, and then on top of that the idea that it's electric and that it's nothing but an electric light, like one you switch on and off.

It is the most she's said so far, the whole time she's been in the house.

Like a whole orchestra at the flick of a switch, I say.

A whole huge orchestra inside one light bulb, she says. It's really clever to do that like with just writing some words together, it's really good the words doing all that by themselves. I really like it. Do you know that thing about that phrase written water?

No, I say.

That thing about the historic poet John Keats Miss Aberdeen in English told us today, she says.

The tragic pop star of the Romantic period, I say. Did Miss Aberdeen not say that?

Yeah, but when he died, my fourteen-year-old self says, like, before he died, the poet John Keats, right, apparently he said to someone, put it on my gravestone that here lies a poet whose name is written water. Not written down, but written water. Water that was written on. I think that's really beautiful. Here lies a poet whose name was written water.

One, I say. Not a poet. It says on the stone, here lies one.

Well, same thing, she says.

And it's writ in water, I say. It's three words, not two.

No, it's written, like one word, she says.

It isn't, I say. It's writ. Then in. Then water.

Yeah but writ isn't a word, she says.

It is a word, actually, I say.

Yeah like half a word, my fourteen-year-old self says. It doesn't mean anything.

It's a real whole word by itself, I say. You can find it in any dictionary. It's changed its meaning over time and at the same time it's kept its meaning. We just don't use the word exactly like that, in that form, any more these days.

I can hear her kicking at the bar under the table.

Don't do that, I say.

She stops it. She goes silent again. I look out over the darkening grass. I don't have to look round to know what she's doing, still swinging her leg under the table behind me but just above the bar, just expertly missing it every time.

He did die unbelievably young, you know, Keats, I say.

No he didn't, she says. He was twenty-five or something.

A joy forever, I say. Its loveliness increases. I can't remember what comes after nothingness. God. I used to know that poem off by heart.

We did a poem by him, she says.

Which one? I say.

The one about looking in an old book, she says. And oh yeah, I forgot. Because when I got into school this morning, it was really appalling because the art teacher made me take off my clothes. In front of everyone.

I turn round.

He what? I say.

Not he, she says. Miss MacKintosh. Weirdo.

Don't call Miss MacKintosh that, I say. Miss MacKintosh is really nice.

She's a weirdo from weirdoland, she says.

No she isn't, I say.

Like, she said to me you've to take off the soaking wet things and put them on the radiator and you can wear my coat. I had to sit in her coat the whole way through double period art. My hands were freezing, I had to put them in the pockets a couple of times. My tights were ripped though, from the stones on the way down on the Landscaping. Then Laura Wise from 3B said she wasn't cold and gave me hers. She saw it happen. She said John McLintock was spazzodelic.

Wait a minute, I say. First, I don't think you should use that word. And second. What stones? Soaking wet, why exactly? I say.

That boy John McLintock pushed me down the Landscaping, she says.

I remember the Landscaping; we used to hang around the Landscaping a lot. I don't remember anything about this, though. We used to pass the Landscaping every day on the way to school then home again. It was the green slope at the back of the houses where they kept what was left of the original wasteground they built the two estates on. Presumably there was some planning prohibition and that was why they couldn't cover the whole thing with houses; instead, they pulled up the trees and grassed over the stubby bushes all the way to the new car park. The Landscaping was quite steep, if I remember rightly.

A boy was pushing people off it? I say.

Just me, she says. He only pushed me off. Nobody else. There were loads of us.

And you were up on top of the Landscaping because? I say.

Because of the new snow, she says.

Let me get this right, I say. He pushed –

It was slippy, she says.

She covers her face. She's smiling under her hands, still sitting at the table with the cold coffee in front of her, swinging her leg underneath the table just above the bar of it. I realize I don't know whether she's smiling because a boy pushed her down a hill, because a girl picked her up at the bottom of it or because an art teacher I know she's got a crush on asked her to take off her clothes.

Then I realize it's because of all three. I remember my hands in the warm pockets of the adult coat. I realize that my fourteen-year-old-self will be fine, she's absolutely fine, and more, she's in my bones.

It moves me. She can see this on my face and she gets annoyed again. Her smile disappears. She scowls.

Written is so much better than writ, she says.

It might be better but it isn't what it actually says on the gravestone, I say.

Weirdo, she says.

Don't be rude, I say.

From weirdoland, she says almost under her breath.

She gives me the quick look and then, with perfect timing, the artful look away. Completely night now out beyond my house and only six o' clock in the evening. All the streetlights are on. All the cars in the city beyond are nosing their ways home or their ways away from home, making the noise traffic makes in the distance. Closer to home, out on the unlit common, under a sky that promises frost, someone invisible to us is rattling across one of the nearby paths on a bike, shouting and shouting. I love you, he shouts, or she shouts, hard to tell which, and then calls out what sounds like a name in the dark, shouted into the starry air above all the thousands of old dead, and then the words I love you again, and then again the name.

My fourteen-year-old self looks towards the window and so do I.

You hear that? we both say at once.

Breaking the Pig

Etgar Keret

Translated from the Hebrew by Miriam Shlesinger

Dad wouldn't buy me a Bart Simpson doll. Mom really wanted to, but Dad wouldn't, he said I was spoiled.

'Why should we?' he said to Mom. 'Why should we buy it for him? He just snaps his fingers and you jump to attention.' Dad said I had no respect for money and that if I didn't learn when I was little when was I going to learn? Kids who get Bart Simpson dolls at the drop of a hat turn into punks who steal from convenience stores, cause they wind up thinking they can have whatever they want, just like that. So instead of a Bart doll he bought me an ugly porcelain pig with a slot in its back, and now I'll grow up to be okay, now I won't turn into a punk.

Every morning now I'm supposed to drink a cup of hot cocoa, even though I hate it. With the skin it's one shekel, without the skin it's half a shekel, and if I throw up right after I drink it, I don't get anything. I drop the coins into the slot in the pig's back, and then, when you shake him you can hear them jingle. Soon as the pig is so full of coins that it doesn't jingle when you shake it, I get a Bart-Simpson-on-a-skateboard doll. That's what Dad says, that way it's educational.

The pig is kind of cute actually, his nose is cool when you touch it, he smiles when you drop the shekel in his back, and even when you only drop in half a shekel. But the nicest thing is how he smiles even when you don't. I made up a name for him too. I call him Margolis, same as the man who used to live in our mailbox and my dad couldn't get the sticker off. Margolis isn't like my other toys. He's much more easygoing, without bulbs or springs or batteries that leak inside. You just have to make sure he doesn't jump off the table.

'Margolis, be careful! You're made of porcelain,' I remind him when I spot him bending over a little and looking down at the floor, and he smiles at me and waits patiently for me to take him down myself. I really love it when he smiles, and I drink the hot cocoa with the skin every morning just for him, so I can drop the shekel in his back and watch how his smile doesn't change at all.

'I love you, Margolis,' I tell him then. 'Honest, I love you more than Mom and Dad. And I'll always love you, no matter what, even if you become a punk. But don't you dare go jumping off the table!'

Yesterday, Dad came in, picked Margolis up off the table and started shaking him upside down real hard.

'Be careful, Dad,' I told him. 'You're giving Margolis a tummy ache.' But Dad didn't stop.

'It isn't making any noise. You know what that means, don't you, Davie? That tomorrow you're going to get that Bart-Simpson-on-a-skateboard doll.'

'Great, Dad,' I said. 'A Bart-Simpson-on-a-skateboard doll, that's great. Just please stop shaking Margolis, before he starts feeling sick.' Dad put Margolis down and went to get Mom. He came back a minute later, pulling Mom behind him with one hand and holding a hammer in the other.

'You see I was right,' he said to Mom. 'This way he'll know how to appreciate things, won't you, Davie?'

'Sure I will,' I said. 'Sure I will, but what's the hammer for?'

'It's for you,' Dad said and put the hammer in my hand. 'Just be careful.'

'Sure I'll be careful,' I said, and I really was, but a few minutes later, Dad lost his patience and he said, 'So come on. Break the pig already.'

'What?' I asked. 'Break Margolis?'

'Yes, yes, Margolis,' Dad said. 'Come on, break it. You earned your Bart Simpson, you worked hard enough for it.'

Margolis gave me the sad smile of a porcelain pig who knows his end is near. The hell with Bart Simpson. Me – hit a friend on the head with a hammer?

'I don't want Simpson,' I said and handed the hammer back to Dad. 'Margolis is good enough for me.'

'You don't get it,' Dad said. 'It's really alright, it's educational. Come on, let me break it for you.' Dad raised the hammer and I caught the tired look in Mom's eyes and the broken smile on Margolis's face, and knew it was all up to me now. Unless I did something, he was dead.

'Dad,' I said, grabbing him by the leg.

'What is it, Davie?' Dad said, still holding the hammer high in the air. 'Could I have one more shekel, please?' I begged. 'Please give me one more shekel to drop into Margolis, tomorrow, after my hot cocoa. Then I'll break him, tomorrow, I promise.'

'One more shekel?' Dad smiled and put the hammer down on the table. 'You see? The boy has developed an awareness.'

'Yes, an awareness,' I said. 'Tomorrow.' There were tears in my throat.

Soon as they left the room, I gave Margolis an extra-tight hug and let the tears pour out. Margolis didn't say a thing, he just trembled quietly in my hands. 'Don't worry,' I whispered in his ear. 'I'll save you.'

That night I waited for Dad to finish watching TV in the living room and go to bed. Then I got up very very quietly and sneaked out through the balcony, with Margolis. We walked together in the dark for a very long time till we reached a field of thornbushes.

'Pigs love fields,' I told Margolis as I put him down on the floor of the field, 'especially fields with thornbushes. You'll like it here.' I waited for his answer, but Margolis didn't say a thing, and when I touched him on the nose to say goodbye he just gave me a sad look. He knew he'd never see me again.

Clowns in Clover

Nadine Gordimer

Most women have a parting shot, the eternal revival of a past injustice which they use ruthlessly and indiscriminately, to end all arguments.

My mother's was our Uncle Chookie. No matter how wrong she was (and being daily indoctrinated by her in the absolute rightness of everything she said and did, we children, Barbara, Bernard and Katie, never dreamt of thinking she was wrong) she put herself in the right at the end of the argument by flinging at my father:

'And in ten years you never thought to send my poor brother a ten-shilling postal order!'

There, of course, she *was* right. He never had. And so, whatever the matter of the argument, we saw from my father's inability to counter the fact of this one neglect that he was wrong, wrong again, and my mother the injured.

The silence of the end of the argument hung in the air like steam in the street after a summer rainstorm. The silence of Uncle Chookie, produced in all its unfailing power. For of course we knew it was of Uncle Chookie whom my mother spoke, although she never mentioned him by name, and she had two other brothers. Uncle Chookie's real name was Bernard, like my brother's, but I suppose the childish appellation had been given him when he was a baby, as such names are given to so many, pending the time he should grow up into the other. He is about forty in my memory, so that must have been about the age he was when we began to notice him first, but because we had never known him any younger, or by any other name, there seemed to us nothing incongruous about knowing as 'Uncle Chookie' this tall, already grey-haired man, bent – like our tall hollyhocks, not of their own volition, but after hard rain – and with long hands that touched everything, even your own when you greeted him, uncertainly, and did not smell, as our father's did, of tobacco and newsprint and petrol, but of soap, like a woman's. Uncle Chookie had large grey eyes – mournful eyes we called them, like my mother's and mine, and round them a recess of shadowed skin. But that was as far as the family likeness went; he was loose-boned, where she was small and neat, he was slow of movement where she was quick, and above all, he was silent; my mother had a high clear voice and talked all the time.

When he was in our house on his yearly visit he seemed like a shadow of my mother; a silent creature, looking out of her eyes, sitting where she sat, following her quietly from room to room.

He came to spend a fortnight with us in Johannesburg every year, and in between we rarely saw him, though once a month or so my mother would bake a cake the night before, put out her things for an early start in the morning, and say – to our maid, or an aunt, on the telephone – 'I'm going to poor Chookie tomorrow, you know. I feel I must, though it's such a drag – ' Then before we left for school in the morning she would be gone to catch an early train to the Northern Transvaal town where Uncle Chookie lived; rather poorly, we gathered, but decently enough: 'Of course, he's got his own room,' we had overheard her telling someone once, 'a few of his own things and a spirit stove for tea and so on, and there's another man next door, a schoolteacher he was, I believe, also very nice, poor thing, and Chookie shares a bit of cake with him, and if *he* gets anything he always takes some in to Chookie...'

We children looked forward to Uncle Chookie's fortnight; though once it came, there was little to distinguish it from any other fortnight: it merely had its place in the marking-off of the year into birthdays, Christmas, school- and holiday-time. It helped, along with the other events, in the gradual relating of the timelessness of childhood to the rigidly time-conscious adult world. Once really with us, Uncle Chookie was scarcely there. He liked to stand in windows, coat peaked out at the back because of his stooping shoulders, watching. If we came past, chasing one another in some game, he appeared to be watching us. If we were not there, he might be watching the birds on the lawn, or the clouds. He ran his hand stiffly over the spine of the cat; at meals he hardly spoke. And my mother

did not make any plans while he was with us. 'I won't be going anywhere much just now, while I've got Chookie with me, you know,'
she would apologize, on the telephone. Then she would come into
the room where he stood, and, her head consideringly on the side –
the way she would come into a room and ask you what you fancied,
when you were sick in bed – say to him: 'I think I'll get the man to
fillet us a couple of nice soles, shall I? They would be nice for lunch.
Would you like them fried, or would you rather I did them with a
white sauce?'

He would sigh, and stare back at her with that anxious, affronted
look that came to his face whenever he was spoken to, as if being
addressed was a burden on him, a responsibility he didn't feel he
could take. 'I don't mind, Babs. Fried will do for me. With a bit of
lemon… I don't mind. Fried or boiled. I don't mind how I take it.'

And they would stand held in the anxiousness of each other's eyes
for a moment (you almost expected to see them sway, their eyes
were so dark and big and fascinated), before my mother murmured
heavily, 'Right then… Right…' and went off to the kitchen.

The only time Uncle Chookie ever really made the fortnight his
own was when he sang for us. My mother – who, difficult though it is
to believe now, must have been a young woman still, and interested
in such things – had mastered a kind of hop and thump in the bass
that was known at the time as 'syncopation'. On top of the highly-
polished upright on which my brother Bernard and I practised 'Für
Elise' there was an untidy pile of popular music – albums of songs
from the Hollywood musicals that came so thick and splendid in the
thirties, 'selections' from London and Broadway successes. We liked
to stand round her after supper, following the curious hobbling-out
of the tunes with much thin volume but little 'voice', my elder sister
Katie, at fifteen, managed quite sweetly on the lower notes, but disappeared entirely out of normal hearing range, perhaps into that
supra-human register which dogs are said to be able to hear, on the
higher ones.

Yet my mother's brother was attracted by this gathering round the
piano. He would be drawn to it, rather than consciously join us of
his own free will; one moment he would be sitting in his chair, the
next we would feel his coat-sleeves, smell his linen-cupboard odour,

among us. And he would start to sing, and we would slowly stop. He sang on alone, in a slightly husky, mellow voice, and when one song was finished he went on to another. My mother turned the pages and changed the tune without speaking or moving her head; as if she were partaking in a spell. We fell back, literally. First our voices went, and then we ourselves, perching on the arms of chairs or lying down to listen from the old moulting kaross. Uncle Chookie, who apparently could bear to speak only under cover of the conversation of others, and who fell instantly silent, died out in the middle of a sentence, in fact, if he heard his own voice speaking out loud, he would sing on for half an hour in the centre of everyone's absolute silence and attention. He, who looked at everything from a bus ticket to a fork as if it presented some menacing challenge to him, glanced along the music sheet now and then to verify a coming note, or a word of the lyric, as if the printed sheet were to him, as it would be to everyone else, merely a piece of paper. He was casual. Standing up singing alone in an attentive room, he met our eyes.

I remember particularly a song from an old English revue called 'Clowns in Clover'; you could be sure that if he had not joined us at the piano before, he would do so when we reached the point in the 'selection' when this song began. We children would waver through the 'chorus' numbers, the novelty number, and what was, I think, a kind of tango, and then, with the first notes, his voice would be there:

I've got those Little Boy Blues…
My heart's right down in my shoes…
Just for that little boy who's
For-getting me…

I realize now that this must have been a curiously inappropriate song to be sung by Uncle Chookie: so obviously meant for a Gertrude Lawrence or a Mary Martin. Yet we did not find it in the least incongruous; so I am sure that, for some equally curious reason, it wasn't. We should have been amazed too, if anyone had found it funny. It couldn't have been that either. Children are usually right about these things. Now, of course, I find the contrast between Uncle Chookie and his song ironic; but if children have any sort of innocence in the mind left them by the time they are twelve, it is innocence of irony, so we could not have been expected to notice that.

❧

It happened when the McKechnies moved away from the house two doors up. We children hung about watching the new people move in. I saw two boys about Bernard's age, with ears like the handles of pitchers, and then rather a strange-looking little girl, younger than I, with a thick neck and a babyish bow in her hair, who called out to me something that I didn't seem to hear properly, because I couldn't understand what it was that she said.

Bernard was not slow in getting to know people. Later in the same afternoon, he came back from playing with the two new boys.

'What's the matter with the sister?' I said. 'She said something to me that I didn't hear, and then she slammed the door.'

'She's loony,' said Bernard, with relish. He rolled his eyes, clutched the front of his hair, and lolled his tongue out.

'You know you're not allowed to use that word,' said Kate, looking at him with her customary disgust.

'Her brothers told me she's loony,' said Bernard indignantly. 'You know what? In their old house, she tore the pages out of the telephone book and stuffed them in the lavatory. You should just hear her – she makes the most awful noises – like an ole cat.' He gave a demonstration, brushing aside Katie's protests with: I'm loony, o-oh, I'm loony, I can't help it, I tell you, I'm loony...'

He and I fell upon one another, shrieking; I lay laughing, but he was too delighted with the idea of pretending to be mad – he kept his tongue lolling out at Katie.

'Just you let mother see you carrying on like that,' said Katie. 'Just you let her see you making fun of that kid.'

'Look, my tongue's got all dry – feel it,' – in his interest, Bernard forgot to be mad. When his tongue was comfortably moistened again, he said. 'They'll have to send her to a loony-bin when she's grown up.'

'*Bernard!*'

'Frightened of your mommy, what will mommy say?' mimicked Bernard.

Katie got the look on her face of having something behind her back that she didn't want to show anyone. 'You know it's not that. You'll just hurt her feelings that's all.' She sat there looking at us.

'Why?' I asked, suddenly feeling awkward.

'Because,' she said.

'She'd just say it was unkind to talk that way, that's all,' I offered.

Katie shook her head. A hangnail on her thumb caught on the silk of her dress, and she lifted her thumb and bit at it with fierce concentration for a second or two. 'You know why. Because of Uncle Chookie. Uncle Chookie's in one.'

Bernard shot her a fast, aghast, derisive look. '*He's not!*'

'Oh yes he is,' she said conversationally. 'A mental hospital. Where d'you think he is, all the time, and why don't we ever go to see him?'

'But he's not mad,' I said, looking from Katie to Bernard, seeing him as he had been a minute before, with his tongue hanging out and his eyes rolling. 'Uncle Chookie's not mad?'

Katie shrugged. She put her smarting thumb to the warmth of her neck and looked at us both with a kind of ashamed satisfaction at the sight of her handiwork.

I spent a great deal of time trying to find out if it was true. I did everything but ask. That was impossible. Impossible, too, to speak about it to Bernard, who must be as bewildered as I, or to Katie, who had accepted it and was apparently calmly going on with her life. It was true, of course, that my mother did not allow us to talk of 'loonies'; but then we were not allowed, either, to call black people 'niggers' or 'Kaffirs', nor could we be overheard referring to someone who squinted as 'boss-eyed'. So how was one to tell?

I went along the road many times to stare, fascinated, at the thick-necked child in the garden two doors away, grunting in the dust where she wandered all day long, shut out of the house like some small noisome animal. I watched her brothers when they came to play at our house with Bernard. I listened to my mother, chattering to the native servant girl above the thick sound of batter being beaten in the kitchen.

I went into the bedroom I shared with Katie and looked at my eyes in the mirror. My mother's eyes.

His eyes.

And when the voices of the others came out, very jolly round the piano in the evening – … heart's right down in my shoes… / Just for that little boy who's, / For-getting me… – I dropped out of their circle, their jollity, and went off to my room, where I lay on my bed, eyes open in the dark, still hearing it.

One afternoon when I had finished practising I took 'Clowns in Clover' out of the pile of music on the piano and hid it in an old box of my father's technical books.

I never really found out. Gradually, as I grew older my mother began to talk as if it was accepted that I knew that Uncle Chookie was in a mental hospital – as, I suppose, she had begun to talk before Katie, when Katie was my age. And no doubt she expected that, like Katie, I should accept it simply as a piece of rather sad information. She never noticed the cold blankness with which I came to meet the mention of his name; she never once sensed the hostility I felt – towards Uncle Chookie, for linking me inescapably with a world of horror and confusion that I half-sensed, half-imagined out of my fear? – towards my mother, until now my shield against all that was painful, for exposing me to this ugly awareness by having him for a brother? – towards myself, for carrying in my veins the blood of this gentle, kindly creature?

As we children grew up, the yearly visits were dropped. It may have been because my mother's brother, like a prisoner who learns to prefer the safety of prison to the bewilderment of the world outside, no longer wished to come, or maybe my mother felt that with Katie a young lady and suitors about, his presence might be an embarrassment. I remember what must have been the last time he came, though; and the last time I saw him. Immediately I had heard he was expected for the usual fortnight I had announced casually that I would be spending that particular time with a friend with whom I often exchanged visits; I was at the age when girls have violently secretive friendships. But unfortunately he arrived a little earlier than he had been expected, and I had to meet him, after all. At the top of the stairs, in fact, just as I was coming down with my suitcase and my tennis racket in its initialled drawstring cover.

I had thought about him such a great deal and had not seen him for such a long time that the sight of him, like opening one's eyes into the plain calm daylight of a room that has just been swollen and twisted as the *mise-en-scène of* a nightmare, shocked me into anti-climax. I stood there at the top of our stairs and he stood a few steps below, holding an umbrella and a neat shabby portmanteau that accentuated the curve of his stoop. Each held back, waiting for the other to get out of the way first, like two nervous animals who do not recognize the scent of the other. He was afraid, always afraid, and perhaps for him it was merely a confirmation of what he *knew* to find that someone else, one of the others, outside of what he knew, was afraid too. We met on his ground that day. Looking at him, a greying, never-old, never-young man, guilt inflamed through all my veins, as adrenaline comes with anger. But all that I had wound about him came up to obscure me from shame; guilt hardened into hostility and revulsion. Without a word, I bolted past him down the stairs.

In the fifteen years since, I have never had a chance to say that word, smile that smile. He died years ago, out of sight, as he had lived.

But the other day when I turned on the radio I heard the song, the song from 'Clowns in Clover'. And I found myself remembering with real pleasure that slightly husky, mellow voice; the voice of Uncle Chookie.

So perhaps I have made it all right, if such things are possible between this world and the next, between him and me.

The Submarine

Uri Orlev

Translated from the Hebrew by Leanne Raday

'Are you asleep?' asked the little boy.

His older brother turned over in the next bed.

'No,' he answered.

The moon had not yet risen. The two children knew from experience that it rose later and later every night. The room was cloaked in darkness. The two beds were close to the wall, facing each other, a square table separating them. The table was placed underneath the window, its surface touching the edge of the windowsill, and on it were an unlit oil lamp and a box of matches. The little matchbox was completely hidden, but the two children knew exactly where it was. The lamp, on the other hand, was visible against the background of the night outside, because the darkness outside was a little lighter than the darkness inside the room.

Suddenly, a siren sounded. Both children sat up in bed and listened. The doors in the apartment house all opened, and the residents of the eight-storey building started walking down the stairs.

'Going to the shelter,' the older child said.

The commotion of the people walking down the squeaky old wooden steps was joined by the distant hum of the aeroplanes and the booming machine guns. The older child got out of bed, sat down on the table and looked up into the sky.

'Come on already, get up, the spotlights are on!'

Long strips of light appeared in the darkness – the German searchlights were scanning the sky in search of Russian aeroplanes.

The little one got up and sat on the table. Well, he didn't actually sit on the table, but on the deck of the submarine. The two children would pad the floorboards underneath the table with blankets, take their oil lamp and light a small flame in it, then dive down into the depths of the sea on their submarine and float up every so often, climbing on deck to look out across Warsaw's sea of roofs.

'Why are they bombing us?' asked the little one.

'Because the Germans are here,' the older one explained.

'And can they tell the difference?'

'No, they can't tell the difference. Or maybe they can. Maybe they look for certain signs...' Yurek stopped talking because he heard someone running up the stairs.

'Christina,' guessed the little one. 'She is coming to take us. Let's get dressed.'

'No, we're not going down,' Yurek said decisively. 'They'll spot us straight away.'

Miss Christina jiggled the handle of the door in three series of three – the signal they'd always had. The older boy opened the lock immediately, since he'd been waiting behind the door.

'Children, get dressed and come quickly,' said Christina as she came in. 'You can't stay here on the roof. Come down to the shelter.'

'Christina, we can't. The neighbours will know.'

'No,' Christina replied, 'I'll say I found you on the street...'

'No, we're not coming down,' said the older one determinedly.

'But...' Christina hesitated. The buzzing of the aeroplanes was drawing nearer and they could already hear the bombs whistling, and the explosions, too.

Christina crossed herself and kissed them both. 'May the Virgin Mary watch over you.'

She left and the older boy locked the door behind her. The two children listened to the sound of her steps as she ran down the stairs and crossed the yard. Then they climbed back on deck to look at the spectacle of lights. In the background, the blasts of the explosions kept coming closer and closer, along with the clatter of the machine guns and the roar of the German defence canons, which were now trying to shoot down the Russian planes.

'Please God, don't let them hurt anyone,' Yurek pleaded.

Suddenly, the two boys squatted down, jumped off the deck and hid underneath the table. A bomb exploded very close by and the shock wave shook their little room. Pieces of plaster fell off the ceiling and a picture of one of the saints fell down on the floor.

'Mum's watching over us,' said the little one.

Little by little, a hush came over the city, until the all-clear was finally sounded. Yurek, as Captain, brought the submarine back up to the surface of the sea and both of them climbed back on deck. They listened to the sound of neighbours going back into their houses, climbing lazily up the stairs. Someone was talking about a bomb that fell close by and hit the next-door building. Another person talked about the Russians:

'Maybe they'll finally defeat the Germans and free us,' he said.

A conversation about the uprising of the Jews in the ghetto started.

'I hope,' someone said, 'that the Germans manage to solve our Jew problem before the Russians come.'

'Yes,' said another. 'They're burning them, burning those vermin over there.'

'It's such a pity about the children,' commented one lady.

'A little Jew turns into a big Jew,' said another man.

'You're a Christian, how could you say such a thing?' the woman asked angrily.

Then the doors were shut and everything was silent again.

The two children climbed down from the deck of the submarine, went back to their beds and tucked themselves in. Some time passed. Then Yurek spoke.

'Kazik, do you feel like talking?'

'Aren't we going to sleep yet?' asked the little one.

'Not yet. Let's talk a little.'

'Okay,' said Kazik, 'but I'll go first today.'

'Okay, so tell me what you're doing right now.'

'Where?' asked the little one.

'Don't be stupid. I know you're lying in bed right now, but what are *you* doing – your army, or you and your generals.'

Silence.

'If you haven't got anything to say, then I'll talk.'

'No, I'll say something,' said the little one. 'We have a little house…'

'Where?'

'In the snow,' a hesitant reply came out from the darkness.

'That snow has to be somewhere,' said Yurek insistently.

'We're sitting around a table, starting a resistance movement,' said the little one, trying to defend his honour.

'Do you have electricity?' asked Yurek.

'No, just candles.'

'And where are my generals and me?' asked Yurek.

'You're not my brother yet,' replied the little one.

'So what am I?'

'I don't know. I didn't know you yet.'

'You see!' the older one said in delight. 'I knew you had nothing to say. You always start and get me all worked up and then you don't know how to continue. Now I'll talk.'

Nothing happened for a while. The little brother was silent. Yurek was afraid that his little brother was fed up of the talking game. 'Are you asleep?' he asked worriedly.

'No,' came the answer. 'But don't scare me today.'

'Okay,' said Yurek.

He got out of bed, wrapped himself up in a white sheet and started dancing around the room. His little brother managed to make out the strange white figure that kept growing bigger and smaller while the floorboards squeaked.

'What are you doing?' asked Kazik worriedly.

'IT'S THE TERRRIBLE MONKEY WHO IS MY SERRRRVANT...!'

'So why do you keep falling over?'

'Oh, you're so stupid! You always ruin things with your questions. You have to talk to me as if I was the monkey!'

Silence.

'Are you in bed again?'

'Yes, it's impossible to play with you.'

Kazik changed his mind.

'Yurek?'

'What is it?'

'I won't spoil it anymore.'

'Okay, listen then.'

Yurek felt his way to the matches and started shaking the box rhythmically.

'Kazik, do you hear? Those are my troops. They're marching now. They're walking into my bed. Look at how the blanket's puffing up!'

'Do they have tanks?'

'Yes, but they left them in their camp.'

'And horses?'

'They left them in their camp, too.'

'Do they live in the camp?'

'Yes, and I can call them whenever I like.'

Kazik thought for a moment and then asked, 'So why don't they come save us from the Germans?'

'You're spoiling it again!' exclaimed Yurek angrily.

'I'm not. I was just asking! Dad could've saved us. He had a sword.'

'Mum could've too,' said Yurek. 'Mum was smart.'

'But Dad was an officer and he could have made the white horse all better,' said Kazik. 'The horse that belonged to the soldiers.'

'Dad cures people,' said Yurek.

'But he can cure horses too!'

'No he can't!'

'Yes he can!'

'Can't!'

'Can!'

'Can't!'

'Can't!' said the little one by mistake.

Yurek burst out laughing.

'You should have said "can", stupid!'

'You're stupid!'

The talking game was over. They both lay quietly and listened to the noises in the courtyard of the building. The windows of the apartment house – and the same went for the whole city – were blacked out because of the war between the Germans and the Russians. But not all the windows were shut, so the sound of a conversation, of someone's laughter, of a baby crying or of a man shouting could be heard from time to time. The children got used to hearing these noises, especially at night when the street was empty and very still on account of the curfew the Germans imposed on the Polish neighbourhoods.

'Yurek, are you asleep?' Kazik suddenly asked nervously.

'No, what is it?'

'I'm afraid of witches,' whispered the little one.

'There are no witches, I keep telling you that,' Yurek said, trying to soothe his brother, but he wasn't absolutely sure of it himself.

'Yes there are! They… they… they…'

'I can't hear what you're whispering over there, speak up!'

'But the neighbours… they'll hear and tell on us…'

'Don't worry,' Yurek said confidently.

'I need to pee,' said the little one, 'and I can't find the pot.'

'Have you looked for it already?'

'Yes. I want you to give it to me.'

'I can't.'

'But you said there aren't any spies and witches,' whispered the little one.

'Not because of that. Look again. Feel around under the bed.'

Kazik gathered up all his courage and moved his hand underneath the bed until it finally bumped into the enamel chamber pot.

'I found it!' he said proudly.

Yurek listened jealously.

'I need to go too. Push it over to me.'

'I'm afraid to put my hand so far out.'

'I'll give you… my Last Mohican General tomorrow.'

'All right, but be sure you remember that promise,' said the little one. 'I don't want you to go back on it tomorrow.' He closed his eyes and moved the chamber pot as far towards his older brother's bed as he could. 'And don't forget – you have to give me General Last Mohican!'

'All right, all right!' said Yurek, already starting to regret their pact. 'I heard you already.'

Yurek placed the pot under his bed and tucked himself in. He listened to the sound of his brother's breathing to try to tell if he was already asleep. Suddenly, he heard strange squeaking noises in the room.

'Kazik, are you the one squeaking on the floor like that?' he asked in a whisper.

'No,' said the little one in alarm.

'So what is that sound? Maybe someone got in?'

The squeaking stopped and then started over again, a little further away.

'It's mice... isn't it just mice?' whispered the little one anxiously.

'Come sleep in my bed,' whispered the older one.

'But I'm too scared to move over.'

'I'll give you Captain Nemo too.'

'Only if you light a match,' said Kazik.

Yurek groped around for the matches. A little flame gleamed in the darkness. Kazik leapt over to his brother's bed in one jump. Yurek moved against the wall to make room for him and gave him part of the blanket.

Now, they both fell asleep.

❧

In the daylight, everything looked different. The room was flooded with sunlight. It was spring outside and the sky was blue. Miss Christina had already brought their breakfast in – fresh buns and milk. She had carried it to them in a bucket, hidden underneath wet laundry. She'd also brought them a little flowering branch of lilac and had stood it in a jar with water. The boys sat facing each other across the table, each sitting on his bed, eating breakfast. Christina had gone out to the stairway and climbed up to the attic to hang the laundry. By the time the children had finished eating, she had also finished her hanging. She returned to collect the dishes. She put everything inside her bucket and covered it with a towel.

'We've finished reading,' said Yurek. 'Can you bring us some new books?'

'Not today,' said Christina, 'you read so quickly... By the way, they were asking about the mythology book in the library.'

'I'm reading it to Kazik little by little.'

'That's very nice of you.'

It was always a day of celebration for the two boys when Christina went to the library to take out new books for them. The children would smooth their hands over the cover, open each book very slowly and smell it; they would hide part of the title, then try and guess the rest, check if there were any pictures and see how many pages there were. There was only one problem – Kazik read very slowly and Yurek, once he had finished his own book, would pester his brother to finish his and would get very irritated when he had to wait. The books weren't only about reading; they were also an endless source of heroes that each boy could choose for his army.

Yurek and Kazik were two countries. They had armies, governments, heroes and generals. They'd play with either small lead soldiers or with soldiers Yurek would cut out of cardboard, glue together and colour with the crayons that Christina had brought him. When they didn't have these sorts of soldiers, they'd play with anything they could put their hands on – anything that could stand by itself on the floor and be knocked over with a 'shooting coin'. They'd indicate the generals, the heroes and themselves. Yurek was Tarzan, Commander of the World. His brother was his brother in times of peace and his enemy in times of war. Yurek read more, so he had many more heroes in his army. For example, he had General Napoleon, General Nelson, General Stalin, General Gordon, General Captain Nemo and General Socrates. He even had dibs on General Moses, whom he took from a story that his grandma had told them before she was caught. But his brother called dibs on Robin Hood when their mother was still alive and told them that story back in the ghetto. Kazik had suddenly jumped up and called dibs before it even occurred to Yurek. Since then, Yurek had been trying to convince his little brother to sell Robin Hood or swap him for almost anything, but Kazik always refused. Kazik also tried to call dibs on generals from the Greek mythology book that Christina had taken out for them – he tried to add gods to his army, but Yurek teased him about it, so he gave up the idea.

Before leaving, Miss Christina reached up to the shelf for the jar with the lilac and held it near their faces.

'Smell,' she told them, 'and you'll be able to feel spring coming in from outside.'

They smelled obediently.

'Good smell!' said Kazik.

'Good smell!' agreed Yurek.

She put the jar back in place.

'Now, wash up quickly,' she told them. 'Tadek needs to go into town today.'

Tadek, her brother, would come upstairs every morning to empty their bucket after they washed. He'd cover the bucket with dry clothes, to make it seem as though he had just taken the laundry off the line in the attic. Christina, Tadek and their mother owned a launderette that was located in the basement of the building.

Yurek washed first. He went behind the curtain separating the washing corner from the rest of the room. There was a bowl placed on a stool there and an enamel jug filled with water. Yurek poured some water into the bowl and quickly washed his face and hands. He washed his mouth but was too lazy to brush his teeth, and he didn't feel like putting the bowl on the floor so that he could really bathe himself.

'Are you finished already?' asked the little one suspiciously.

'Yes. I'll set up the game while you wash.'

'Don't cheat. Fair shares!'

'Don't worry!' Yurek reassured his brother, whose concern was quite justified. 'When you finish washing up,' he added, 'pour the water from the bowl and the pot into the bucket, so that everything will be ready for Tadek and he won't get cross.'

'You pour it!' said the little one irritably. 'Why does it always have to be me?'

'Because you always wash after me.'

'Okay,' said Kazik, 'then tomorrow I'll wash first. And don't forget the two generals you gave me last night!'

Yurek didn't answer. He kneeled down on the floor and organized the game. He placed the soldiers on both sides of the floor, protected by domino pieces and blocks, and built a fortress on each side of the room. He made them from blocks, tin and cardboard boxes, and overturned cups. Bottles turned into towers and brushes became forests where soldiers could hide between the stiff trees. Finally, a few pieces of soap were transformed into houses.

The door handle was jiggled in three series of three. Yurek twisted open the lock. Tadek came in and saw that everything was ready for the battle. He took the bucket, smiled at them and said, 'Don't make any noise now, remember?'

'Yes,' the two boys answered in unison.

Tadek went out. Yurek locked the door behind him, and the game began.

Each boy could move all of his soldiers across the wooden floor up to the length of a pencil. Each had three 'canon shots' – heavy coins – and three 'gunshots' – small coins – when their turn came. They'd shoot the coins off between their finger and thumb.

Yurek placed a book on the floor, chose the heaviest coin in his stock of shells and blasted it off towards his brother's fortress. The coin hit the block wall and the blocks scattered around, hitting noisily against the wooden floorboards.

'I've wrecked your wall!' Yurik exclaimed.

'Never mind,' said the little one.

'Now the guns,' said Yurek, and he shot three little coins, one after the other, towards a small group of his brother's soldiers.

'I killed Robin Hood!' cried Yurek in delight.

'No you didn't! He wasn't there.'

'Liar, you said the one inside the hat was Robin Hood!'

'Did not!'

'I'm not playing with you,' said the older brother, 'you keep changing the names around to keep everyone alive – that's not allowed!'

'No I don't,' said Kazik. 'It's my turn now.' He held up one of his soldiers and said, 'Ironhand is charging forward on his horse!'

'He doesn't have a horse,' said Yurek scornfully.

'He does – you can't tell me what to say. Now it's my turn to shoot.'

Kazik shot three little coins at his brother's troops and cried out with joy, 'I killed your General Gordon!'

'Dream on, the one you hit is just a soldier.'

'And that one in the corner also fell over, and the third one and the one behind the post!'

'But none of them are important. Now it's my turn. My soldiers are surrounding Ironhand. Surrender!'

'Ironhand will never surrender!' replied Kazik proudly.

'Give him to me – I'm taking him captive!'

'You'll have to find him first, he's gone into hiding!'

Yurek charged his brother, twisted his hand and pulled Ironhand out of his brother's clenched fist. Kazik was almost in tears.

'Give him back!'

'No, he's a prisoner of war!'

'Give him back, you pig, give him...'

Yurek ignored his brother's whining.

'My soldiers are leading him to me – on your knees, you coward...!' he said, raising his voice.

'He's not a coward!' said Yurek, gritting his teeth.

'Beg for your life before Tarzan, the Commander of the World!' cried Yurek.

'He won't beg. He's not afraid of you!'

'They force him to the floor, and I get up and slap him right across the face,' said Yurek, and he slapped his brother.

'Ouch! Why did you hit me?'

'Well, I can't hit a little piece of wood, can I?'

'So just say it!'

Kazik got really angry and pounced on his brother, trying to take Ironhand back by force. Yurek pushed him and the two children began fighting.

'You can't have him!' grunted Yurek. 'He's a prisoner of war. Let go! You'll be sorry!'

'Give him back!' cried the little one. 'I'm telling you... give... give him back...'

'Idiot, cry more quietly, the neighbours will hear!' said the older one and added: 'All right, I'll give him to you, but you have to agree that I execute him honourably, and then we'll play a new game.'

'Okay,' said the little one calming down, 'I agree.'

Yurek quickly built a wall of blocks.

Kazik hid the little soldier behind his back. 'I'll make him ready myself,' he said.

'All right,' replied Yurek.

'All my soldiers and officers are present,' said Yurek triumphantly while gathering his soldiers around. 'General Napoleon will be the shooting squad and I...' Yurek became silent. He heard the sound of marching soldiers from far away.

'Germans!' said the little one enthusiastically. 'Come see!'

'Don't you dare go to the window!' Yurek told him in a harsh tone.

A company of German soldiers was marching down the street. They were still quite distant, but the sound of their rhythmic steps could already be heard quite clearly, and when they passed by the building where the children were hiding, they started singing a cheerful marching song. Both children stood and listened.

'It's nice how they sing,' said Kazik.

'You shouldn't say it's nice,' said Yurek.

'Why?'

'Because they're Germans.'

'So their singing isn't nice?' asked Kazik in surprise.

'No. Maybe it is, but you can't say it is.'

'Why?'

'Because.'

The company of soldiers moved on, and there was no longer anything special about the street. Yurek returned to the game and declared authoritatively, 'I'm blindfolding Ironhand's eyes.'

'No need. Ironhand fears nothing.'

'What is your last wish?'

'That you send this letter to my wife.'

Yurek burst out laughing. 'You have a wife?'

'Now look who's spoiling things! Stop asking questions!'

'All right, all right... My soldiers are raising their guns. And General Napoleon is raising his sword to give the order to fire.'

'Wait, what about the drums?' asked the little one.

'The drums are pounding...'

'For liberty! For the homeland!' declared the little one.

Suddenly, the two boys could hear the sound of heavy steps coming up the stairs. They froze. They'd learned to recognize their neighbours by the sound of their steps and their voices. There was the lady with the quick steps and the high-pitched voice, and the drunkard who sang and cursed at night. But the steps now were unfamiliar. They'd never heard them before, and the steps kept coming up and up until they reached the floor beneath theirs.

'Maybe he's going to see the neighbour downstairs?' said Kazik hopefully.

But the stranger continued walking up until he stopped outside the door to their room. He jiggled the handle in three series of three.

'We've been given away,' said Yurek. He walked up to the door, hesitated for a moment and then unlocked it. A tall stranger wearing a long coat, a stiff hat and a fancy walking stick in his hand was standing in the doorway.

'Hello children,' he said, and he walked in, crossing the tiny room with only a couple of steps and sitting down on Kazik's bed. The children were so scared that they didn't notice the stranger had been careful not to step on their soldiers. He placed his hat and walking stick on the table and turned round to Kazik.

'You... not you... I mean the little one, come here. Stand facing the light so that I can see if you're lying or telling the truth. What's your name?'

Kazik said nothing.

'His name is Kazik – Kazik Kosopolski.'

'Shut up!' said the stranger. 'I didn't ask you. Where did you come from, Kazik?'

Kazik said nothing.

Yurek answered in his place again: 'We come from Lvov.'

'I asked you not to talk! I'm warning you for the last time.' He turned to the little boy again. 'When did you leave Lvov, Kazik?'

Yurek interrupted the questioning a third time. 'We left a year ago. Mother and Father...'

The stranger slapped Yurek across the face. The boy cried out in pain.

'Now shut up!' said the stranger.

'But he's little... too shy to talk...' explained Yurek in a broken voice, his hand holding his cheek.

'Don't worry about him,' said the stranger, and he turned to Kazik again. 'You're Jews. You can tell me the truth, Kazik.'

Kazik said nothing.

'No!' cried Yurek, and a second slap landed on his cheek.

'If you dare disobey my orders one more time and answer for him, I'll thrash you with my stick.'

'But he's just a little boy,' said Yurek sobbing.

'I've already told you – don't worry about him.'

The stranger kept his eyes on the older brother and asked him: 'Are you brothers?'

'Yes'

'When did you get out of the ghetto?'

'We're not Jews! We came here a year ago from Lvov. Mother and Father… Father is an officer in the Polish army and he was taken captive in Russia. Mum was sick in the hospital and sent us over here to our aunt. Since then we've been living here with her.'

'Do you go to school?'

'Yes… no. We don't go.'

'Why?'

'We don't want to. We want to go to our school in Lvov, when we get back. We'll go back soon. The war will be over and we'll go back to Lvov.'

The stranger smiled. 'What's your name?' he asked.

'Yurek Kosopolski.'

'How did you get from Lvov to Warsaw?'

'By train.'

'And how did you come here from the station?'

'By coach.'

'Which city is prettier: Warsaw or Lvov?'

'Warsaw is much prettier!' exclaimed Yurek, but then he realized he had fallen into a trap. He lowered his voice and said, 'No, Lvov is actually prettier…'

The stranger started laughing and then, all of a sudden, Kazik opened his mouth and asked, 'Who are you?'

'I was starting to think you were mute,' said the stranger. 'Come here. Don't be scared. Are you hungry?'

'No,' said Kazik.

'I'm from the police. I came to pick you up because you're Jewish.'

'Are you going to take us away now?' asked Kazik.

The stranger paused for a second and then said, 'No.'

'Why aren't you taking us away? Aren't you a bad man?'

The stranger collected his hat and walking stick from the table and started making his way out. He walked towards the door, and this time the children noticed that he was careful not to step on their soldiers. He opened the door, was silent for a moment and then turned around and said, 'I *am* a bad man.' He went out and closed the door behind him. The children just stood there, listening to the sound of his steps going down the stairs, then crossing the yard, until they could no longer be heard. Yurek lay down on the bed.

'Well… he's gone.'

'You see?' said the little one.

'See what? I got slapped because of you.'

'Because you answered instead of me.'

'So why did you keep your mouth shut?'

'I forgot.'

'Forgot what?'

'The story Mum taught us in the ghetto.'

'Since I was smacked because of you,' announced Yurek, 'you'll play war with me now and give me Robin Hood too.'

'I won't,' said Kazik stubbornly. 'Besides, I knew nothing would happen. Move over a little, I want to lie down too.'

'How did you know?'

'I dreamed it.'

'What did you dream?'

'I dreamed we were running down the street with Mum, and the two Germans that caught us then, the grey and the brown, they were chasing us. We ran up the stairs and came here and they were after us, and then, suddenly, the ceiling opened up and God came in.'

'God?' asked Yurek. 'What did God look like?'

'Naked,' said Kazik, 'with lots of hair on his body and lots of light on his face.'

Yurek laughed.

'A naked and hairy God?'

'Yes, but it was God!' said Kazik, insulted. 'Why should he care about being naked? All the gods in the *mytlology* book were naked.'

'It's called mythology, silly. But what about all that hair?'

'He's God. Why should he care about having hair?'

'Okay, what happened next?' asked Yurek very seriously.

'The Germans became smaller,' continued the little one, 'smaller and smaller until they disappeared into the floor.'

'When did you dream that?'

'Last night!'

'You haven't made it up?'

'No.'

'Swear it!'

'I swear!'

'Don't just swear. Swear on Mum and Dad.'

'I swear on Mum and Dad.'

'What else?'

'That's it. So when that man came here I knew nothing would happen.'

Yurek sat up. 'Get up! Let's start the game over!'

'Okay, but only if it's peacetime. You always want it to be war and more war.'

'Okay,' said Yurek, 'we can play a little at it being peace. I'll come visit you in your country and you can throw me a welcoming party and prepare a parade in my honour.'

'All right, but can't we just lie on the bed a little bit longer?'

Yurek lay down again beside his brother. 'Sure,' he said.

'Tell me about what we'll do when we're giants,' asked the little one.

'When we're giants,' Yurek started, speaking in a storyteller's voice, 'we'll be able to become bigger and smaller whenever we like.'

'No,' said Kazik, 'start with how we save Mum and Dad.'

'At night, we'll become huge,' said Yurek, speaking expressively. 'And we'll go to Mummy and Daddy and put them in our pockets – each one in a different pocket because they won't fit together in just one. We'll take along Grandma too, and Aunty Stepha, and Aunty Eva...'

❧

And it was night again. Yurek brought the submarine up to the surface, and both children sat on the table, knowing they were on deck. They sat without saying a word. Everything was different. The two children knew that well. Their submarine was the one that floated on the surface of the sea, a sea whose colour was that of the night sky; and their submarine was drifting through the water, moving slowly from chimney to chimney.

Pink Shoes

André Brink

The last day of the architects' conference in Kraków has been set aside for excursions, but by that time several of the delegates have already deserted. For Johann Alberts from South Africa, the conference has become an endless series of long-winded papers, and he cannot wait to get back home to his wife and his seven-year-old daughter, Tinka: a sweet little fairy-girl with blonde hair and huge blue eyes, the joy of his life. For him, the only highlight during the dreary papers and discussions has been meeting the diminutive, intense Miriam from Paris, barely thirty, quietly spoken, although it soon becomes evident that she doesn't hesitate to take on even delegates with well-estab- lished reputations. The crunch comes as early as the second day when she tackles an arrogant and boring professor emeritus from Oxford, and stomps out in disgust. Johann, increasingly annoyed with the rambling talk himself, finds himself following her to the symmetries of the old quadrangle, where she is lighting up a cigarette.

'Bravo!' he says with a smile. 'You certainly spoke for most of us. Where does your chutzpah come from?'

'That's exactly the right word.' An unexpected glimmer in her dark eyes. 'I'm Jewish.'

Over the next three days they make a habit of spending most of their free time together. He can feel the barriers between them slowly going down. But in the evenings, when he escorts her up to her room, she deftly manages to avoid him every time. Until, on the penultimate evening, he once again drops her at her bedroom door and she unexpectedly asks, 'Would you by any chance care to go to Auschwitz with me tomorrow?'

'I've actually been looking forward to seeing the salt mine at Wielicka,' he confesses, hesitant. 'Why don't you rather come with me? Or we could go the castle.'

She shakes her head with unexpected urgency, 'No. I *have* to go to Auschwitz. But I'm scared of going on my own.' Adding after a moment, 'You see, my great-grandmother died there.'

'Oh.' He still hesitates, then shrugs. 'If you're really sure.'

'I am.' Unexpectedly, impulsively, she stands on her toes and kisses him. 'Thank you, Johann.' Then she unlocks the door, and prepares to go inside.

'Two of my grandfather's sisters also died in a concentration camp, you know,' he says quietly.

This time she does look at him. 'How come?'

'In the Boer War. The Germans learned a lot from the British, you see.'

There is a very long silence. To his amazement Miriam puts out her hand to open the door more widely for him to move past her, into the room.

Their bus arrives at ten the next morning. Her generous mouth is drawn in rather tightly. At the camp, she sets off on her own, leaving him with an eerie feeling of distance, of remoteness, almost of absence as he passes through the stark entrance with its infamous legend: ARBEIT MACHT FREI. And it persists all the way as he does the rounds: as if he is not really there, as if nothing of all this is real. It belongs to a different dimension altogether. Not even the grim space between Blocks 10 and 11, which evoke the worst excesses of punishment and execution, can shock him into an awareness of the present. He is aware of only one desire: to be somewhere else, not here. He thinks of his wife, Alison, of his little girl. For a moment he even has to grope for their names in his memory.

Why has he ever allowed himself to be dragged to this improbable place, so dark grey, even on a day of sunshine, as if an eclipse has cast its shadow over the world?

It is near the end of his tedious round from one block to the next, avoiding the gas chambers and the crematoria with their tall towers, that he stumbles into the spaces dedicated to things, objects, mementoes taken from the dead. Suitcases, each marked precisely with a name and an address. Hair. Combs. Spectacles. An entire room filled with chamber pots.

And shoes. Women's shoes, men's shoes. Children's shoes. In the midst of all of this there is, suddenly, like a scream, like a knife in the guts, a single pink girl's shoe. It could have fitted a child of six or seven.

Now he thinks of Tinka. Remembers the particulars of her feet. How small and narrow and exquisitely vulnerable they are. How neatly they fit into his hands. Tinka running in the garden. Tinka bending a dusty leg to let him kiss a bruised toe. Tinka doing ballet. *Look, Daddy, look!*

At the entrance to the main building, he sits down to wait for Miriam.

When she turns up, much later, very pale, they do not talk. Together, they go to the exit and find their air-conditioned bus.

The next morning, before they are taken to the airport, he strolls through the streets one last time. Inside the Cloth Hall, opposite the statue of Adam Mickiewicz, he finds a shop with clothing and knick-knacks for children. They have a pair of pink ballet shoes in Tinka's size. He buys them without even asking about the price.

Tinka is so delighted with her shoes that for the first night they have no choice but to let her wear them even to bed. And soon, for the inevitable Christmas performance of the 'Nutcracker Suite' in the Artscape, she will dance the Sugar Plum Fairy in them.

It is when they prepare to leave for the theatre that Alison ingenuously asks, 'Johann, who is Miriam?'

He feels a numbing sensation spreading through his body.

'Miriam?' he dumbly mouths the name. 'I have no idea.'

'That's strange,' says Alison. 'She does seem to know *you*. Rather well.' And she puts before him an opened envelope, and the letter she has taken from it.

He stays at home, alone. The woman and her small daughter, both in tears, leave for the Artscape. When they return, Alison has regained her composure, but Tinka is still sobbing – with renewed vigour. Because now something else has happened. In the middle of her dance, it turns out, the strap of her left shoe broke and she fell on the stage, and everything ended in an unmitigated shambles.

'We'll get you new shoes,' he promises. 'Tomorrow night you'll be perfect.'

'No, I won't,' Tinka sobs. 'I'll never dance again.' Exploding with sudden vehemence. 'And it's all *your* fault!'

'Now please, lovey,' he asks, a throbbing headache behind his eyes. 'Calm down, it's not so bad.'

'It's *your* fault, Daddy!'

He turns to Alison. 'This is getting ridiculous. Please calm the child down.'

'I won't calm down!' screams Tinka. 'It's your fault, Daddy. It's *your* fault!'

That is when he hits her. With such force that she crumples to the floor, now yelling blue murder. He has never lifted a hand against his darling daughter, but this is too much for flesh and blood. And it becomes even worse when Alison goes on her knees beside the child to press the sobbing little body against herself.

The ballet shoes are passed on to Ntombi, daughter of the house-keeper. She is a year younger than Tinka and small for her age. Somebody repairs it, not very neatly, but well enough to be worn again. Ntombi curtseys and claps her small hands together. She takes the shoes to Khayelitsha with her.

Between Christmas and New Year the black township is convulsed in the grip of too much festivity, too much heavy drinking, too much violence, but resolute about seeing it through to the explosive end. On the third day of Christmas, a day of torrential rain, Buyiselo, the best friend of Ntombi's father, comes round to their shack in Khayelitsha, and the men start drinking. When Buyiselo prepares to leave, little Ntombi grabs him by the hand and begs him to take her to his home with him, so that she can play with his youngest daughter, Nomfundo. At first he refuses, but in the end he goes off with the little one. Happy in her new pink shoes, she skips along. Buyiselo allows her to wend her own way, proceeding next to him but taking her own shortcuts and detours in the deepening dusk.

And somewhere along the way he loses her. After half an hour of stumbling through increasingly unfamiliar alleys among the shacks, he begins to panic. Ntombi loses her way among the hovels. She starts shouting for Buyiselo, but there is no sign of him. And then there is a strange man who looms before her in the dark. Tearful by now, Ntombi tells him what has happened and begs him to take her home. No problem, he says. He takes her by the hand, rather too tightly for comfort. But when she starts squirming and whining, he gives her a clout that sends her sprawling. It is a part of the township she doesn't know at all. And everything is soaked with the rain.

'Please,' begs Ntombi, 'please take me home.'

'*Tula!*' he snarls. 'You come with me. And not a fucking sound, okay?'

Soon there are no more houses or shacks around, only the rustling and soughing of a bluegum plantation.

She starts fighting, vicious as a cornered meerkat. Her clothes are being torn from her.

It is so dark by now and Ntombi is fighting so furiously that the man loses his balance.

She starts kicking him with her new pink shoes. She feels one of them being torn away from her small foot.

And then she is free. Scuttling on all fours through the mud, she blindly storms into the night, hearing him bellow in pursuit.

At last, too tired to move any more, she collapses in a little heap and loses consciousness.

At some stage – Ntombi will never know how or when – she will be found by strangers, and tended in a shack where a blunt candle is burning in a chipped blue saucer. Much later she will be taken home again, her whole body aching.

She recognizes the voices of her father and her mother. But Ntombi remains inconsolable. She has lost one of the pink shoes, and she knows she will never find it again.

Shame

Judith Ravenscroft

Muffled sounds, a deep distant rumble punched by short high-pitched squalls, reached her through the water. Her eyes fixed wide, she saw the sand floor in elegant swathes, dappled with gentle ridges; dead-white as if boneless hands, hers, cutting through the limpid water. Then her eyes began to smart, worse if she tried to close them; and her lungs ached, craving air. She reached upwards, kicking her legs hard, arms outstretched above her head to break the surface. Her coming up made a spray of foam – the joy of lungs filling fast and deep. Free now to stand and rub her prickling eyes, she peered in between at the blurry beach, and blobs that slowly took on the forms of people, umbrellas, red, green, and blue. The indigo sky and golden sand of the south, dreamt of through her northern winters.

A group of men gathered in the shallows, all types, old and young, in shorts or swimsuits, or trousers rolled up above their knees. Others ran across the beach to join them. She watched them take each other's hands as if to play a game, and form a line, a human chain, ready to broach the sea. Women and children stared, on the beach, or, as she did, chest high in the choppy, late-morning sea. Her hands clasped her face where they'd wiped the stinging water, in suspense, perhaps, and trepidation.

'Ellen!'

She turned distractedly to where her mother stood ankle-deep, clutching her skirt with one hand, Stella with the other. Max, up the beach, resisting her anxiety, lolled about under the umbrella.

'Come in!'

Ellen dropped her hands, turned away, but then obeyed, respond-ing to a hint of panic in her mother's voice. She walked, leaning for-wards against the tide, feeling the resistance of the water, and then stepped more forcefully, as if her mother's fear, and the strange urgency of the line of men, had infected her. Once out of the water she slowed and, reluctant to mimic her mother's scrambling speed, walked, dignified, sedate, to the umbrella. She took the towel her mother offered but refused to rush herself.

'What's happening?'

'It's lunchtime.'

'But what's happening?'

'Someone's drowned,' said Max.

'Ellen, pick up your things and come.'

But she didn't, not at once. Wrapped in the towel, she watched the men walk out to sea. She heard the cry go up as they bunched in one spot, and then three or four of them lifted a body, carried it through the shallows and on to the beach. She ran forward with the others who waited, and shoved and was pushed until another cry went up for air, let the poor man have air. And only then, when they all backed away, did she go to gather up her things and follow her mother and Max and Stella over the dunes to the house.

'Did you see it?' Max wanted to know.

'See what?'

'The body.'

'Yes.' And left him, not having seen enough to describe it; only felt the sinking sense in her stomach and a small burst of excitement.

Later they learned that no amount of air could have saved him, a young soldier, they said, from the camp inland, who'd swum too soon after a hearty breakfast.

No mention was made of a friend. Ellen saw him that evening, in no doubt that that was who he was, for who else but a dead man's friend would sit alone on a bench, in the midst of the evening promenade, his head in his hands, the slump of his shoulders expressive of nothing so much as a recent and shocking loss. And then, shortly after the moment of her seeing him, the only one, it seemed, in that holiday crowd to do so, she felt the bitterness of regret, that she'd failed to approach him, to reach out and touch him, to communicate her sorrow. Perhaps she'd faltered, stopped in her tracks, or at least slowed down, but then she'd done nothing, she hadn't put out a hand, but instead picked up speed again in pursuit of the others. And then in the bar – where they went for a treat some evenings to drink

Fanta – she felt impatient to return, to make good her omission. But by the time they passed the spot again, an elderly couple sat on the bench and the dead man's friend was nowhere to be seen.

She imagined telling someone; in her disappointment she was moved to tell her mother, a better choice than Max, because she'd listen, so long as Stella didn't distract her, but then she'd say too much, ask too many questions. And Max, too, would be all over it, but he'd have plans, fantasies, centred on dead bodies, and she'd regret ever having mentioned it, whatever it was, another fantasy perhaps, that the tragic man and the drowned man were somehow connected.

Then she saw him again, a few evenings later, in the bar. She sat as she always did on the tall stools so that she could swivel – and it seemed to her that his very solitariness had drawn her attention.

He was just sitting, a glass on the table before him. He faced into the room, not out towards the terrace and the sea, and he didn't look as if he was waiting for someone. Nor even as if he was passing the time of day, because he didn't seem to be watching the scene, taking things in, but it was as if he was somewhere else, deep inside himself, or perhaps nowhere, perhaps just vacant and empty, as if his grief had burned a hole inside him.

Suddenly he reached for his drink and gulped at it, then stood up as he put the glass down, and left. Ellen slithered off her stool and followed him out of the bar. She stood on the terrace and watched him walk along the promenade until she could see him no longer.

The man was a foreigner, not as she was, but in the sense that he didn't, it seemed to her, belong in that place either as a holidaymaker or as someone there to serve the holidaymakers. It was as if he didn't know what he was doing there, as if fate had led him to that stretch of coast, for a swim that would drown his friend, and then for some reason he was stuck there, forced to live out the time he was obliged to spend in that place.

Ellen now felt caught up in his fate, so that when she saw him for a third time it was as if she had been waiting for the inevitable to happen.

Her mother, Max, and Stella had returned to the house, leaving Ellen on the beach to watch the sun go down. She wanted to see the moment when it dropped, as it seemed, into the sea, slipped below the horizon leaving a green glow behind. The moment would be brief, and she sat cross-legged by the umbrella, which had been closed and tied for the night, staring with as much concentration as she could summon. But then she missed it, distracted by a figure who walked across her vision and sat down on one of the pedalos drawn up on the beach. She glanced, then pulled her attention back to the sun, was distracted again as the figure, a man, leaned forward, his arms resting on his knees. She recognized the pose of the dead man's friend, and forgot the sun, intent only on watching him, his back, which seemed to hold no kind of tension, to be wholly inert, as if he'd been dealt a body blow.

But then, suddenly, he seemed to find a purpose. He jumped off the pedalo, turned his back on the sea and the sinking sun, and strode up the beach. As he passed her, a few paces away, he glanced in her direction, but without any sign of interest or recognition. Perhaps that was why she followed, because he'd not seen her as she had seen him, and there might not be another time.

It was easy enough to keep him in sight. He crossed the road as she reached the dunes, and was halfway up the main street as she passed their house. She saw her mother through the window of the lighted dining room, laying the table for dinner, as if in another, remote world that Ellen had now passed out of. She kept on, past the shops and bars and the people who thronged, and it was as if both he and she went unnoticed, like ghosts who could be seen only by those who were gifted to see them.

At the top of the street he turned right. It was quiet there, and dark. So as not to alert him to her presence she slowed, stopped at the corner, saw him disappear up a track off to the left. At the turning point she waited, hesitant to follow him into what seemed to be an edge-of-town scrubland. For a while she heard his footsteps, and saw the flicker of a light as if he had a torch to show him the way. Tentatively she began to follow, picking up speed as she found her feet, and watching for the light.

It was because of that that she stumbled, watching the light instead of feeling her way, fell headlong, face down in the dust. Then the bark of dogs went up, a terrible racket, and she thought it was because of her, her stumbling, and she lay there petrified, waiting for the dogs to find her. But, then, when nothing happened and the barks tailed off into whimpers, she lifted her head, got up gingerly, and saw a steady light ahead of her.

It was light from a window, some kind of house, his home, and it was he perhaps who had set the dogs off, the sounds of his arrival. And the dogs weren't there, they were further off, in the woods beyond.

She crept up to the window and peered in and saw him: he stood with his back to her, in front of a large, open fridge, pouring a drink from a bottle. As he swung the fridge door closed and turned, she ducked and ran away.

She was late for supper, and slipped into her seat as unobtrusively as she could, though she was out of breath from running and smeared with dirt. Max guessed at something. He came to her room later, an alcove off the kitchen. A pull at the curtain and then his low confiding voice: 'Ellen?' His face appeared, all inquiry, wanting to know but knowing better than to ask. 'The sun was a long time going down.' She'd already decided not to tell, not yet, when so little had happened and it was all in her head. So she went on reading, ignoring him till he went away disconsolate, knocking over the pile of her books as he went, a gentle kick to get his own back. She reached out to grab him but he dodged out of her grasp and scuttled across the kitchen jeering.

A rough path took her through straggly trees. She walked slowly, quietly, felt the closeness of the air, a clamminess, early as it was. Soon the path curved and it came into view, a one-storey structure, roughly plastered so that brick showed through in places. She stopped, stepped sideways to watch from behind a tree: it looked like a place things were stored in. The door was closed, with an unlocked padlock hanging down from the bar. She waited, watched for some sign of him – in vain.

Lying on her bed after lunch, her eyes closed, dazed by the morning's sun, by the heavy silence of the house, she held her body in a slight tension of expectation. The sigh of her breath, the whine of a wasp, the half-imagined pad of footsteps, the displacement of air as the curtain was twitched, and the wheeze of slightly bronchitic breath.

They waited, but not too long; when she heard the creak of a bone she opened her eyes and leapt. She grabbed him, they grappled, entangled in the curtain; they fell to the ground, he, the smaller, pinioned by her, both spreadeagled, choked by the dusty curtain. Then he did what he always did to unnerve her, he acted like a corpse. Not a sound came out of him, not a breath or heartbeat or twitched muscle. Lifeless. She got off him, pulled at the curtain, her breath shallow, her face flushed. Then at last he opened his eyes, a coy grin, as if he liked it, inert in an after-ecstasy. She fell back on the bed and kicked him.

❧

Max had constructed a racetrack in the sand. He flicked several small, variously coloured plastic balls around it, in competition with himself. Ellen lay on her side watching: Max, the sea, and then a man who stood by the water. She watched without Max knowing that she watched, and felt an uncanny intimacy with the man; he was oblivious of her, but she rejoiced in her secret knowledge of him.

When she sensed Max's glance she turned her gaze to meet it, betraying nothing on her face. He didn't look where she looked, hadn't seen who she'd seen, and she kept her face vacant as she held his eye, and he held hers, waiting for who would turn away first. It was her, because the man moved then, behind Max's back, and she saw him walk up the beach and pass them, and then she dropped her gaze and, disdainful, rolled over to lie on her front, her chin in the sand, but watching, without Max knowing that she did.

She wanted to follow him, at once to get up and follow, but she knew that Max would come too and nothing would stop him. She dropped her face on to her folded arms and looked down at the sand, at the little peaks and dips, and the grains so many millions of them, and as if at a distance she heard the flick of a ball and the murmur of voices pierced by an eerie cry. She felt the nausea of tedium, the endlessness of a hot summer's day in which nothing needed to be done and the only constraint was her family, these people chance dictated she share her life with, who surrounded her, hemmed her in, and it was then that she got up and walked away, not towards the dunes in pursuit of the man, but along the beach past the pedalos, and when Max got up to follow her she turned on him, and with all the ferociousness of a cornered cat, spat and hissed her venom at him, so he slunk away, wounded, and ran off, head down to hide his tears.

He stuck to her like a leech. Evading him became part of it, an irritation that brought its pleasures in the plotting of devious strategies to get away to watch the hut without his knowing. So the habit was set in her, of watching and waiting and seizing her chances.

Once she went at night. She simply walked out of the house after everyone had gone to bed. They went early, at nine most nights, so people were still about in the street, children too, and no one took note of her. She didn't look back to see if Max followed her, trusting that he hadn't, that he was exhausted by the strain of his constant alertness to her movements and had fallen asleep.

Later she was to feel an overwhelming sense of shame at what she might have done, as well as regret at not having done it. It was as if, in her mind's eye, at the moment that he opened the door to her knock and peered through it and saw her she would realize the folly of her going there, her lack of tact and discretion, her ignorance in not anticipating that by turning up on his doorstep at night she made them both vulnerable.

And so she didn't knock; she stood as she always stood, not daring to approach too close, but watching from behind a tree, seeing only an edge of light round the door, waiting for something she was unable to articulate.

Then, the next time she went, he'd gone. It was obvious he'd gone. The door was open, the lock hanging down uselessly, and when she dared to look inside she smelled the air of abandon.

Her grief became a murderous anger directed at Max. At first she ignored him, brushed him off like a fly. She refused to answer when he spoke to her, turned her back and walked off when he approached her, looked into the distance rather than catch his eye. But then, when he came up behind her in the sea, she turned and he was there, shivering, his arms wrapped round himself, the anger burst out of her, and she sprang on him, pushed him under the water and held him hard as he struggled, struggled more and more desperately. Still she held him, taken over by fury and revenge, wanting to kill him – until he went limp beneath her, suddenly withdrew his protest, or the life went out of him, which brought her to her senses, and she pulled him up and still he lay slack and she thought he was dead.

But then his eyes opened, in the sly way that was his, and she knew he'd tricked her, had known in his desperation the one thing that would make her stop. 'You almost drowned me,' he blubbered, and there was amazement rather than horror in his voice.

She went on going to the hut, just in case, and because it didn't matter any more she became careless so that one evening before dinner Max followed her and suddenly, as she stood looking at the open door and the lock hanging loose, was beside her. She didn't fight him. And when he asked what it was she was looking at, she said it was a hut, and when he asked why, she said it was a man's hut, and the man had gone, so that now it was just any hut, of no interest. She pressed her lips together in a thin line so as not to answer any more questions, and stalked off. After a while Max followed.

Personal Fulcrums

Richard Zimler

I was looking at magazines at the San Francisco Public Library a couple of weeks ago and happened upon a contributor's note in which the author said that all his stories were about an innocent paralyzed when confronted with trauma. In my memory, I was a seven-year-old boy with long blond bangs standing frozen in front of a skinny man in blue pyjamas sitting on a hospital bed. The man had gaunt cheeks and sad eyes. His skeletal hands were sticking out of wrists wrapped with gauze and bandages.

The little kid was me. The withered guy on the bed was my father. My mother says that he got that way after losing two quarts of blood. Most of it soaked into the bathtub, and by the time paramedics reached him the water was clouded pink. She also says that I was found trying to pull him out. I'd called 911, then gone back to him. I don't remember any of it.

I wasn't supposed to be at home, of course. But my Little League baseball game had been called in the second inning. It was only a drizzle, but home plate was a bit lower than the rest of the field and had become a puddle.

My mother never even tried to get the blood off my uniform. And we never bothered ordering another one. She was able to find work again as a saleswoman at Magnin's, and we were able to keep the house, but we really didn't have extra money for hobbies. I suppose if I'd begged... But playing shortstop for the Giants was no longer a dream.

Dahlias bloom in September in the San Francisco Bay Area. Each year, on my father's birthday, the 27th, I put some big violet ones like pompoms from my garden into a vase and sit it on my mantel. I suppose this ritual is insane, but what do you do for a father who simply got into his Rover one fine day in May and disappeared without a trace?

One of my earliest memories is of him clipping a flame-coloured bud from a rosebush in the backyard of our house in the San Jose Hills and asking me to bring it inside to my mother. 'Tell her I'll be in for lunch in a minute,' he added.

Why do I remember that simple line and not anything whispered to me at the last minute? All my life it has seemed that I never got the secret advice or password from him which I'd need to make me a man.

After the wounds on his wrists had healed, he came home. I remember meeting him at the door, standing with one foot on each of his, then walking together into the kitchen. He had great black boats for shoes. Two days later, he was gone. No note. No clues. He left while I was at school and while my mother was shopping at Safeway.

The morning after our first night without him, my mother said, 'He'll be back, don't you worry.' The ash was curling at the end of her cigarette. She was sitting on her bed in her nightgown, nursing a brandy in her mouthwash cup. Years later, when I was in junior high school, I asked for a possible explanation. My mother shrugged. She said he was simply a car mechanic who liked to cultivate flowers. A normal guy. He watched Giants' games on Channel 2, bought a Rover because he'd seen Laurence Harvey driving one in some English movie. His favourite foods were pot roast and shish kebab. On Sundays, he liked to read the *San Jose Mercury* in bed, then take a long shower. She didn't know if he'd been unhappy. He certainly never said anything.

'Didn't you ever discuss his suicide attempt with him?' I asked.

It was then that she lost control and screamed: 'Goddammit Charlie, he ordered seeds from a hundred different fucking seed catalogues!'

This must have meant something special to her, but I never found out exactly what. As a teenager, you think your parents are weird and inexplicable, even the ones who don't abandon you. Too late, I realized that you'd better ask questions like this while you've still got time.

My mother died four years ago this June, occupies one half of a dual plot she reserved in the Hillcrest Cemetery in Los Gatos. I suppose she still believed right up to the end that he'd come back. But I don't think that the other half of the plot is ever going to have a body. He's just not going to call and warn me that he's on his deathbed. Or make some pilgrimage home like a lost elephant to its ancestral burial ground. Even so, you'd have thought in the thirty-two years he's been gone that he'd have sent me at least a postcard saying that he was fine and working at a botanical garden in South Carolina, or at a tropical nursery in Maui, or wherever it is that gardeners who are also car mechanics go to really get lost.

Each year, at Christmas, I send the Filipino family who bought our old house a card and remind them to forward to me any letters my mother or I might get. They must think I'm some lovelorn nut hoping to get a letter from the girl who got away.

When I can get beyond my white-hot anger, I confess to myself that he might have been an interesting person. *He ordered seeds from a hundred different seed catalogues.* I would have liked to have known him.

After I read the contributor's note about innocents paralyzed by trauma, and after I thought, *this poor guy must write about schmucks like me*, I remembered a time several years back when Lana, my wife, and I were walking on Castro near 18th Street. It was spring, sunny. All the Victorian houses seemed to possess the proud and colourful promise of homes in a naïve landscape. We were happy, had just bought scones at the Cheese Board and an autographed copy of *Flaubert's Parrot* at the Walt Whitman Bookstore. As we passed the Elephant Walk bar, we saw a pregnant woman panhandling under the awning. She must've been at least seven months along, looked haggard and hopeless, like one of those dirt-poor Appalachian mothers photographed during the Great Depression. My heart leapt against my chest as we passed, and I felt as if I'd swallowed poison. Tears started as soon as we got into our car. Lana got pissed off. 'So instead of sitting there and bawling like you always do, why don't you *do* something!' she yelled.

I just looked at her. I mean, what was there to do? This was 1987 in Ronald Reagan's America, and if a pregnant woman was homeless and begging, then that's the way people obviously wanted it.

Lana has large brown eyes so dark and stunning that that's all you see when you first meet her. She was staring at me with them then like I was her enemy, was making me feel impossibly heavy – like a huge boulder that won't be moved no matter what.

'I'm going to call the cops,' she said. 'They have an obligation to do something for her, to take her to a shelter or something.'

Lana called the San Francisco police from our house, a stucco cottage on the southern slope of the hill separating the Castro District from Noe Valley. Then she tried three shelters. When she reported back to me, she said, 'The cops won't go help her and the shelters can't send anyone to pick her up. She has to present herself at one of their doors and ask for a bed.' Lana was livid. 'It's fucking unbelievable,' she kept whispering to herself.

I was feeling kind of justified knowing that there was nothing you could do even if you tried. I patted the couch next to me, but Lana wouldn't sit. She ran her hands back and forth across her short brown hair, mussed it up into a tangle. Then she started pacing. I stayed put where I was; she's petite and lean, but you don't want to get in front of her when she's angry.

When I met Lana I didn't know anything about that rage of hers. I thought she was reserved. You only find out about people's wounds a few months later, after you begin sleeping with them. She had long hair back then, wore only jeans and loose-fitting sweaters, was studying for her master's degree in gerontology at UC Berkeley. I'd just gotten back to San Jose after four years in New York. I'd earned a bachelor's in classical guitar from the Manhattan School of Music.

Lana always had a lot of interest in elderly people because her Grandma Winky, her mother's mother, was the bright spot in her life. Winky was from Oxford, Mississippi, and when Lana was a kid she used to sit her on her lap and tell her stories embroidered with antiquated words and people. One in particular I remember was about an elegant octoroon from New Orleans who worked as a butler for cousins of William Faulkner. One day this 'gentleman of impeccable manners who spoke French better than any French ambassador' just up and disappeared without a trace. The other I always remember was about an eighteen-year-old white girl named Irene 'with curls in her hair like Mary Pickford' who'd had a baby out of wedlock by the first black paediatrician in Lafayette County. Irene had been sent off to live with her father's sister Harriet in Little Rock. She never saw her lover again. Her baby boy, called Isaac, was given up for adoption in Memphis. Irene's heart had been broken.

Winky told us that she and her parents left Mississippi during the Depression and found migrant labour work in the peach orchards that then covered San Jose. Only much later on did we figure out that that was a lie. Eight years ago, when she died, we found a canvas suitcase at the bottom of the linen closet of her apartment in Menlo Park, and in it was a photograph of a wrinkled old woman wearing a dark, high-collared dress. On the back was written in Winky's scrawl: Aunt Harriet, March 1933. We also found a couple of dozen letters written to Winky from her parents, all with Oxford postmarks and all addressed to 722 Clarion Way in San Jose. Obviously, her family didn't move out with her to California. As for Aunt Harriet, she was undoubtedly Winky's aunt, not some relative of any Irene. In fact, there never was any Irene. Or rather, we figured that Irene was Winky, that she'd been exiled to California after having a child by a black man to whom she wasn't married. None of the letters from her parents made mention of any of this, but, of course, any 'proper' Southern family would have done its best to forget that such events ever took place.

We confirmed one part of this story by checking in a 1940 San Jose phone book that had been put on microfilm by the public library. Morgan was the last name Winky had had before she married Grandpa Don, the father of Lana's mother. On the microfilm, we discovered the name Harriet Morgan. That must have been Aunt Harriet, because the address given was the same as on the letters, 722 Clarion Way. We drove down the forty miles from San Francisco to San Jose, got lost on a ghastly strip of car dealerships and gas stations, and eventually found a tiny old clapboard house with hydrangeas out front, smack dab in the centre of a run-down Chicano neighbourhood. It was here, and not in Little Rock, that Winky as Irene 'had spent years staring out of the window, always facing east, toward Oxford and the life from which she'd been severed'.

We wrote to the Memphis police and some hospitals in the area, but we never learned what happened to Winky's baby. Maybe he wasn't given up for adoption in Memphis. Maybe his name wasn't even Isaac. But somewhere near Oxford, Lana must have a great-uncle and maybe some second cousins we'll never find.

Lana's mother and father claimed that they'd never heard anything about Winky's life before she'd married Grandpa Don. We didn't believe them, but we weren't going to press the issue.

I suppose I take these things too personally, but all these discoveries about Winky really upset me. Not, of course, because she'd had a baby out of wedlock. Or because she fell in love with a black man. It was that she had to give up both him and the baby and move clear across the country to escape her past. And I admit that I was hurt that she had lied to us about it. Lana wasn't. 'You really thought all of Winky's stories were the whole truth and nothing but the truth?' she asked, so much disbelief in her voice that I didn't even bother answering.

When I first met her, Lana wasn't just studying gerontology in Berkeley, but was also waitressing in San Francisco three nights a week at Paprikas Villa in Ghirardelli Square and doing stand-up comedy on Friday and Saturday nights. In May of 1977, we decided to rent the cottage together in San Francisco that we ended up buying three years later when the owner died. An incredibly busy girl, Lana was at the time. We hardly had time for lovemaking. But it was exciting, too. She opened a few times for Robin Williams at the Holy City Zoo, did improvisations with Dana Carvey at Fanny's. Later, when she realized she wasn't interested in putting in the decade of club work it took to make it to the *Tonight Show*, she began working on a screenplay. Then, after she got her master's, she bought a video camera and an editing machine and started making videos of weddings and bar mitzvahs. 'Nobody realizes it, but I make Andy Warhol movies,' she used to tell me. 'Avant-garde oral histories.' At first I wasn't convinced, but it's really true. Because along with the usual shots, she interviews the close relatives of the bride and groom or bar mitzvah boy so that the people watching learn something about the history of families involved. She's got an Italian grandmother singing threshing songs she learned back in the hills of Calabria; a ninety-year-old Jewish tailor describing the Warsaw ghetto uprising;

Irish old buggers talking about garment industry strikes in New York when they were beaten by their cousins on the police force. We've been married seventeen years now, and I'm her biggest fan. I like it most when the people in her videos talk about the events around which their lives turned. That's the information she really tries to get. I dream that someday she'll be discovered and that they'll do a retrospective of her films at the Pacific Film Archive. I've already come up with the title for it: *Personal Fulcrums: The Videos of Lana Salgueiro Sanderson.*

Lana likes classical guitar music on her productions. So she records me in her editing room playing Bach suites or Villa-Lobos preludes or whatever it is she wants, then transfers the music to the videos. Other than that, all my income comes from teaching individual guitar classes at UC Berkeley and San Francisco State. I garden on the weekends, cook Thai food at least once a week, watch the Giants on Channel 2. I love living near Castro Street and being able to sit outside at the Café Flore. From the wooden patio there, I watch things that are unusual elsewhere in America – gay men kissing in public, college students with pink-tipped hair sipping espresso, fog ribboning through the Twin Peaks in the late afternoon. I enjoy browsing in bookstores and walking downtown amongst the businessmen. I like looking at skyscrapers. I'm happy. In all the years Lana and I have been married, I haven't once been tempted to take a razor to my wrists or off myself some other way. So maybe we can downplay the possibility of a genetic cause for my father's suicide attempt and disappearance. Maybe he just got sick of us. Once, on the *Phil Donahue Show*, I heard a father who'd abandoned his wife and kids say just that. It sounds absurd, but it's got to happen sometimes.

I've been thinking about my dad and Lana and my past a lot more than I like of late, not so much because of the contributor's note I read at the San Francisco Public Library, but because Lana's baby brother, Denny, was kicked out of their parents' house a week ago and disappeared for a few days. I don't think I've slept more than four hours a night since then. I get too hot under the covers, then too cold. And then the muscles in my legs begin to stiffen and ache. Pretty soon, all I'm doing is thinking about my father.

Apparently, Denny robbed a corner grocery store. The owner didn't press charges for some reason, so he didn't have to worry about prison. But Mr Salgueiro, Denny and Lana's father, decided he didn't want to risk any more visits from the San Jose police to his house and told his son to clear out. The boy only disappeared for a few days. The parents never called to tell Lana. When she telephoned them as she does every other Sunday, her mother explained the situation and said, 'He's seventeen. We've done what we can. It's his life.'

Denny returned still barred from his parents' house and began sleeping in the garage. Lana drove down to San Jose to speak to him and try to broker a compromise with her parents. When she asked him where he'd left to, her brother said, 'I just went away,' and wouldn't say more.

Negotiations never really got started. Mr Salgueiro said, 'I don't want that *filho da puta*, in my house', took himself a beer from the refrigerator, dropped down in front of the TV and that was that. He lapses into his first language, Portuguese, when he's pissed off or drunk. Lana tells me that *filho da puta* literally means 'son of a whore', but is equivalent to our 'son of a bitch'.

I suppose my father would also be vague about where he disappeared to if I could find him. Though by now he might be pushing up imported tulips or antique roses in some finely landscaped cemetery in La Jolla reserved for gardening mechanics. Apparently, such cemeteries for specific kinds of people are the new thing; the last time I was at the Gaia Bookstore I saw an advertisement in *America Yoga* magazine for a cemetery in Orange County for New Age worshippers of the Goddess and another one in the *Vegetarian Lifestyles* for a cemetery outside Austin, Texas reserved for people who'd been vegetarians and non-smokers. Stuff like this makes me think sometimes that things are more than a little wrong with America these days. Like we've all just snapped under the pressure. Though maybe my father is an exception, is married with three lovely children and a collie, living a Leave-It-to-Beaver life in some Midwestern town where people still leave their front doors open at night. Maybe the problem was us, after all – me and my mother, I mean. She implied that to me once. We were over at my Aunt Liz's house for dinner, and the two of them had gotten smashed on gin and tonics. I must have been about sixteen, was trying to watch a Warriors basketball game on TV. 'Before we were married, Charles was great,' my mother said, talking to Aunt Liz about my father, loud enough so that I was sure to hear. 'We used to bum around together. Go dancing in North Beach. Eat burritos in the Mission. He was fun. Really fun! Then we got married and suddenly I'm living with an impostor. Angry all the time. Mean. Doesn't like all the things about me he used to like. Even started saying my tits were too big! When we had Charlie, it was all over. He wouldn't touch me. It was like he realized only then that you got a kid from fucking.'

One night just before she died, my mother was staying with us and came into our bedroom crying. Lana was in her editing room. I was alone with my guitar, reading through a new piece by Leo Brouwer. She stood before me, tears streaming down her cheeks. By then she had jowls, brittle grey hair which she let down at night. 'I feel so cheated,' she whimpered. 'I was a virgin when I married your dad. Look what he did to me.'

I was about to say, 'You think *you* feel cheated…' But I shut my mouth and went to her. Lana says she can't believe I didn't tell her anything about my feelings. But what would've been the point? I mean, once my dad left, my mother couldn't see or hear me any more.

✤

Three days ago, the night after Denny moved into his parents' garage, Lana woke me up at two in the morning and said, 'We've got to do something.'

'About what?'

'My brother.'

The clanging sound of the raccoons trying their best to knock over our garbage cans reached me. I got up. The back yard was real dark, but I could see the white spathes of the calla lilies sticking up from behind the lawn like so many ears listening for my response. 'Those little bastards want our garbage again,' I said. 'There'll be coffee grinds everywhere.'

'Charlie,' she said, 'we've got to help him.'

'What can we do? He's seventeen. He lives with your parents. And we've got Caroline.'

Caroline was an old friend of mine from my days as a music student in New York. She'd been staying with us for a week and would be with us for another five days. I love her dearly, but she requires a lot of attention. I didn't need one more responsibility.

'We still have to do something,' Lana insisted.

'Such as?'

'We could take him in.'

'Oh no, this is between him and your parents. I'm not getting caught in the middle.'

'In the middle of what?'

'Your family.'

She knew what I meant by that only too well. A long time ago we decided that if her parents had been born as plants, they'd be thorny old weeds putting burrs in everything that passes. I could tell from the way her jaw was throbbing, however, that she was about to start screaming, so I said, 'Look, when Caroline leaves, we'll talk about it. We'll go down and visit your parents and talk it all out like adults.'

'It's just that Denny's all alone,' she said.

'We'll figure something out. I promise.'

But I was lying. I didn't intend to figure anything out. I figured that after a few more days, the parents would let him back in, or he'd run away or something would happen to take us off the hook. It was a mistake; Lana can always tell when I'm lying. I don't think she's got any special radar. I just think I'm no good at it. My voice must change or something. So she started yelling after all, accusing me of being a coward and not wanting to confront her parents. It's an argument we've had before. Usually I just sulk. But this time I told her the honest truth. I suppose it was my lack of sleep. 'You're the one who's the coward,' I said. 'For the last twenty years you've been avoiding telling them what you really think.'

Lana looked out the window for a long time at the calla lilies. After a while, I crept up behind her and together we listened to the raccoons jumping against the garbage cans.

The next day I woke up and found the oven top cleaned. It's aluminium. It was shining like a newly-minted coin.

'I've cleaned it with this solution I make out of baking soda and vinegar,' Caroline explained.

'Looks great,' I said.

Caroline has a lot of extra energy these days for cleaning because she's recovering from bulimia. She used to vomit as much as eight times a day and spend a good deal of the rest of her time thinking about her illness. How she managed to keep giving a full load of viola classes I'll never know. Anyway, now she's down to twice a day. And she *is* looking better. Goat-ribbed, she was. Now she's got some gentler contours. Though she's still got that gaunt face, those bug eyes. Her closely cropped grey hair doesn't help – it just seems to accent all her bony angles. The new hobbies she's taken up to fill up her spare time are knitting and pottery-making. The red vest she started making for me three days ago has a front already. As for her cleaning, all the cans in our pantry have had their tops washed; our steak knives are newly sharpened; and our bathroom looks like something in a TV commercial. She even bleached the shower curtain and ironed the fluffy throw rugs on the floor. I didn't even know you could iron them. You want a hygienic house, Caroline and I decided, then hire a recovering bulimic. I've already asked her to paint the outside of the house next year. Free room and board for as long as it takes.

Lana and I are the only two people Caroline has told about her bulimia. Aside from her shrink and the members of her help group, that is. I don't remember exactly when she told me. She thought I'd be horrified, but those kinds of things don't horrify me. I don't think I'm very judgemental about people. Except for my father, of course. Maybe all my judgement focused on him, and there isn't any left for anybody else. So once Caroline knew she was safe with me and Lana, details of her life started coming out. She tells us more each yearly visit she makes. First, there were stories about her abusive grandmother who raised her. Caroline's father had been killed in World War II. And her mother, I suppose she was working all day. Caroline speaks English perfectly, so I tend to forget that she's actually German, from a small town outside Bonn. She came to the United States thirty-four years ago on a scholarship when she was just twenty-one. Went to the University of Virginia of all places and did a bachelor's in history, only later started taking her viola-playing seriously. I suppose because her family was German, I always picture her grandmother like the witch in *Hansel and Gretel*. She used to beat Caroline black and blue. With wet towels because they don't leave permanent marks. The biggest villain, though, was her stepfather. He forced her to suck his cock. That's the terminology Caroline uses, so that's the way I say it, too. Just this year we learned that he was the town doctor, *Herr Doktor*, a well-respected man. It was just after World War II in Germany and people were living on turnips. The family got meat and sugar through the good doctor and he got Caroline in exchange. From age twelve to nineteen, he forced her to suck his cock while the family fattened up on veal and *apfel strudel*. Two days ago, Caroline confessed to us that when the bastard died, she sobbed. I asked why, of course, and she said, 'I guess I loved him.' But she said it as if it were a question.

Apparently, the relationship between abusers and the abused is more complicated than I ever thought. I suppose I'm pretty innocent about that sort of thing. I was spanked a few times, yelled at frequently, but never treated roughly. So I think I'm pretty naïve about people's shadow lives. Like when Lana told me that her brother Denny must have had a different father than her. I was floored. Then it made sense, of course; he's twenty-one years younger than she is, and I don't believe for a moment that her parents were still having sex by then. So my mother-in-law must have had an affair when she was about forty, probably thought she could never get pregnant. Though I can't imagine who would want to touch her. When I told Lana that, she said it was probably the guy who was their mailman at the time. Apparently, she was only half-joking; she says he had Denny's shade of red hair.

Lana and I didn't speak about it, but we both know that her mother's affair was the real reason Mr Salgueiro called Denny a *filho da puta* when Lana went down to San Jose to try to broker a truce. What he was really saying is that he thinks his wife is indeed a *puta*, a whore.

Caroline told us a few days ago that before she vomits she feels like her skin is crawling with bugs. She wishes she could shed it and step out all nice and new. She meets in a group with other bulimics once a week at North Shore Hospital on Long Island. All of them want to have new skin.

೩೬

I've been thinking about all this tonight because I've been unable to sleep. From about two to four in the morning I just listened to the raccoons in the backyard and lost myself in thought.

When I look over at Lana on nights like this, I realize how lucky I've been. For so many years I never thought I'd be capable of loving anyone. People always said I was a cold person. A guitar teacher I had in high school told me that I had no passion. My mother told me once she thought I was dead inside.

There have been many times when I've broken out into a cold sweat thinking that they might be right about me. That maybe I've ruined Lana's life. After all, she wanted to have kids and I never agreed. She's thirty-eight now. In another two or three years it'll be too late. She says that she has no regrets, but sometimes I'm not sure.

This sort of guilt began to invade my thoughts at about four in the morning. It must have been the power of suggestion, but I felt a little like Caroline, like my skin was too confining. So I dressed real quietly and crept downstairs. When I closed the front door behind me, it felt right. The air was fresh and cool. Castro Street was empty. I got into my Honda and started driving.

I drove down Market Street to Highway 101 and headed south. My parents' old house is just off Lafayette Street in San Jose, right near the airport. I thought I'd take a look at it, but when I reached the exit about forty-five minutes later, I just kept on going. That felt good, like I was released from a servitude I'd never really agreed to. I wondered if my father had felt like this.

೩೬

All of San Jose's peach orchards are gone now, and the city has sprawled into a tangled mess of fast-food strips and residential neighbourhoods – like Los Angeles without UCLA or the County Museum or the beaches to redeem it. I've absolutely refused to orient myself on the visits Lana and I make to her parents' house in one of the new 'suburban dream' neighbourhoods down by the

Los Gatos hills. So I wandered around for an extra half hour before I found Alpendra Drive. When I parked in front of Hell House, as Lana, Denny and I call her family home, I still didn't know what I was up to. I thought I wanted to tell Mr and Mrs Salgueiro that they were assholes who had no right to have children and then not love them. But that wasn't it.

I found the garage door closed. I gripped the handle and lifted it up. 'Who's there?' came Denny's voice, all rushed and frightened.

'Your idiot brother-in-law.'

'Charlie?'

'You got another one?'

I heard the sound of feet on cloth, then the light came on. Denny was in his underwear, standing on his sleeping bag. He's a skinny kid. Too pale for California. True, he has beautiful green eyes, but he does everything he can to make himself look awkward. Like his hair; it's dyed black as can be, clipped close around the sides but left bushy on top. And he's got a quarter-sized enamel earring shaped like a garlic bulb in his right ear. Bought it last summer in Gilroy when me, Lana and him went to the Garlic Festival.

'What are you doing here?' he asked in a hushed voice.

'You can't keep sleeping in the garage.'

'Whisper, you'll wake my parents,' he told me.

'You think I care? I haven't slept well in a week. Why should *they*?'

'You mean you haven't slept well because of me?'

'Because of you and Lana. And my own past. Sometimes with me everything gets all mixed together.'

He looked down, considering his options. 'Did my sister send you?' he asked.

'Nope. I take responsibility for this. So put your clothes on. I'm tired.'

'I can't go with you.'

'Why not?'

'School. I've still got two months of school left.'

'You can go to school in San Francisco.'

'I can't transfer at this point of the year. And I'll have to repeat the year if I quit now. I won't be able to start college in the fall.'

'We'll worry about that later.'

'No, I can't go,' he said definitely.

Mr Salgueiro's old black Pontiac was parked in the garage. 'That is one *ugly* car,' I said to Denny. He smiled. He's got a nice smile. He's a good kid, a little lost and lonely, but who wouldn't be in his position? I realized for the first time how much I loved him. Strange how you can live for years not really knowing things like that. I said, 'Listen, have you got your driver's licence yet?'

'Why?'

'Have you got it or not?'

'Yeah, I got it.'

'Good, then you can get up a bit earlier than usual and drive to your regular school from San Francisco. It'll take you less than an hour.'

'Using whose car?'

'Mine or Lana's.'

'How will you get to work?'

'Denny, we can stand here thinking up questions all night long. Just put on your damn clothes and come with me. Seventeen years of this is enough. I'm not saying you have to give up on your parents. But Lana's got a good heart. And she loves you. I can't say either of those things about the occupants of Hell House. Can you?'

'I think they love me,' he said.

'Maybe. Maybe I don't understand love. I don't know. I don't even care. The point is, you're locked out of your house, and your father isn't going to let you back in. You want to live your life like a refugee you can. You want to come home with me now, you can do that too. Your choice.'

Kids will put up with too much from their parents, and I could tell he was about to refuse my offer. So I told him to just try it with us for a week and see if it works. In the car, we talked about his robbery. Turns out, things were a lot more complicated than I thought.

He said, 'You'll be the first person I've ever really told about it.'

Sometimes I wonder why it is that people will open up to me. Caroline says that it's because I never show surprise on my face. When she's in one of her esoteric moods, she says I'm the reincarnation of a very old being who has seen everything. When she's like that she calls me 'The Watcher.' I suppose I should be flattered, but I don't particularly like it.

'Go ahead,' I told Denny. 'It can't be that bad.'

He shook his head. 'It's worse.'

'So... what is it?'

'You can't tell my parents. Or even Lana.' His voice was imploring.

'I won't say a thing to your parents. As for Lana, I can't promise. When we lie in bed at night I say things I...'

Before I could finish my sentence, he said, 'I'm... I'm gay.'

He squeezed it out of him like he expected me to slam on the brakes or start pulling out my hair. I can't say I'd ever suspected it, but on the other hand I wasn't floored. I said, 'Denny, you live in the Bay Area you stop thinking that being gay or straight is any big deal.'

'You're wrong. It's still a big deal in San Jose. It's not like San Francisco.' Denny's hands had formed fists. 'People here... it's like San Francisco's an island with pretty houses and cafés and book-stores and a thousand fucking Chinese restaurants. San Jose... San Jose, man, it's... it's got people who watch Monday Night Football and drink beer and just want to get through their days without having too many hassles from their kids. It's all people who would hate Lana's videos.'

I knew what Denny was saying was mostly true, but that he was talking more than anything about his father. I said, 'Just tell me what being gay has to do with your robbing a grocery store.'

'It's not just a grocery store. It's got a section where people can rent videos. It's a weird little place.'

'Go on.'

'I don't know,' he said. 'I just did it.'

'Not good enough.'

'It's the new manager. He's a Turkish immigrant. Maybe thirty. I was buying cigarettes there one day... '

'You've started smoking?'

'They were for my father.'

'And what happened?'

'And we started talking. It was during the day, but nobody was there. We were talking about Turkey because I noticed his accent.

He said he had some photographs of Istanbul on the wall of the stockroom. He locked the front door and we went back there. Then he just sort of reached down and held my cock in his hand. I mean, he felt through my jeans.'

'And then?'

'Well, he sort of gave me a blow job. It was the first time... the only...'

His voice was choking up. To put him at ease, I asked if it had been any good.

He laughed like people do who've been close to crying. 'Not really. I was too nervous. Afterward, I figured I wasn't really gay because I didn't really enjoy it.'

'My first one was awful, too,' I said. 'I think you can still see the teeth marks on my cock if you look closely.'

Denny didn't laugh this time. He asked, 'Charlie, do you think I'm really weird?'

'No.'

He was biting his thumbnail and staring out the windshield.

'Look,' I said, 'you want to make being gay a big deal, you can. I'm just glad you discovered it now and not later when...'

I was about to say, '... when you're married and have a seven-year-old kid.' I surprised myself with that. But being gay suddenly seemed like a possibility for my father. Maybe he left us out of guilt. Maybe it wasn't me and my mom, after all. Maybe he thought that *he* was the one at fault, that he was ruining our lives, was going to make me gay if he stayed. *He ordered seeds from a hundred different seed catalogues. He began to say my tits were too big.* Was that my mother's crazy way of saying... ? Was it possible?

'When what?' Denny asked me.

I was disoriented and didn't answer, so he said, 'Why are you glad I discovered it now? I want to know.'

'It's just that the sooner you understand that sort of thing the better. Cuts down on the complications.'

'I'm not sure what you mean by complications,' he told me. 'It seems pretty complicated to me.'

'It doesn't matter for now. We'll talk about it later. Anyway, you went back to see the Turkish guy.'

'Yeah, a few days later. And he did it again.'

'And this time you liked it.'

He smiled shyly. 'But on the way out of the store, I don't know why, I was angry at the guy, stole some videos from the shelf. And ran. It was like I had to get back at him. He called the police to get his videos back. But he didn't press charges. I suppose he didn't want the story about us coming out.'

❧

The sun was just coming up over the bay when we got home to San Francisco. Lana and Caroline were already at the kitchen table. Coffee had been served, was steaming out of the ceramic mugs which Caroline had made for us this year. They're tawny-coloured, with purple irises glazed on the outside.

Caroline was wearing her pink kimono, was stirring in a bowl the mixture of yoghurt, yeast and powdered vitamins which she eats each morning to make up for the nutrition she loses into the toilet twice a day. Lana was in her sweat pants and one of my Giants baseball shirts. When she saw Denny, she jumped up and hugged him. While she danced him around the kitchen, I told Caroline a bit of what had been happening. Then we sat around talking about Lana and Denny's parents. While I was starting on my second piece of toast, Caroline tilted her head like she does when she's about to spring a real direct question on you and said, 'What made you go down now and get Denny?'

So I told her and Lana and Denny about the contributor's note I'd read at the library. I said, 'Apparently, this author writes about people like me – who cry now and then when faced with bad situations, but who don't *do* anything. So I finally decided to go ahead and do something.'

'That's bullshit!' Caroline told me.

'What is?' I asked.

'Are you blind? Who do you think got a scholarship to music school, who plays like an angel, who scraped together enough money to put a down payment down on a cute little house? And who made your marriage work – your mother? And why do you think I'm here? Because you're some passive asshole?'

What she said upset me. I guess I never thought of myself as so responsible for the way my life had gone. I made believe I was tired in order to escape the pressure of her stare. I stood up and said, 'I'm going back up to bed.'

'You're not angry with me?' Caroline asked in a hesitant voice. Her shoulders were hunched, and she looked like she might cry.

I was gripped then by a really strange sensation – that I'd brought her, Lana and Denny together that morning for a reason that went far beyond Denny's trouble with his parents. It felt as if I were in need of their protection. 'No, I'm not angry,' I replied. 'A little confused, I suppose. I guess I'll have to think about all this when I'm more awake. Maybe it'll make sense then.'

Lana took my hand and led me to the stairs. We left Denny with Caroline. She was explaining about why she puts yeast in her yoghurt. Then Denny called my name. 'Thanks for coming to get me – for rescuing me from San Jose,' he smiled.

I didn't respond with words, just nodded. Looking back at him made me lose my voice. Because it was then that I realized that what hurt the most is that my father never said anything to me about calling 911 and saving his life, never even thanked me. It was as if I'd made some sort of mistake I was going to pay for for the rest of my life. And that I would pay for it by never being able to have a family of my own.

Rudolf's Secret

Karina Magdalena Szczurek

> like a dead spider's, her legs and arms
> curl around her body, hidden under
> a battered blanket of shattered dreams
>
> (from 'The night is everywhere the same' by Anne Keru)

Some things are still very clear. Saturn, the bruised sky, Anele's unmatched socks, her wrists, or even the smell of Granny's hands when she drew for me. Rudolf was there, of course. But strange, how after many years, I do not recall the scene itself, how it is blurred in my memory like a photograph out of focus. Sometimes, I imagine the bathtub full of red water. Sometimes, I try hard to make it look transparent.

I remember Rudolf sitting in the morning on the little suitcase which Mom had prepared for me in the night. I saw her packing it and crying silently. She thought I was asleep, but I only pretended. It must have been very early when father came into my room and told me he was taking me to Granny's again for a while. Mom wasn't feeling well and needed rest, he explained, but this time I knew better. He wouldn't let me see her before we left. Maybe she preferred me not to see her, I don't know, and now that she is gone all but my memories are gone with her.

I know now that it wasn't the first time, but it was the first time I saw it. She made sure that it was the last for all of us. It took me a while to remember all the other times my mother had sent me away, or the way she winced when I sometimes wanted to cuddle, or the heavy make-up and the dark glasses, and all the other obvious signs.

It all happened shortly after my sixth birthday. The morning after I saw them, I carried Rudolf to the car and Father took the suitcase.

After the sleepless night, I must have drifted off during the drive because I only remember arriving at Granny's house. Father didn't even want to stay for tea, he left immediately. I didn't want to hug him, so I just waved and ran into the house with Rudolf under my arm. I asked Granny to be bathed the moment she followed me inside. When I insisted on taking Rudolf into the bath with me, she suggested to put him in the washing machine instead. I didn't care how, I just wanted us to be clean. I didn't know then that some words are waterproof; they do not come off in the wash.

It was during that weekend that Anele brought her sadness over for sharing. She came while I, unable to share, sat cross-legged on my granny's kitchen floor, watching Rudolf through the small window of the washing machine. He showed up every now and then among the grey foam bubbles and the dirty laundry. In between, I sometimes saw my own face reflected in the glass surface, my curls all fuzzy around my head, still a bit wet from the bath.

When the doorbell rang, the chicken Granny was preparing for lunch was abandoned on the kitchen counter, naked among garlic cloves and rosemary twigs. It looked lonely. I could hear the sounds of a warm welcome in the passage. I peeked around the corner to see the visitor. When the phone sounded its shrilling ring I got such a fright that I sprang back into the empty room, and when I dared another look again I saw Granny picking up the receiver while a young woman in a long grey dress disappeared into her studio. I sneaked past Granny down the passage. I can still walk like a cat, softly and unnoticed. That's how I saw what I saw, even if I was not supposed to. The young woman also didn't see me watching her. I remember how pretty she was. The grey dress came down to her ankles. Standing there, I noticed how her socks did not match, one was black with a red flower on the side, the other plain dark blue. She was holding a parcel in her hands which looked like a present. I heard Granny's voice behind me, 'Yes, don't worry. It's really fine. You just get better.' I guessed it was Mom on the phone, lying to Granny about being sick. If only I had spoken to her when she had asked for me…

The young woman stared at the painting on the easel in the centre of the room. 'This is Saturn,' I told her and she jumped around like a frightened squirrel to see me. 'He is trying to swallow his children. But they are running away.' Granny liked painting gory stuff. She had a soft spot for myths and legends. Maybe because she knew how true they are. In a way her gruesome stories prepared me for what had happened; because of them I also knew about Saturn. 'Hello there,' she said putting the parcel she was holding on Granny's table and tugging one of the many braids falling over her face behind her left ear. As she was about to reach for another, the long sleeve of her dress revealed a bandaged wrist.

'What happened to you?' The question was out of my mouth before I could think about it, but she did not seem offended. She just whispered, 'It's a secret,' and pulled both sleeves over her hands. The other one was also bandaged, I saw. I felt guilty about asking, so I offered something in return, 'Rudolf's also gotta secret,' I whispered back and ran out of the room. I heard Granny calling me, 'Lena, Mommy wants to speak to you... Lena!... Lena?'

But I didn't want to speak to her. And I have regretted it ever since. I went back to the washing machine and pretended not to hear. It was difficult to hold back the tears pressing on my eyes, big and brown in the reflection of the washing machine window. But I was glad that at least soon both of us, Rudolf and me, wouldn't be dirty.

In the afternoon, Rudolf was dangling from the washing line by his wings outside the kitchen window. The sky looked bruised; I was worried it would rain before Rudolf was dry. The air in the house was filled with rosemary. I sat in Granny's lap at the kitchen table and her hands still smelled of garlic as she drew ponies and donkeys in the sketchbook in front of us.

'You know,' she began while she was working on the fence of the enclosure for the animals in the drawing, 'when Anele was here, your mommy phoned. She sounded very weak. But I told her she mustn't worry, the two of us are just fine.'

'Dad says Mommy is sick,' I probed.

'She will get better soon. It must be the flu everybody's getting now,' she added and touched her upper lip with the tip of her tongue before finishing the drawing. 'There. How do you like it?'

She couldn't have known, and no matter how much I wanted to

tell her, I didn't know how to begin. That's how I learned the pain of secrets. I asked about the young woman with the bandaged wrists instead, 'Is Anele sick too?'

'No. Not really. She is just very sad. That is why she needed a little chat today. To share her sadness. She used to be one of my students. She paints, too, you know.' I nodded and thought about Mom who had no one to share her sadness with. I turned to the sketchbook again, 'Now please draw Rudolf for me.'

'Let's see if he is dry first. Maybe he can pose for us properly before the rain gets him. And we must find a spot for this,' she pointed to the content of the parcel Anele had brought with her. It was a small painting, full of reds and dark blues smudged across the canvas. 'What is it?' I asked Granny.

'These are Anele's feelings. She is sad and angry. That is why she paints these at the moment.' At first she hung it up in her studio, but after that weekend, it ended up in the shed; because it was too much to take, she explained to me later. Now, it hangs in my study, sometimes to remind me, sometimes to reflect my own anger. Anele went on to become quite famous. I attended a few of her exhibitions, at first with Granny, then after she too had died, on my own.

That day when she brought the painting to Granny's house, my world was already shaken but not yet completely shattered. The painting remained on the kitchen table for the time being while Granny and I went outside and collected Rudolf with the rest of the laundry. The first raindrops fell to the ground as we were returning to the house. He was all clean and smelled of softener. Like Mom, I thought at the time. Most people laughed when they saw him, but back then I didn't think he was funny. Guardian angels are not supposed to be funny, they're just supposed to protect you. I'd had him since I was born; he was really just a teddy with wings, round soft brown body with a red heart stitched onto his breast and big white wings – well, they were grey until Granny washed him. When we were in the kitchen I whispered into his ear so Granny wouldn't hear me, 'You're clean now, too.' But she picked it up. 'That he certainly is,' she said. 'What's this obsession with cleanness today?' she asked, but I just shrugged and told her, 'It's Rudolf's secret.' An awkward silence followed, which Granny broke, sizing me up: 'I won't interfere with secrets. So, let's see what a model he will make, shall we?' She put the washing basket on the kitchen table and made her way down the passage. I followed, hugging Rudolf to my breast.

In the studio, Granny removed Saturn and his children from the easel and placed Rudolf on a high stool in front of it. 'Now,' she began, while I stood behind her looking at the running children, one covered in blood, another screaming. 'I think he is too small for this canvas,' Granny continued. 'What do you say?' She looked around at me with a funny smile. I didn't know what to say. 'I think you will have to help him out. How about the two of you posing together?'

I looked at Saturn, then at her and Rudolf, and suddenly the question just popped out of my mouth, 'Granny, what is a bitch?'

'What sweetie?' She was obviously shocked.

'A bitch,' I repeated. To cover up my confusion I climbed onto the stool with Rudolf and tried to pretend nothing had happened.

'Where did you hear that?' The smile in Granny's eyes flickered, as if hesitant whether to stay or go.

'What is it?' I insisted.

'Well, it's the name for a girl dog. You know how one calls a girl horse a mare and a boy horse a stallion. So, a bitch is a special name for a girl dog. And,' she added with that voice, I recognized, adults use when pretending that something wasn't important, 'it is an ugly word for a wicked woman. Where did you…'

'We are ready now!' I told her, interrupting and straightening my back with Rudolf poised on my knees, his plush wings all clean on his back.

I still have that portrait Granny painted of me and Rudolf; it hangs next to Anele's anger. That night I asked Granny to put the portrait next to my bed and to leave the bedside light on. I felt safer with two Rudolfs with me in the room, even if one was painted. But I couldn't sleep, the words *dirty bitch* hammering in my head. That is what he had called her the previous night. He repeated the words over and over again like a harsh whisper with every blow. Bitch. Dirty bitch.

Wicked woman. A dirty wicked woman.

And all I had wanted was to go and pee in the night when I saw the light in the lounge and went to have a look. I stood in the shadows, unable to move. The memory of what I saw probably blurred because of tears in my eyes. What I never forgot was the sound of his voice, those words spoken so quietly, but with the force of a whip.

I ran. They never saw me, and never knew what I had witnessed that night. In the safety of my room, I slipped back into bed, trembling, the need to pee all forgotten. My limbs were calm when Mom came in some time later. She packed my suitcase in the dark. I saw her silhouette against the window, she was sobbing very quietly as she went about the packing. Before she left, she whispered something to me and caressed my cheek with a cold hand. I wish I could've asked her what it was she'd said. I never saw her again.

The following night, my mother was much more successful than Anele. While I was hugging Rudolf and looking at his image in the portrait at Granny's house, Mom decided to wash off her life. Father found her the next morning in a bathtub full of blood.

Yes, I remembered that weekend when Anele came over to share her sadness with Granny. If only I could've done the same, Mom might have been still alive; I reproached myself for years to come. After her death, Father took off, and Rudolf and I came to live with Granny. Sharing sadness wasn't always easy; I don't know how old I was when I was first able to talk about what had happened. It was also much later that I remembered Anele and asked Grandma about the reason she had sliced her wrists open. Rape is also a waterproof word.

Many years afterwards when I was looking for a name for my own daughter, I also found out that, in Xhosa, Anele's name meant 'enough'.

De-Luxe Model

Adam Thorpe

My schoolfriend Hugh Gould had a big old house in Chorley Wood. I liked being invited there and to stay overnight, which happened every so often. He had a huge bushy garden with real trees, whereas ours was small and bare; his house included a drawing room, a dining room, a kitchen, a scullery and something called a utility room, with five bedrooms above and an attic where we plotted impossible schemes. There was a posh wireless, but no television.

The kitchen and scullery had floors of uneven brick, worn down by centuries of use, that were useless when it came to racing our Dinky toys. We couldn't race them anywhere else because the house was carpeted from wall to wall, and the only strip of exposed parquet was in the study; Ronald, Hugh's father, worked there all day as a representative for a Peruvian gold-mining company. Or that's what Hugh claimed. Ronald also had his own dressing room, which I thought was a good idea, as I hated dressing in front of my twin brothers. Hugh was an only child.

Hugh's mother, who was much taller than her husband, looked after the house with the help of her charlady. Compared to my own mother, who worked as a nurse, Mrs Gould had an easy job, but she never stopped saying how tired she was. I was a bit scared of her, because she was bad-tempered and strict and would point out that my socks had fallen, that my shirt was hanging out of my shorts, and that my hair (which was clipped to just above the ears) made me look like a beatnik – this last comment pleased me. We had to unbuckle and remove our shoes if we came in from the garden, in case a single grass blade or a speck of mud should 'soil the impeccable interior' – as Hugh put it, mockingly, once we were safely upstairs.

The one advantage my cramped and messy modern house had over Hugh's, apart from having a telly, was the lino in the kitchen:

smooth enough to race our Dinky toys on. This advantage was cancelled when Hugh's mother decided to redo her kitchen from top to bottom. I couldn't visit for several weeks as a result, but Hugh said it was the biggest building job since the Pyramids; his jacket's leather elbow patches were marked by white dust. Finally it was over, and by now I was very excited because Hugh told me that the new kitchen had been kitted out with the latest space-age equipment, including a robot to wash the dishes very like the one featured in a recent copy of *Look and Learn*, to which Hugh subscribed. He was deadly serious about this, and my initial scoffing dwindled to keen anticipation.

Nothing prepared me for the change. The scullery wall had been knocked down, so it wasn't even the same room. Walking into the kitchen by the new glass-paned door was like being transported to a different dimension – or at least to a different house. All the old wooden cabinets and shelves had been torn out and replaced by new, off-white melamine units with metallic handles like grinning lips. The table was also melamine, surrounded by yellow stools with plastic cushioned seats that sighed when you sat on them.

In one unit sat a white machine with a square door, a golden handle and three buttons.

'The robot,' said Hugh.

'That's just an ordinary dishwasher,' I scoffed – although I had never actually seen a real one before, or not up close.

'Ordinary? This, folks, is a de-luxe Colston with every imaginable luxury feature,' Hugh cried, in an American accent. 'Needle-jet spray, swivelling basket, two full rinsing cycles, leaving your dishes super-dry and sparkling clean,' he squealed, dancing about on the orange lino.

I had only just noticed the lino: it was incredibly smooth and we were in socks. Hugh's mother came in and told us off for using the kitchen as a skating rink and making an awful racket. Her glasses magnified her eyes and had curly bits over the top like extra eyebrows. She gave us tea and sponge cake eaten with little forks and then, drawing deeply on her menthol cigarette, she ordered us to 'load the dishwasher'. This involved taking our tea things to the sink, rinsing them until all the crumbs and clots of jam had gone, then placing the plates, cups and cutlery inside the machine in exactly the right position as dictated by her. Hugh was reminded to flick what he called the 'turbo-jet blade' to check it didn't catch on anything: this was really important, apparently. He asked which setting and she said 'heavily soiled'.

The machine was now ready to go, and I was allowed to fill the detergent compartment with white granules, tipping them out of the plastic flask so carefully that Mrs Gould said we would be here all day. But I had been told not to go above the line, and not to touch the granules with my bare skin.

'It's really quiet,' Hugh said, pressing one of the buttons – the top one. 'Space-age techonology. They'll take one with them when they go to the moon.'

The machine coughed, shuddered, and made a sound similar to that of our lavatory filling up, except that it went on and on. Then about ten minutes later – during which time Hugh and I chatted while Mrs Gould wiped the gleaming surfaces around us, sighing above her plastic pinny – it shook violently and I thought it was about to blow up. The shaking calmed down, but it still sounded as if every dish inside was being methodically smashed by an army of miniature men.

'It's considerably quieter than Mrs Mallinson's older model,' said Mrs Gould, settling down to another cigarette in her rubber gloves. Mrs Mallinson was the next-door neighbour, whose husband commuted to the City and drove a Jaguar. Both the Mallinsons smelled of gin and laughed aloud in their garden.

'Considerably quieter, Mummy,' said Hugh. I was never sure whether or not he was mocking someone.

We were allowed to go upstairs to play, but only on the understanding that, in about forty minutes, we would descend for the unloading operation. I was desperate to slide down the banisters, as on my last visit we had only got to the semi-finals of the world cup – with the Soviet Union in the lead, unfortunately. If Hugh's mother stayed in the kitchen, deafened by the dishwasher, and Ronald remained shut up in the study as usual, we had a chance of succeeding without being detected.

We were about to begin after the opening ceremony when, on the landing, Hugh suddenly seized my arm and whispered in my ear that he had something incredibly secret and exciting to show me, that he only showed trusted friends and that, if he did show me, I would have to swear on my own blood never to tell anyone else.

I instantly agreed, my heart hammering, despite the unpleasant idea of spilling my own blood. This visit was turning out to be the best yet; I needed it. Since my father's fatal crash in our Hillman Minx two years before, I had existed in a bubble of misery disguised by a grinning mask and silly pranks at school. My marks had plummeted. Perhaps Hugh was about to show me a secret door in his shadowy tangle of a garden, a door leading to somewhere you could kick a ball around with the dead.

We slipped into his room, however. He reached under his bed and pulled out a shoe box, its lid secured by a rubber band and pierced with tiny holes. It smelled of my grandfather's rabbits and something scrabbled about inside. Very carefully, inch by inch, Hugh lifted the lid. A tiny pointed nose pushed out, then a beady-eyed face. It was a mouse, with pink forepaws that grabbed the side as if on a boat.

'Basildon,' said Hugh. 'Basildon Ebenezer Bond.'

I was disappointed. We had mice at home, the white kind from the pet shop that kept dying. This was a wild mouse, Hugh informed me; it had somehow survived his mother's chronic hygiene campaign, which included the sprinkling of poison pellets at strategic points. Its parents were probably dead.

'Or its children,' I suggested.

'It's too young for children,' Hugh snorted.

The lid was pressed down again and the broad rubber band snapped back.

'It must feel a bit trapped in there,' I said.

'I'm training Baz to behave like a pet,' Hugh said. 'Once I've trained him, he can play in my room and sleep on my pillow and do whatever he wants.'

'A bit lonely in there,' I persisted.

'Oh shut your cakehole,' Hugh snapped, and shoved me onto his pillow where I pretended to die in agony.

His mother's familiar command called us down like pigeons to a crust. I was surprised to see Ronald there, blinking through his thick spectacles, his oiled hair swept back from his forehead, exaggerating his baldness in the same way my own father's haircut had. Ronald was at the new sink, receiving the dry contents of the dishwasher from his wife. 'Here they are and about time,' sighed Mrs Gould, frowning at us.

I replaced her at the dishwasher while Hugh was given the tea towel and stood on the other side of his father. Mrs Gould watched, like a foreman or a manager, blinking furiously. I was surprised to see that Ronald was rinsing the utensils over again, handing them to Hugh to be dried. Then I understood: everything I took out of the machine had a horrible, warm feel to it, a roughness sickeningly combined with a dry slipperiness, a dreadful texture I had never experienced before in my entire eleven years. Once dried again by Hugh, they were handed over to Mrs Gould, who examined them carefully then put them away in drawers or in one of the new cupboards that all looked the same.

'It's like a factory belt,' Hugh pointed out.

'More like a chain gang,' murmured his father. Ronald looked strange in rubber gloves and a pinny, with his bristly moustache; he wasn't much taller than me. He had panned for gold in Peru and sheltered in a cinema doorway during an earthquake that had killed twenty-two thousand people in a few minutes. 'We'll have to invent some slave songs, boys.'

'Stop talking rubbish and get on with it,' snapped his wife. It amazed me, how she treated him. It wasn't normal. Then she would suddenly be nice and soft for a few minutes, as if letting go of something, and a smile covered her face like a dazzling sun on a rainy day. It never lasted. The whole unloading operation took twenty-five minutes. I calculated that the Colston de-luxe model had added another hour to washing the dishes, but somehow that seemed part of its power, the power of progress.

Hugh had two beds in his large room. I lay in one of them that night, after a bout of ghost stories, and failed to drop off. It wasn't the ghost stories, it was Basildon Ebenezer Bond. Baz scrabbled about under Hugh's bed, I could hear his desperate little paws. I found it difficult to breathe, thinking of him stuck in the tiny box and its awful darkness relieved only by pin-pricks in the day, like stars. Gradually, a new plot evolved in my mind. I pictured Basildon living a happy life in Hugh's huge garden – his home a hole in a tree, with rooms for all his family. I had always wanted to live in a tree. Our garden had no trees.

❧

While Hugh was in the bathroom after lunch the next day, brushing his teeth prior to going outside, I pulled out the shoe box and slipped a practised hand inside. Within seconds Basildon was wriggling inside my jacket (my school jacket, with its deep pockets, doubled as my coat), ready to be released into the fresh air. All would have gone well, except that on our way out Mrs Gould asked us to stack the dishwasher. She was training us, she joked. It was almost ready to go again, because supper had involved large pans and it needed an empty space or two to really foam freely, as she put it.

As I knelt down to the machine, nervously placing the rinsed frying pan where Mrs Gould had directed me to, I felt something soft tickle my arm underneath the sleeve; a shadow crossed my hand. I straightened up, startled, as Hugh poured in the granules. I checked my inside jacket pocket: Basildon was no longer there, but now there was a hole at the bottom through which I could tickle my armpit. I wanted to say something as I scanned the Colston's interior, the unwashed plates and cutlery like the workings of an evil time-bomb, but before I could summon enough courage, the door slammed shut and the button was pressed.

'Bombs away,' said Hugh, as if he could read my mind.

I played explorers among the evergreen bushes in a zombie-like daze, but Hugh didn't notice. I could hear the dishwasher rumbling and gasping away from halfway down the lawn: Basildon might not have run into it at all, of course. Or he may have escaped.

When the last cycle came to an end, I could hear the breeze and the birds. Our play was interrupted, a few minutes later, by a piercing scream from the house. We ran into the kitchen without removing our shoes, scattering tiny clods of earth over the shining linoleum. Mrs Gould was shivering and whimpering at the table, clutching her face as if she had seen a ghost; Ronald was perusing something in his hand, which he then held out flat towards us. Lying on his palm was a formless brown object with a string attached to it. Hugh pulled a puzzled face. Thankfully, Basildon was no longer recognisable as a once-living creature.

'It's a mouse,' said Ronald. 'A mouse in the dishwasher.'

'In the dishwasher!' wailed Hugh's mother. 'Oh God! Nowhere, nowhere is safe!'

'That's what they said after the earthquake,' murmured Ronald, as Hugh shot upstairs to check and I followed meekly, preparing my mask yet again.

Swan Sister

Katherine Vaz

My sister, Rachel, was born wrong. There was a mistake in every cell in her body. She lived for a while in an incubator at St Vincent's Hospital in New York City and looked so tiny in her glass nest. 'She's our little swan,' said my mother. Rachel was wild, and beautiful, and seemed ready to fly away. She stared upward, each of her eyes just one drop of pale blue. 'Hello,' I whispered. 'Don't you want to stay with me?' I was eleven and had been waiting for a sister for a long time. She was rose-pink. Her head was like a soap bubble, the kind that has panes the colour of a rainbow on it. My father put a toy elephant on the top of the glass, to lasso her with its trunk if she tried to float off before we said goodbye. She was going to leave us very soon.

One night while holding Rachel, I saw my Uncle Jack tapping on the outside of the window of the intensive care unit. He and my mother had not spoken in years. He walks fast, talks fast, reaches high; my mother is slow. She's a young spirit with no sense of time. Sometimes instead of going to work, she decides to go to Central Park and sketch the trees, and my job is to call the pet store where she's a cashier to say she has the flu. Thin as one of her drawing pencils, she forgets to untangle her short black hair. Humming, staring into space, she escapes in her mind to places I can't always reach, and when my father comes home from working at his fruit stand, he helps me make tomato soup filled with carrot pieces cut into daisies. Mother taught me how to twirl around until I'm too dizzy to stand; she made us both necklaces from chains of paper clips.

Uncle Jack is an old spirit who decided he didn't have the patience for us. But there he was in the hospital with his arms around Mother. Rachel had worked a miracle in summoning him back to us. And suddenly our mother was calm and strong, so the little swan must have performed wonders inside of her as well. Uncle Jack was the one to cry. Mother said only, 'She's my joy for as many hours or days as I have her.'

'You have me now, too,' he said.

When Rachel was allowed to come home, I invented a plan. I would show her New York. It was the city of my birth, and my mother's birth, and my father's. If Rachel saw how astonishing it was, and how much I loved it, she would decide she could not possibly leave us. We lived in our own small nest on West 18th Street, high enough to see the river turn into melted silver when the sun went down. I held Rachel up to our window and said, 'It's so exciting here your heart won't ever stop beating!' The clouds were like white wings drifting along, above the wide world, bird-high.

The doctor said it was a fine idea to help Rachel enjoy every single minute. We were given permission to take her out. She had a tube attached from her nose to an oxygen machine that was green and thin and had wheels and a handle so that we could push it around. Mother offered to steer the machine and I could carry Rachel. One bright morning, the light dripping gold, we bundled her in a blanket covered with sailboats and took the elevator down fifteen flights. The first man to fall in love with my sister, other than my father and Uncle Jack, was Rafael, the doorman. 'Who is this angel?' he shouted when we crossed the lobby.

He took my sister from me and said, 'She's a sweetheart.'

'Oh, yes,' said Mother, happy as a breeze. 'Jessica and I are going to show her the city.'

'Will you marry me?' Rafael asked Rachel.

Her face was too weak to smile, but she politely shined some light off her eyes.

We made a strange parade, Mother wheeling the machine and my sister in my arms and the tube connecting her to the canister of air, as we strolled slow-motion down West 18th and stopped at Tillmore Bakery Supplies, with its ballerinas for cakes, candles with sparkles, and sugar roses. She would have no birthdays, but we wanted her to see a giant store that held out the promise of every celebration that anyone could imagine. In the narrow aisles, shoppers stepped aside as I showed Rachel the bins of confetti, party hats (I put one on), and the books on how to make wedding cakes that looked like white temples. I showed her cookie cutters shaped like half-moons and turkeys. Rachel slept. 'Please try and pay attention,' I said. It was almost like our first sisterly quarrel. Mother giggled and took the party hat off my head and pretended it was a megaphone that she held to her mouth to boom out, 'Earth to Rachel!'

My sister perked up and grabbed my finger with her right hand as we went back onto the street. Summer was already tipping toward fall. The leaves were turning their usual fire colours, and they scuttled through the streets until people, or taxis and cars, crushed out all that fire under their feet or tyres. Maybe it was Rachel's second miracle (or third, fourth, one hundredth) that when people saw us walking at half-speed with the oxygen machine and my sister attached to it, instead of being in a hurry (like my Uncle Jack), they also slowed down and said, 'oh, heavens' or 'oh, my' the way people sound the first time they see a tide pool – how pretty, how easily crushed.

We walked under some scaffolding around a bank. 'Look, Jessica! Look, Rachel!' said Mother. A construction worker had taken off his metal hat and was bowing at us.

We turned down Sixth Avenue so that Mother could show Rachel the pet store, Animal Kingdom, where she worked. Chihuahuas jumped at the glass in the window display when I lowered her into view. My sister's legs had no strength but I felt a tremor in her, telling me that she would kick with pleasure if she could. She had raw, thin skin so much like the flesh of these puppies that they forgave her for being a bird. The pet store smelled of grain, leather, newspaper, and the milky scent of baby animals. My mother introduced Rachel to her boss, Doris, who had red hair that she brushed upward into a flame. She was the person I lied to whenever I called to get my mother out of work, and I often feared that Doris would explode into a torch that would burn its way to the truth.

Instead, Doris gave us a toy cloth mouse with a small bell attached to its collar. I shook it in front of Rachel and her head tilted.

'You taking care of yourself, sweetie?' Doris asked my mother. Doris has a voice like a volcano erupting.

'Rachel is taking care of all of us,' said Mother.

We visited Mr Wing, who runs the stationery store where I buy pens and notebooks for school and fold-out maps of the subway. I call him my 'Quarter Friend' because one day I was fumbling with my money, and customers were impatient behind me, but I could not bear to use my special quarters with the mementos of the states on them. Mr Wing laughed and said, 'I'm also a collector.' He likes Georgia with its huge peach, which leaves me no choice but to roll my eyes and say, 'But Mr Wing, how common!' He never fails to act like this is the richest joke he's ever heard. He keeps a shrine with joss sticks and oranges on a shelf with a red paper poster of the Double Happiness symbol. 'Ask for happiness, and also a long life, Jessica. A long life without happiness is useless, and a happy life that isn't long is not good either,' he once explained to me.

Today he gave Rachel a red envelope with a dollar in it and said, 'For good luck.'

Oh the wonders we took in, my baby sister and Mother and me! We saw fish with open mouths, like trophies, in the window at Balducci's, and the bricks and spires of the old courthouse that makes me think of a palace in Moscow. It's now a library. Rachel whined and fussed; was she sad because she could not read books? Mother said, 'I'll take you to the big public library with its stone lions, and Jessica and Father and I will read to you at home.' I would take her to art museums and show her Monet, who paints the world as if it's melting. And to gardens with birds-of-paradise, lilies, and other children.

We backtracked to West 14th Street for a surprise visit to Antonio's, my father's store, where he sells fruit, vegetables, bread and candy. Sometimes in the alley behind, the pale green and yellow wrappings from the apples and pears get loose and fly about. They look like the moltings of canaries. When I handle the fruits there, I imagine them full of bird-singing. I put them to my ear and listen. Today I held one to Rachel's ear; she'd been born knowing the language of the skies.

Father was cutting open a burlap sack of lemons when we walked in, and he stopped and smiled. The world froze. 'My girls,' he said.

He helped Mother steer the oxygen machine around a stand with a pyramid of red apples. They gleamed. They had white kisses on them, from being polished and stacked in the light.

Father said, 'Rachel isn't too tired, is she? Are you, dear?'

He wiped his hands on his apron. He is skin and bones, and his hairline is already receding. Even his moustache is thin. He handed me a caramel and suddenly, unwrapping it, I was struck as if I had been sleepwalking through my many foolish days and now I was jolted awake – because all of us were here, my sister fluttering against my chest, my mother exhausted but at peace. There was sweetness in my mouth. We were surrounded by fruit that could be split open to hear better the bird songs inside them. My father is quiet (Uncle Jack once said he had no ambition), but on the day of Rachel's great adventure, I put my head to my father's chest and discovered that there was singing, loud birdsong, inside my father, too.

The weather turned colder after that, and we agreed to keep Rachel inside. But I longed for the day to take her out again, and I began to knit a jacket for her. Mother bought me thick yarn, blue and white. I wanted to work small waves of blue into a white background. I sat by Rachel in her crib and my needles clicked out a little music that made my heart sing. They made a tap tap that lulled her to sleep – but many nights she fussed and many mornings she awakened short of breath. 'That's part of a swan's story, Jessica,' said my mother when she saw me worrying. 'Swans disappear at night and perform bold deeds and must race back by daylight, panting.' Mother taught me a cable stitch, and I kept unravelling my work until it came out just right. I did a front panel, the blue yarn peaking along, and started one of the sleeves – not easy! 'You'll be wearing it by Halloween,' I told Rachel.

I imagined the night as a swarm of crows, biting at her feathers. They must have nipped her without mercy, because often at first light she was red and crying. I finished the collar. It was rough, not as smooth as it should have been, but I knew I had to hurry.

We ventured into the city one more time: Uncle Jack called to say that he was getting an award for the best sales of stocks and bonds for his company that year. Invitations engraved in gold arrived, including one for Rachel. And one for me: I ran my fingers along my name, indented on the page: Jessica. We took a taxicab because we thought Rachel's life would not be complete without a genuine ride in one. The driver kept saying, 'Poor child, poor child,' until Mother said: 'What are you going on about? Sir? She's off to Wall Street. She's in heaven.' Mother was in her black velvet dress, and I wore my cranberry velvet one with a matching sash. Rachel was in green togs that made her skin less yellow.

Uncle Jack was wearing a black suit in a theatre-like room. When he saw us, he stopped talking to some people and came to hug us. He took Rachel in his arms and said, 'It wouldn't be the same without you here.'

We could not stay long because Rachel began to cry again, but Uncle Jack ordered a limousine to take us home. I said, 'Rachel! Maybe people will think we're rock stars.' I'd brought along my knitting in a brown paper bag, because I knew that time was running short. I still needed to fix the hem, and one more sleeve was left to knit.

That night I sat up even though my eyelids kept dropping. I stitched the hem in place. Just as I was starting on the right sleeve, Rachel returned early from her night flight, wailing, and I had to comfort her. Father got up; it was almost his usual time. There's a courtyard below us, and I showed Rachel that pieces of the moon had gotten caught in some of the bramble bushes. Father nursed a cup of coffee and stood with us. The sky flipped stars into his cup, tiny ones, a size that could fit over Rachel's eyes. He said, 'It's my favourite time. The night is finishing and the day is starting, and they're both together for a moment, right now. It's like there's no one else awake.'

'Almost no one,' I said.

'Right,' he said. 'There's us.' It was four in the morning. Rachel screeched worse than ever, and he took her from me to see if he could quiet her. Her screams brought Mother to us. We tried to pat Rachel, sing to her. She hollered, she raised the roof. She hit high notes and then low ones and started in all over again.

'She's in pain,' said Mother.

An ambulance took Rachel and Mother to the hospital, and Father and I rode in a police car, but I was frantically knitting. I needed to finish the jacket. Hospital clothing is so horrible and unpretty, and Rachel liked to look nice.

When Father and I got to St Vincent's, Mother met us in the

emergency hallway. She was serene, so I thought Rachel would be fine. I had ten rows started of the last sleeve. I'd been getting the thread wet with sweating. The soles of shoes in the corridors made a squishing sound, and some nurses were laughing and I almost yelled at them to shut up. I was still hearing Rachel's screaming inside me.

'They tried to revive her,' said Mother. 'But they couldn't.'

Her insides were too small and too wrong for her to live.

Father and Mother did not want me to see her, but I said I needed to. I had that jacket to give her.

She was lying alone on a table in a room without much light. A white plastic tube like a pretend-cigar was still in her mouth, and Father took it out. He was weeping, but Mother was quiet. I stared into Rachel's blue eyes. They were half-open, looking at me – didn't that mean she was alive? Mother closed them with her finger. That's when I began to cry and bellow. I was going to be sick. I'd failed her. I hadn't taken her to the museum, or the library. I hadn't even finished her autumn jacket.

'Never mind,' said Mother. She took the jacket from my hand and threw the ugly white hospital blanket off my sister and dressed her in the white-and-blue knitting. I shrieked enough to shatter walls and take the colour out of paint. A sleeve was missing! I hadn't been fast or good enough!

'Let me tell you the last part of Rachel's Story,' said Mother. 'It goes like this: Everyone knows that swans only sing once, the most stunning song of their lives, but unfortunately, it's right before they die. Remember how she screamed tonight? Well, it's only because we're people and she's a swan that we couldn't tell at first that it was the most beautiful song in the world. And the mistake, the terrible mistake, that most people make when a swan dies is that they wrap it completely up tight. They cover its wings! And so, in the grave, a swan turns into a skeleton of a person, nothing more.

'But Rachel has a wing free. That was very thoughtful of you. Now she gets to fly wherever she wants. You'll have to look carefully; she's blue and white, so she's in the ocean and the sky. She wants to stay with you, and do you know why? Because it was brave of you not to turn away from her. You gave her a full life.

'She went to a place of many parties and a hundred candles. A

117

man asked to marry her! Friends greeted her wherever she went. Like a wise old woman, she soothed me and then won over your Uncle Jack. Can you believe he loves us again? That was Rachel's doing. Most people in a long life don't do as much good as she did in thirty days. She made the crowds stop and gape at her: What fame! She dressed up for fancy financial-street events. The city was at her feet; she was already soaring above it. How can she give that up?'

Uncle Jack came to the funeral at the cemetery, and I thanked him for walking in step with me, gripping my hand, because I kept shutting my eyes not to see the graves.

'She won't be able to breathe in the earth,' I said.

He pointed at the sky. 'She's everywhere now,' he said.

Nowadays, the subway rumbles and I think, 'Listen, there's life underground.' I see a white cloud and it's Rachel's swan-like wing, waving to me. Her blue and white jacket fills the air, but it's her bare wing that I want to touch when my feet feel like stone. I'll have to rethink the idea of Double Happiness: One can have a complete, amazing existence in just a few days, and it's joy as big as the world. Rachel is a generous sister, because often, as I walk along, she dips down to let me catch hold of her feathers. I lift my sad face and gaze around. The buildings here, they want more and more of the sky, past the simple blue of it. They wear that blue on their collars, and keep on stretching. I want the sky of New York, too, and beyond it. I sprout wings on my back, wings on my ankles. My swan sister, Rachel, whispers, 'Hold on tight,' and what a shock. What a surprise. I'm the one flying.

The New Sidewalk

Dorothy Bryant

'No. I want it smooth.' Louie Rocca thrust his belly forward and shook his head. 'Smooth, like glass.'

'Yeah, but you know, it gets a little wet from the rain, somebody's going to slip and break their neck.'

'What's the matter? You can't do it smooth? You don't know how?'

The workman flushed. 'Don't worry, mister. I'll make it like frosting on a cake.' He inched his knee boards further forward on the wet concrete. As he bent and reached for his trowel, I heard him mumble, 'And I hope you fall on your fat ass some foggy morning.'

I stood leaning on the wooden barricade with the other children and watched him work. His right arm smoothed the metal trowel back and forth over the thick grey ooze in a long sideways figure eight. Bubbles and swirls erased as he ironed them out in steady, rhythmic movements.

'And you kids, you keep off it, see?' I jumped at the sound of Louie Rocca's voice behind me, and, as I turned, my nose almost hit his belly. I looked up at his face, trying to match his hard look with a defiant look of my own. I knew the other kids were watching, and Louie Rocca was our enemy. We never played ball in front of his house; if the ball went up over his roof to his back yard, he would keep it and say that would teach us to keep away from his property. There were so many children on the block that someone's father was always replacing a broken window. Louie Rocca's window had been broken only once, and that time it had been his own son Dominic who was at bat. Dominic, to our disgust, had been terrified and had sworn on the Blessed Virgin that he hadn't done it; his father believed him and called us criminals, destroyers of property who would all end up in prison some day.

He pointed his finger at me. 'First kid who touches it before it's dry, I'll use a two-by-four on him.'

I took a step back, but Roy stood still and stared back at him through his thick glasses. 'Who's going to touch your lousy old sidewalk? Besides, my father says you touch me and he'll get the police on you.'

'Hah. Sure, the police. They know you, huh, Roy? The young Mafia, that's what we got on this block.'

He was right about the police knowing Roy. Roy's parents had never gotten over the surprise of becoming parents when they were nearly fifty years old. They shrugged in confusion as he ruled them and terrorized the neighbourhood. Once he had thrown a lighted firecracker into our mailbox, starting an interesting, if small and quickly quenched, fire. The BB gun he received one Christmas equipped him as the neighbourhood sniper. The police had taken the gun from him, and he turned to knife throwing. An accident ended this phase before he managed to hurt anyone but himself. He had been practising throwing his knife against a fence. The handle of the knife hit the fence, and the knife bounced back, hitting Roy in the left eye. Three operations had saved his sight, but he now wore thick glasses. The experience had not changed him, and the glasses, instead of making him look studious or vulnerable, only made his fierce eyes look bigger. No one ever called him four-eyes.

Louie Rocca turned away and began to walk around the wooden barricades as he had been doing since the concrete had been dumped. For another hour he harassed the finisher, talking about pitch and drainage and joints while the man silently did his work. Louie smiled only when adults stopped to look. Then he would point to the square in front of his house. No halfway patch jobs for him, he would say. Rip the whole thing out and do it right, he repeated over and over. His words implied an affluence rare in 1938, when the other fathers on the block were patching and painting only when necessary, counting themselves lucky to have met last month's payment on the mortgage.

The adults would nod and walk on. We children were the only constant audience, and we gave all our attention to the workman, asking him questions and envying his being paid for enjoying such an orgy of mud moulding. Finally he finished, cleaned his tools, and loaded them onto his truck, saying, 'Just keep off of it till tomorrow.'

Louie Rocca nodded impatiently and looked relieved as the man drove away. Then he turned and looked at the slick surface, delicately jointed in neat squares. Now it was all his. He owned the best sidewalk on the block.

The other children had been called in to dinner, but Roy and I still leaned on the wooden barricade.

'What you waiting for? Go home. You kids go home.'

I moved one foot, but Roy stood still, as if he had heard nothing. Louie Rocca moved closer. 'You think I don't know why you hanging around? Soon as my back is turned you figure to write your name or some dirty thing in my sidewalk.' He walked carefully across a plank to his front steps and sat down. 'You might as well forget it; I'm going to sit right here and keep an eye on you.'

Roy nudged me, and we turned and started walking slowly up the block.

'How long do you think he'll stay there?' I asked.

Roy smiled. 'He can't sit there all night. See you later.' He ran up the stairs and into his house.

I could hear my father washing in the bathroom as I walked into the kitchen. My mother turned from the stove. 'You're late. Wash your hands. Dinner's ready.'

I washed my hands at the kitchen sink and dried them on a dishtowel. My father came into the kitchen and we sat down. My mother ladled pale yellow broth into our soup plates.

'I was watching the man put in the concrete,' I explained.

'Is it finished?' asked my mother.

'Yes,' said my father. 'A nice job too. I saw it on my way home. Slick as glass.' He laughed. 'That guy doesn't know what he's letting himself in for. The way he hates the kids playing around his place. Why, when those kids see how smooth it is for roller skating, they're going to play all their hockey games right smack in front of his house.'

I hadn't thought of that. Where had I left my skates? I began to eat faster. I wanted to suggest a hockey game to Roy before someone else got the idea – and the credit.

My mother sighed. 'I don't know what that man has against the kids. It's a disgrace, a grown man yelling at them the way he does.'

'He's a big bully, that's what.'

'Eat your soup.'

'He likes to be the boss, all right,' said my father. 'He runs that house of his like he was Mussolini himself.'

'And he gets to look more like him every day,' said my mother. 'His wife and the kids too. They're all round as barrels. Why, his wife told me he has a fit if they don't have pasta every day.'

'He told me if you would fatten me up I wouldn't catch so many colds,' I said.

'I guess I know how to feed my family without that big mouth telling me.' The bowl of stew clattered as she set it down hard on the table.

'Take it easy,' said my father.

'All I ever hear from him or his wife is how they bought this and they bought that, and how they got such a good price because they know somebody who knows somebody.'

'And how much land he had in grapes near Lucca, and how many people worked for him,' added my father, then laughed. 'The guy next door asked him, "Then why didn't you stay there?" They don't talk anymore.'

'I heard a woman at Saint Anthony's say she had known him in the old country – no family, lived on the streets, half-starved. She didn't even know his name. Everyone called him "ghitarra" because he played and sang for pennies.'

'Pathetic. You gotta feel sorry for him.'

'That's no excuse for the way he acts. If everybody who had a hard time back there acted the way he does –'

'Can I go out now, Mom? I'm finished.'

'What about your homework?'

'No homework tonight.'

'After the dishes. And just until it gets dark. Don't forget your sweater. It's not summer anymore.'

I hurried through the dishes while my mother put the leftover stew in the ice box and swept the kitchen floor. Louie Rocca probably was inside, still eating. I didn't want Roy to get to the concrete before I did. I hung the dishtowel on the rack, grabbed my sweater, and ran.

A dozen or so kids were already playing one-foot-off-the-gutter, but I shook my head when they called me. I ran to the wooden barricade where Roy was already leaning.

Louie Rocca was still sitting on the steps. Next to him was a plate with a fork and one or two strands of pasta on it and a half-empty glass of red wine. He had eaten his dinner on the steps. As I reached the wooden barricade, I saw something resting across his knees.

'That's right, kid. See? I got my shotgun here. I'm gonna shoot the first *bastardo* touches my sidewalk.'

Roy's eyes met his defiantly. 'You don't dare or my father will –'

'No?' He picked up the gun.

I pulled at Roy's arm. 'Come on. Let's get in the game. I have to go in when the streetlights go on.' Roy let me pull him away, but he wouldn't play. He just sat on the curb until his mother called. As he waved good night, the streetlights went on. Louie Rocca was still sitting on the steps holding the gun when I went into the house.

'He's got a shotgun,' I told my mother as I undressed. 'And he's going to sit there and watch. And anybody touches his sidewalk, he's going to shoot them dead.'

'Did you hear that?' my mother said. 'That crazy man. He's going to hurt someone.'

My father didn't answer her, but I heard him open and close the front door. I got into bed, and my mother turned off the light. In a little while I heard the front door open and close again.

'It's all right. It isn't loaded. He showed me. But he says he's going to sit out there all night until the concrete is hard. He's afraid one of the kids will mess it up or a cat might walk across it or something. It's his business. Let's go to bed.'

That night I dreamed of Louie Rocca. He was standing on his steps holding his shotgun. On each step behind him was a row of balls. One of the balls I recognized. It was the one I had lost over his roof a few weeks before. I was standing with twenty or thirty children, a single row surrounding the fresh concrete. The wooden barricade was gone, and each of us had a toe touching the edge of the wet sidewalk. Roy was standing next to me. I looked down and saw that he was wearing roller skates. We all began to chant, 'Give us the ball, Louie, give us the ball.'

He raised the gun with his right hand, and with the other hand pointed to the balls. 'I grow the best grapes in Lucca. Anybody tries to take just one, I'll shoot him.'

Roy crouched, then pushed himself forward. He spread his arms and glided in a wide arc on one skate, across the soft grey surface, cutting a deep track and stopping in front of Louie Rocca. Louie raised the gun, pointed it at Roy, and pulled the trigger. From the gun oozed one string of spaghetti. Then the balls began to roll down the steps. I looked at the sidewalk; it had turned into a sheet of glass. As the balls bounced down the steps, each one cracked the glass with a sharp clink, clink, clink.

Clink, clink. The sound came from the kitchen. The edges of the window shades were light. I dressed as fast as I could, not stopping to tie my shoes.

'Where are you going?' asked my mother as I ran through the kitchen. 'Breakfast isn't ready yet. Take off that dirty shirt. I ironed you a clean one for school.'

'I'll be right back.' I ran out the front door. I was still half in my dream and almost believed I would find glass in front of Louie Rocca's house. I nearly fell running down the front steps. As I reached the sidewalk I looked down the block and saw that there were, as in my dream, a row of children surrounding the square in front of the Rocca house, leaning on the wooden barricades. I looked for Roy, but he was not with them.

Louie Rocca was still sitting on his front steps with the shotgun across his knees. His head was resting against the banister. He was asleep. With his eyes closed his face looked softer, worn. His thick cheeks sagged, and his mouth turned down, as if he was having an unhappy dream. No one spoke. No one moved. All the children were watching Louie Rocca and almost holding their breath.

When I reached the wooden barricades and looked down at the concrete, I saw why. Almost every inch of the new sidewalk was etched and lined. There were footprints in circles. There were pictures outlined, cartoon-style: a horse, a gun, a sailing ship, a house with a curl of smoke coming out of the chimney, a knife, a firecracker exploding, a tree. Across the middle of the sidewalk, gouged in letters nearly a foot high were the words, LOUIE ROCCA IS A BIG FAT WOP.

As I turned to look at the frozen faces of the other children, I saw Roy across the street, standing in front of his house. I waved at him to come and look, but he only smiled and went into his house.

I heard a clattering noise and looked back at Louie Rocca. The gun had fallen off his knees. As he opened his eyes, the children ran. I ran too.

❧

Years later, Louie Rocca's sons replaced the concrete, but for as long as we lived there the sidewalk remained as it was. Neighbours averted their eyes at first, but soon stopped noticing it. We children never mentioned it, even among ourselves, but, for a while we all avoided Roy. Such a lasting symbol of public defeat was more than any of us had wanted. Perhaps we had some vague concept of fair play, even extended to our enemy.

Roy and I drifted apart. He had taken to using his knife on whatever small animals he could capture. That and his studies in the private school his parents put him in began to absorb him and, I guess, led to his later success. He's a prominent surgeon now, the only kid on the block, we often say, who ever amounted to anything.

Square

David Liss

In the front of the bus, Isaac felt each bump as though he were on a roller coaster, making the slow and steady climb, waiting for the big drop. His stomach lurched at every turn, as though they were about to topple, the bus skidding along on its side in a scraping, screaming chorus of twisted metal and broken glass. And maybe it would. Maybe he would be lucky and the bus would crash and he would be hurt – not badly, but badly enough that he might hope for some sympathy. With a broken arm or a piece of metal sticking out of his side, they wouldn't expect him to fight.

Isaac wouldn't look back, but he heard them laughing and talking, laughing at him and talking about him even when they were laughing at and talking about other things. They bounced excitedly in their seats. They bumped fists and high-fived. Justin Rector said, 'You ready, Jewburg?'

Isaac looked across from his front seat, traditional home of losers and rejects and, he had discovered, retards, to the bus driver, an elderly black man with a close cut of steely grey hair. 'Man,' the driver said, shaking his head the way you did when you were both astonished and amused, 'that boy is going to whup you *good*.'

Next to Isaac Goldberg sat the kid they called Dobby because of his supposed resemblance to the house elf in the Harry Potter movies. Isaac didn't see it himself, not really, but Dobby – Isaac didn't know his real name – looked weird. Really weird. He had an unusually long neck and then an unusually narrow head, the same length as his neck, only moderately wider. His ears stuck out, his eyes were wide and far apart, his mouth freakishly long and his lips pencil thin. There was something seriously, birth-defectively, wrong with Dobby. He was in special ed and mentally slow and, Isaac thought, maybe a little crazy. He sometimes spoke coherent if strangely entangled sentences, but just as often he chanted and rocked. Right now he was shifting back and forth, occasionally side to side, saying, 'Jackson minor under out, Jackson minor under out,' in his strange voice: low and resonant and eerily keening. Isaac's first day on the bus had been one horror after another, but when the kids had openly mocked this poor retarded kid – *Dobby, did you get uglier over the summer or just stupider? Dobby, did you crap in your pants again?* – when they'd teased him and laughed at him and thrown balled up pieces of paper at him, it still had the power to shock Isaac. This came after Justin Rector had given him a black eye, on the first morning of his first day of middle school in a new state. It came during the afternoon ride home, just before Justin and his friends had stuck his head outside the window to laugh as they passed a car accident where sweaty EMT guys attempted to fit a neck brace on a prostrate body.

'You better not hurt my knuckles when I hit you,' Justin called out. 'Then I'll get *really* mad.' He was in the eighth grade, and a good five inches taller than Isaac. He had wide, furiously sloped shoulders and thick arms. He played for the football team.

The bus driver shook his head. 'Whup you *good*.'

Next to Isaac, Dobby stopped chanting and rocking. He straightened with sudden force, as though he'd just woken from a nightmare, sitting corpse-stiff for a minute or so and then he pulled on Isaac's sleeve. Isaac did not want to turn and see the look on Dobby's horrible, grotesque, earnest face, the face of the only person next to whom he could sit on the bus. He'd tried sitting next to a fat kid a couple of days in a row, understanding instinctively that fat kids were low ranked, maybe even lower than he was, but that hadn't worked out. On the third day the fat kid had turned to him. 'What, are you a faggot?'

No one had spoken that way back in his old school in Pennsylvania. No one. Not ever. Isaac stood up, but there were no empty seats, and only one empty spot he dared occupy. Next to Dobby.

'Look, they're boyfriends!' the fat kid had called out, sensing an opportunity to improve his stock by depressing Isaac's even further.

Isaac flushed with shame and humiliation, but he hadn't known what else to do. He stayed put, kept his head down and waited for the bus to arrive at school, where he would wait for the school day to be over and then for the bus ride home to end.

Dobby was still tugging on his sleeve, so Isaac turned, trying not to let his eyes focus. They did against his will, and he saw that Dobby had bright green eyes and very white teeth, small and narrow with just a hint of sharpness. His lips, though very thin, were bloody red, and he had snot encrusted under his small, flat nose. His hands were, like his head and neck, very long, not human hands at all, and his fingers, as long and thin and curiously-jointed as a spider's, held a folded piece of paper.

'Take this,' he said in his strange voice, simultaneously deep and shrill, each word drawn out, as though they were uncomfortable in Dobby's mouth. 'Take it, and put it in your pocket and keep it there.'

'You passing notes with your boyfriend?' the fat kid called out. He had too much to gain to miss anything.

Dobby kept the note up, held in a pincer grasp. 'Take it and put it in your pocket. It's protection in your pocket. It will protect you. In your pocket.'

He didn't want to take it, but Isaac couldn't bear to look any longer on Dobby's elongated hands, his freakishly jointed fingers. He took the piece of paper and unfolded it. In the center in small print of ornate letters – the word gothic came to Isaac's mind, though he did not know why – was what looked like a word-finder puzzle.

U	S	M	O	S	O	S
S	M	O	S	O	S	O
M	O	S	O	S	U	S
O	S	O	S	U	S	O
S	O	S	U	S	M	M
O	S	U	S	M	O	S
S	O	S	O	M	S	U

Isaac stared at the table for a moment.

'I made it,' Dobby said. 'I'm giving it to you because I made it, and its yours and I made it.'

Isaac handed it back to Dobby. 'Thanks.'

Dobby shook his head. 'You have to have it,' he said. 'You take it and have it keep it and put it in your pocket and take it. It's yours. I made it. It's for you. Take it.'

Knowing that all eyes were upon him, that Dobby's voice was getting louder, that they had no idea what was on the paper, only that Dobby had given it to him, Isaac slipped it into the back pocket of his jeans.

'Someone's in love,' the fat kid called.

What astonished Isaac most was the cruelty, the pure, wanton, unchecked cruelty, devoid of any internal or external modulation. Things hadn't been like that in his school in his old neighbourhood, a green suburb outside Philadelphia. There had been mean kids, sure. Problem kids. No shortage of them, but somehow the range of meanness had been more constrained, the invisible fence hemming in their acts of rebellion more tightly. Drew Nelson would knock over books in the library, sometimes even smack them out of girls' hands. Carter Rastoff was known to throw food in the cafeteria, and once even hit another kid, but these outbursts were met by teachers, even by cafeteria workers, with swift and definitive retribution. His bus driver there had also been an old black man, named Mr Hawks whom all the children addressed as *Sir*, and, though he never raised his voice in anger, a single look from him could, if he wished it, bring the bus to obedient, respectful silence. Mr Hawks radiated a kindness for children, and he also radiated a kind of suppressed power – a man who had lived a long, complicated, certainly challenging life full of secrets, maybe even some dark ones. The kids sensed all this, and they liked him for it.

Isaac understood that things were now different. His old school had somehow been special. They'd all known it. They'd spoken of their school, their district, with a kind of pride. They were the best in the county, in the state, in their part of the country. They did things right. The new school didn't seem run-down or deficient in any way Isaac could tell. The carpets weren't worn and the paint wasn't peeling. The kids weren't poor, didn't wear old or tattered clothing. The parents who dropped off and picked up their children drove cars as new and expensive and the ones in the parking lot of his old school. Yet this school existed in a different universe, one less organized and definitive. It radiated a kind of ordinariness. And it was middle school. Isaac left his old school after finishing the fifth grade. They'd moved to Florida over the summer, and now, here he was, in sixth grade, middle school. Maybe it would have been like this back home. Maybe kids who'd always been nice and easy to play with would have, over the summer, metamorphosed into vicious, petty, vindictive, unregulated things, but Isaac didn't think so.

Isaac had never had problems at his old school. He'd never been in a fight, not a serious one. He'd never been picked on except in the way that all kids unthinkingly pick on one another, cruel and petty one moment, forgiving and cheerful the next. He was a little short, a little too heavy, but he'd never been teased or made to feel like he didn't belong. He hadn't even noticed that he was short or a little heavy.

In Florida, things were different. On the first day of school he'd climbed onto the nearly full bus, focused on the new kids, the new fashions, the new experience. It was hot, Florida hot, hotter than it had ever been on the first day of school in Pennsylvania. The seats of the bus were brown. They'd been olive green on the old bus. Of course it was full of strange faces. He'd known that and yet, somewhere in his mind, he'd expected these new faces to be just like the old ones, the ones he remembered from back home.

These faces were older. His was older too, he supposed, but these were much older than anything he had anticipated. Some of the boys had dark, menacing patches of facial hair. One had tattoos running along his forearm. The girls had breasts and cleavage and exposed midriffs and pierced bellies. No one, not even the other sixth graders, looked as young as Isaac felt. No one else looked lost or frightened or new. They were locked in conversations, raucous and laughing and vibrating with restless, directionless energy. They ignored him and yet watched him with predatory intent.

There were several seats with only one kid in them, but mostly they sat on the end, and he'd have to ask for permission and he didn't want to do that. In retrospect Isaac realized that everything could have been different if he'd walked over to one of these kids and said, 'Shove over,' in a commanding, if not precisely hostile, voice. Later he saw someone do that, and it worked effortlessly. But how could he have known how to do it? He'd never had to do it before, and no one told him how it was done.

Anyhow, there was an easier option since directly in the middle of the bus he spied an entirely empty seat and, feeling relief flood him, Isaac sat down in it and slid all the way over to the window. He wasn't going to make some stranger beg him for permission to sit. He was generous. He'd let anyone sit there.

Some instinct he could not identify made him turn around and watch a big kid with longish brown hair that fell over his eyes in a way meant to seem both charming and dangerous. He was standing in the aisle, something never permitted on his old bus, talking with one of the girls with an exposed belly. She half ignored him, half flirted with him, not saying much but smiling, occasionally whisking the blonde hair away from her eyes. And then the kid turned away from her, rose to his full height, and took two or three steps over to where Isaac sat.

'You're in my seat,' he told Isaac.

For a few minutes he'd managed to convince himself that he'd disappeared into anonymity, but now everyone was watching him, watching the big kid with his brown hair in his face and his big, sloping shoulders. They were laughing, pointing, shifting excitedly, readying themselves for something unknown but awesome.

Isaac had no idea how to respond. He looked around, waiting for someone to tell him what to do, to find a way out. He said, 'You want to sit by the window? I can let you in.'

The tall kid, Justin Rector, shook his head, letting his hair fly around his face like he was in a rock band. It seemed somehow a practised gesture. 'It's my seat,' he said, still maintaining a kind of light amusement in his voice. He might let the offence pass because it was so absurd. 'The whole fucking thing is my seat.'

'How can it be your seat? It's the first day of school.' He spoke easily and affably. He'd had conflicts with other kids before. Everyone had, but Isaac was used to people liking him, used to them being nice and reasonable. It was the last time he would feel this way, and that's why he later remembered it so clearly, remembered how he was completely unprepared for what happened.

'Are you crazy?' Justin Rector asked him. 'Are you out of your fucking mind. This is *my* seat.'

'I guess now it's my seat,' Isaac said, not trying to be hostile or territorial, but both affable and determined. 'But I'm happy to share.'

'Oh man!' someone shouted from the back of the bus.

'Get up,' Justin said. 'Now.'

It was a test. It had to be. If Isaac got up, he knew the other kids would laugh at him. It was his first day of school and if he got up, everyone could know they would push him around. And what was this big kid going to do to him anyhow? He was bigger, clearly older. He wasn't going to hit Isaac. No way. Bigger kids never hit smaller kids. It was against some unwritten, unspoken and utterly inviolable code. There was nothing to do but stay put.

'I don't see what the big deal is,' Isaac said, more sheepishly than he intended. And Justin hit him, hard, right in the eye. Isaac felt the impact, felt his head strike the window and he felt Justin's big hands grab him by his arms and pull him out of the seat, depositing him in the aisle. He tasted dirt and rubber, and he felt himself crying. He heard laughter and he heard the bus driver say, 'God *damn*,' not with anger, but with a kind of appreciation, the way his stepfather might when watching a golf swing on TV.

Justin took the seat, sitting lengthwise, pushing his feet into the aisle and onto Isaac's back. 'Get the fuck up,' he said.

Isaac spent the rest of the ride standing in the aisle, trying not to cry, listening to the whispers and snickers and insults. He kept waiting for some nice girl, pretty but maybe not too pretty, to offer to let him sit, but no pretty girl came. He felt his face swelling, and he was sure that when he got to school the teachers would demand to know what had happened. He would valiantly refuse to tell, but they'd get it out of some of the other kids and Justin would get what was coming to him. But no one asked about it. By the end of the day, his eye was a sickening black purple, and no one asked.

Later, at home, he sat at the kitchen table eating a pocket pizza while his mother put away groceries. She bought food mostly for Isaac and Hank, his stepfather, because her meals came in special packages delivered by the UPS man. She looked pretty much like she always had, but Hank wanted her to lose weight, and she had to buy special food to do that.

'How was your first day?' she asked him, looking longingly at a bunch of bananas.

'Fine,' he said.

'How were your teachers?'

'Good.'

She paused a moment after putting a box of ice cream sandwiches into the freezer. 'What happened to your eye?'

'Nothing,' Isaac said. Maybe he wanted her to tease it out of him, so he could show that he wasn't a tattletale. Maybe it was pride. But he wanted her to know. He wanted someone to know that an eight grader had punched him in the eye because he'd dared to take a seat on the bus, but he never told her because she accepted his answer.

In his mind he imagined Hank telling her that Isaac had to work out his own problems by himself, but maybe that was too optimistic. Maybe his mother didn't understand that a black eye was a big deal. She was busy. They were both busy. Hank was busy with the new job, the reason they'd moved to Florida, and his mother was busy setting up the house. She still had furniture to buy and wallpaper to pick for the guest room. They were getting ready for a dinner party with people from Hank's new office, and they had to find a caterer. There was talk of getting a new car, maybe a hybrid. They were busy.

❧

The day after Justin Rector hit him, Isaac found all the seats on the bus taken, and everyone looked at him with angry, imperious stares, making it abundantly clear that they would have nothing to do with him. They almost begged it of him. Please don't sit next to me, don't even ask. Don't come near me with your outcast germs.

In school, no one would talk to him. At lunch, no one would sit

with him. In PE, he was picked last for volleyball, and he was delib-
erately kept out of play. As near as he could tell, Justin Rector had
not told anyone that Isaac was off limits, but news of the incident on
the bus had spread with a viral intensity. There were fat kids, dorky
kids, kids who had been last year's victims and who now huddled
together in collectable gaming card clusters, who removed themselves as far as they could from Isaac.

At night he lay in bed and thought that if this were someone else's
life, if it were a movie or a book, the thing that would puzzle him
the most was why Justin would not leave him alone. He had nothing
to prove and nothing to gain, and yet he'd taken a relentless dislike
toward Isaac. They were in different grades, and so they shared none
of the same classes. They ate lunch at different times, but Justin
might see him in the hall and ram him with his shoulder or knock
books out of his hands. He might flick Isaac's ear or give him an
Indian burn or kick him in the back of the knee. Once Justin had
walked passed an open classroom where Isaac sat in the back and
managed to slip inside and pull out Isaac's chair just as he was sitting
down, so he landed hard on his tailbone and had to concentrate not
to cry. The teacher yelled at Justin and told him to get back to his
own class. Then she yelled at Isaac. She said he should stop clowning
around and get back in his chair.

Things like this had never happened in Pennsylvania. No one
had every done anything like that to anyone, except in the most
extreme cases of aberrant behaviors, and then parents would be
summoned, therapists called in. Here, Isaac witnessed a hundred
acts of cruelty each day, and none went answered. He came home
with burns and cuts and limps and his mother only looked at him
questioningly as though waiting for him to volunteer some information, which he never did. Not even when things threatened to
get worse.

In his second week of school, Justin stopped him in the hall. 'I
heard you said some shit about me.'

Isaac shook his head, feeling somehow wronged. If there was one
thing he'd done, one thing to cling to, it was that he had not said
anything to anyone. He'd taken it all in silence.

'Bullshit,' Justin said. He gave Isaac a shove. The vice principal walked past, gave them both a curious glance, but kept moving. 'Bullshit,' Justin said again, eager to pick up where he'd left off. 'You've been talking shit, and I can't let it stand. So it looks like I'm gonna have to kick your ass.'

That was when he started taunting Isaac on the bus, how one of these days he was going to get off at his stop and that was going to be it. That was when it would be time to pay what he owed. What, Isaac didn't believe him? He thought Justin was full of shit. Well, Isaac was going to find out who was full of shit and who wasn't. It went on like that for a week until Isaac began to think that day would never come, that Justin would keep threatening Isaac until he got bored and forgot. The next afternoon, however, Justin announced that today was the day. Isaac sat up front with Dobby, looking straight ahead, trying to ignore the taunts of the kids and of the bus driver. He tried to ignore his own fear and the pounding of his heart and Dobby's concerned glance, making sure that Isaac still had the square diagram in his back pocket.

Isaac reached his stop. He paused a moment and then pushed himself out of his seat, feeling the moisture from the sweat on his legs clinging through the fabric of his pants to the vinyl below. His steps were slow and irregular. His sneakers kept catching on the rubber of the bus floor. And he dared to hope. Maybe it was just more cruelty. Maybe Justin Rector wanted nothing more than to make Isaac afraid, and so as not to stoke the fires of cruelty, he refused to look back.

He didn't need to look, because he heard the movement behind him. He heard the squeak of rubber shoes on rubber floor, and he heard the bus driver say, 'God *damn*,' and he heard the hushed, hurried laughter. He stepped outside and felt the oppressive sticky heat of the Florida late summer, maybe close to a hundred degrees and humid. Above dark clouds gathered, maybe to rain, maybe not.

Isaac stepped off the bus in front of the Date Palm Run apartment complex. His house was about half a mile away, and he briefly thought about running. He was a fairly fast runner, and if he surprised them, took some short cuts he knew, he might be able to beat them to his house. Maybe there would be a cop car along the way.

Anything could happen. But he knew that every kid on the bus was looking at him, and he couldn't bring himself to run.

Isaac turned around to see the bus pull off. He saw the faces pushed up against the window, the shaking head of the bus driver, and Dobby, staring straight ahead, his mouth moving in one of his unfathomable chants. Justin Rector stood in the wake of the bus with three of his friends, all of whom were laughing with jittery excitement. Two of them high-fived.

Justin took a step forward. 'You ready to get your ass kicked?'

What kind of response did he expect, exactly? Isaac thought about how at his old school, only a few months ago, he'd been kind of a funny kid. He'd crack jokes and make the other kids, his *friends*, laugh, maybe at the lunch table or at recess or even in class, when they were supposed to be listening. It seemed strange to him that he could have changed so much so quickly. He wasn't funny anymore. He had no friends, and he never said anything to anyone, not at lunch, not at recess, and never in class.

The old Isaac, who never would have been in this position to begin with, would have made some sort of joke. 'No, I'm not quite ready. Let me pick my nose first, and then I'll be right with you.' But now? He didn't even know what to do. Now that the bus was gone, he could run. That option was still open. There was no shame, he thought, in running from a kid bigger and older, not when he was so obviously outmatched. Or he could fight. He could put up some sort of show, to prove he had heart. In the movies they would see what a courageous, scrappy kid he was, and they would decide he was okay after all, accept him into their gang. Isaac would then either valiantly refuse to join in with them and so achieve a new kind of honour, or by joining them he would transform them from a bunch of thugs to good kids who studied hard and helped out those less fortunate than themselves.

Things like that only happened in children's stories, though, the kind of stories that only made kids feel worse about their sad, hopeless lives. So that left Isaac to choose from the list of things that could happen in the real world. Running, he decided, was his best move. He needed to get out of there, and later he would figure out what to do next. Maybe he would tell his mother, and she could help him. Maybe a teacher. Maybe he would do all those things he'd never wanted to do before, or maybe someone would volunteer to help. Maybe someone somewhere would make things better, but nothing was going to get better now, not if they stayed there.

Except he didn't run. He looked up at Justin. The clouds had grown denser and darker, and he felt a drop of rain, the first footprint of a Florida summer storm – short, sudden and brutal. Isaac looked at Justin, whose long hair was moving around in the growing breeze, who grinned with his strong, charismatic malevolence. Hardly even knowing he was going to speak, Isaac cleared his throat and said, 'Just in rectum.'

Justin had been about to take a step, but now he froze. His friends froze, though one of them let out a girlish titter.

'What?' Isaac said. 'No one's ever brought that up before? That your name sounds like *just in rectum*? It was the first thing I thought of. I mean, what is just in his rectum? And why *just*? Not in the mouth? Just in the rectum, Justin? Is that what it means?'

Yes, Isaac thought. This is the third way. Better than running, better than fighting. He might still run, might still be made to fight, but he was getting in his licks here. Justin's friends were looking around nervously, trying not to laugh.

Justin was now red. 'Motherfucker,' he said.

Isaac understood it all at that moment. Jason's tough guy thing was entirely a defense mechanism, an elaborate security device designed for no other reason than to keep people from saying *just in rectum*. No matter how obvious, how inevitable, he kept it at bay, he kept it unsayable, unthinkable even, with perpetual, vigilant threats of violence. Now it had all blown up in his face. The very system designed to keep those words unuttered had unleashed them into the universe. It was hardly surprising. This was the eternal lesson of history, the message embedded in every monster movie ever made. Science, knowledge, power, nature – only fools and madmen thought they could contain them, and those fools and madmen were always the first devoured.

It was a point well taken, because Isaac was about to become one of those fools himself, destroyed by the force he had unleashed. He watched as his doom approached. It was one of those moments you see in movies and comic books and novels, but never live in real life. Until now. Things slowed down, and Isaac's mind, normally scattered, inclined to miss the obvious, took in everything. The laces to both of Justin's Nikes were untied. He took a step with his left foot and trod on the laces of his right shoe. Then he lifted his right foot, hard and angrily. The laces caught.

Isaac had done this himself a million times. Who hadn't? He'd never actually fallen, however. He'd always corrected himself, and he expected Justin to correct himself now, but he didn't. He did not jerk back or hop or windmill or stumble. He toppled forward like a felled tree, like a statue of Saddam Hussein.

Even then things might have been no big deal. For Justin, that is. For Isaac they were already turned around, and he knew that. He could run, he could be beaten up, and it would not matter. Well, it would matter, especially being beaten up, but not in the same way. Justin looked like an idiot, and all of his friends would go to school tomorrow and talk about how Isaac had scored points off Justin, how Justin had been rattled and turned clumsy, and soon it would be whispered everywhere. *Just in rectum.* Isaac actually began to believe that somehow, impossibly, he had carried the day.

Justin hit the earth. He never put his arms out in front of him, or rather, he wasn't able to. Isaac saw him move his hands forward to break his fall, and then they jerked, as though an electrical shock had run through his body, and his arms shot back to his side, straight and pressed to his body. He hit the ground, the spotty grass and whitish Florida dirt along the roadside, breaking the fall with his face. Isaac heard something break or crack, a sickening sound both brittle and wet, and he felt his stomach lurch. Justin lay there, perfectly still, his face pressed to the ground, arms still at his side, his knees bent, his feet in the air, and he looked so absurd that Isaac felt certain he was faking it. His friends also thought he was faking it, and they laughed and bumped fists. Then they told him to get up. They said their *come on, mans* and *dudes*, and still Justin did not rise.

Isaac stared, unable to move, thinking he ought to run. If Justin were hurt, really hurt, his friends might turn on Isaac. But he kept looking, kept watching to see what would happen next. And then he noticed it. The blood, pooling around Justin's hidden face. It was hard to see at first because the blood seeped into the ground, but the soil was wet from the summer rains, and it began to collect and form dark pools in the crab grass. Isaac understood that it would have to be an enormous amount of blood to accumulate like that. His friends must have realized it too, because they gasped and muttered and stepped back and stepped forward. They turned white in their faces and red in their eyes, and they looked at Isaac, not with anger or blame or even fear, but with a kind of confused awe.

Then it began to rain. The rain came down at once, like a trap-door above them had been released, and this, Isaac understood, was the perfect chance to run.

At home, changed and dry, Isaac knew everything was going to be different, though he didn't know how. Different good or different bad? The outcome of the fight had been too decisive for it to be a bad outcome, but he dared not hope for anything too good. Maybe he might be alone and friendless and ostracized, only now without the threat of violence. That would certainly be something he might hope for. As for getting in trouble, he wasn't especially worried. No one ever seemed to get in much trouble for anything, and besides, he hadn't actually done anything to Justin. That meant he couldn't take credit for knocking him down, but, on the other hand, he'd stood his ground, and he'd come away uninjured. Justin had been the one lying in a pool of blood.

But what if he was seriously hurt? What if he was dead, and they blamed Isaac? If all of his friends said it was Isaac's fault, what could he say to defend himself? Yet, somehow that didn't concern him. He didn't think that Justin's friends, questioned by the police, would be able to keep their stories together. Even if they wanted to blame Isaac, he didn't think they could get away with it, and why should they want to? No one had done anything to Justin. He'd tripped and hurt himself. It was one of those things that had just happened. If one of them had done it to Justin then Isaac would be worried, because then they would need someone to blame. As things stood, they didn't.

Then Isaac remembered the square. He took it from the back pocket of his wet jeans and studied the damp paper, now cracked and ragged along the seams. It was nonsense. It was clear and utter nonsense, and yet Dobby had said it would protect him. Of course a piece of paper with some letters on it could not protect him, but there was no arguing with the fact that Isaac had placed this square in his back pocket and while he possessed it the impossible had happened. It was nonsense, but maybe it was nonsense worth considering.

Isaac felt a sharp tingle of excitement. Not because he was, by his nature, drawn to the fantastic and mysterious, because he wasn't. It was more the novelty of it all. For the first time since his move something interesting was happening, and it wasn't bad.

※

After dinner, Isaac went onto the family computer and did a search on magic squares. At first all he found was some sort of complex mathematical game, the rules of which lay far beyond either his ability or his willingness to comprehend. It took a little more adventurous searching, but in the end he found that there was a long history of making talisman's out of letters, just like the one Dobby had given him, anagrammatic squares that were alleged to contain some kind of power. The word *abracadabra*, favored spell of uninspired stage magicians, originated as such a talisman. There was a whole branch of the occult, called Enochian magic, in which strange and vaguely menacing angels were summoned or controlled or manipulated by making charts out of letters and runes.

How retarded Dobby would know about such things was a mystery, and that was not even dealing with the greater question of how such a square could be real. Isaac had never been inclined to believe in monsters or magic or unseen wonders. Even as a little kid, he'd understood that his mother was the tooth fairy and that nothing hid under his bed or in his closet. And yet there was the square. It made no sense, and Isaac felt himself compelled to dismiss even the possibility that he had been aided by a magic talisman, but he wondered if maybe his sense of logic wasn't failing him. He knew from his reading in kids' science magazines that the world was full of things that made no sense or that science could not explain. No one knew how gravity worked or why bumblebees can fly. He'd heard once that scientists have no idea how cats purr. How hard could that be to figure out? You give a cat some tuna and you do an ultrasound or MRI or whatever it is they do to look inside something. But he figured there were people out there who knew more about this stuff than he did, and surely some scientist somewhere would want to be the guy who discovers how cats purr. Yet no one had done it.

Isaac's family was not religious, and he didn't know if he believed in God or not, which he suspected meant he didn't. But the way he figured it, either the universe was created by God or it wasn't. If it was, then what created God? If not, then how did the universe get here? Everything had to have a cause, didn't it? He understood that religious people would say that God was eternal, that He had always been there, but that made no sense. Everything had to come from something, or so it seemed to him. It actually seemed more logical that the universe could come from an eternal, always existing God than an eternal, always existing collection of matter, because he could not come up with a scenario to explain how matter could be eternal and always existing, unless it came from another universe, which really just deferred the problem rather than solving it. So, if all this was true, then either there was a God, which meant that there were supernatural forces in the world, or there wasn't a God, and the universe came from somewhere or something he couldn't even imagine, and that there were forces, natural or otherwise, out there no one knew anything about. In either case, who was he to say that writing letters in a square on a piece of paper couldn't alter reality? He'd seen it with his own eyes, and surely that had to count for something.

Things *were* different the next day at school. Justin's seat was empty, and Isaac took it, partly as an act of defiance, and partly because he wanted a place to sit. Dobby almost never rode the bus in the morning, and so the front seat was occupied by a pair of pretty, giggling seventh grade girls who didn't quite not look at him. He turned to the back of the bus and saw Justin's friends, and Isaac made himself not turn away from their gaze. He'd find out about their disposition sooner or later, so it might as well be sooner. They didn't smile and wave and beckon him over, but he hadn't expected it and didn't want it. Mostly. It was always nice to be welcome, even if it was with people you didn't like. But they didn't turn away or curse at him or threaten him. One of them gave him a half nod, and Isaac turned away. Maybe he had pulled this off, bought himself some breathing room, a few rungs on the totem pole.

He heard the rumours soon enough. Isaac and Justin had been fighting or about to fight or something, and Justin had fallen down and hurt his eye on a rock or a piece of broken glass or a used heroin needle. Something, but Isaac heard pretty quickly that he was in the clear. Justin's friends had been in the principal's office all morning, and they'd admitted that Justin was being a jerk and maybe giving Isaac a little bit of a hard time – not bullying him, no, because everyone knew better than to bully – but just a little rough play. Nothing major, and Justin had slipped.

Isaac heard all this very clearly. It was Justin's fate that was more ambiguous. He hadn't been faking it. He'd passed out as soon as he'd hit the earth, and even the brief but torrential downpour of rain, raising up pools of bloody water that almost drowned him, had failed to wake him, and his friends had been forced to touch him and stuff, to roll him over. When they saw the damage, they'd had to knock on someone's door at the apartment complex and call 911. No one knew if Justin was going to be blind or partially blind or even lose the eye entirely.

On the way home that afternoon, Isaac sat in Justin's seat again. He walked past Dobby, who sat by himself and didn't seem to mind or notice that Isaac ignored him. He was in one of his fits, and he rocked back and forth gently, his arms folded across his chest. He muttered to himself, and it sounded like, 'Rock, paper, rice. Rock, paper, rice.' Over and over again.

Things were beginning to turn, and so it seemed like being overly solicitous to Dobby, now that he did not have to be, was a bad idea. He was less radioactive, there was no doubt about that, but it wasn't like he was instantly transformed into a cool kid who could do anything he wanted. Isaac was in some kind of border space, some realm between outsider and pariah, and he desperately wanted to remain an outsider, which was bad, but not as bad as being a pariah. That meant that he couldn't dare to be friendly to retarded kids when he had other, better options, like being alone.

On the other hand, he had to find out more about the square. If these things were real and they actually worked, he had to know. Especially, he had to know before Justin got out of the hospital and came looking for revenge, or at least his seat back. On the third day after the fight Isaac heard that Justin definitely was going to lose his eye. On the fourth day he heard he was definitely not going to, but would be mostly blind in that eye. That meant he was going to be disfigured, disabled, and looking for someone to blame. Justin didn't seem like the kind of kid who would, given the chance to reflect, see how it was his own actions that had brought him low. He would blame Isaac.

Isaac knew he had to do something. He asked around. The special ed kids were always kept in some dark, isolated section of the school, and they rarely made contact with the regular population, so Isaac knew he'd have to do a little work. Still, it was not hard to find out Dobby's real name. He just asked the assistant principal when he saw her in the hall. Dobby, it turned out, was improbably named Cavanaugh Philips Jr – incongruously formal for a deformed kid, but also a stroke of good luck. Phillips would not be too uncommon a last name, but the *junior* meant Isaac now knew the father's name. Assuming Dobby's parents weren't divorced, that should make things easier. At home, Issac did an Internet search and found an address for Cavanaugh Philips about three miles away from his house, right along the bus route. That Saturday he rode his bicycle over to Dobby's parents' house.

The first thing that struck him was that they were rich. The house was huge, two stories with balconies and a massive pool and lots of lush lawn with ornate landscaping. He knew the house was what was called Spanish style, and he knew the cars parked out front were expensive, though he did not know what they were called. They looked expensive though – large and glistening with flawless paint jobs. So, if Dobby's parents were rich, why did they send him on the bus? Why did they send him to that school?

Isaac sucked in his breath and rang the doorbell. In a moment a very pretty woman with blonde hair and tanned, well-weathered skin answered the door. She wore a white blouse, unbuttoned maybe one button too many, and she had sunglasses worn on a cord around her neck.

'Is this where Cavanaugh lives? Cavanaugh Jr, I mean.' He felt uncomfortable calling him by his real name. Had they known he was so irreparably damaged when they gave him so imposing a name?

The woman's eyes darkened and she studied him. 'How do you know Cavanaugh?'

'From school,' he said.

'From school,' she repeated. She looked surprised, sceptical, doubtful, and Isaac had to resist the urge to run away. He wasn't doing anything bad, he told himself. He was just visiting.

'Do you have – classes with him?' Dobby's mother asked.

Isaac shook his head. 'I ride the bus with him.'

'And you two are – friends?'

'Sort of,' Isaac said. 'I sometimes sit next to him. I need to ask him something.'

She continued to study him, and Isaac felt exposed, caught doing something wrong, but he knew he didn't look menacing, and whatever natural scepticism she might be feeling, it probably wouldn't be sufficient grounds to deny him access to her son. She took a step back and let him inside.

She called out for Dobby. She didn't shriek or yell like his mother did. Her voice was loud, but pleasing, almost musical, and yet commanding. Dobby appeared from another room, wearing shorts and a loose T-shirt that showed off his strange, long and painfully thin limbs.

'You have a visitor. A friend?' Her voice betrayed just how unsure she was in this situation. It seemed likely that Dobby had never had a visitor just stop by before.

'Isaac,' Isaac said.

'Isaac,' she said, as though trying out the name.

Dobby stood there, nodding his long, strange head. His face betrayed nothing. He nodded, bobbing slightly, as though suspended in water. And then he said one word. 'Square.'

❧

They sat up in Dobby's room, decorated with a heavy bias toward Star Wars. He had a TV in his room and some picture books, and lots of toys, especially electronic toys full of urgent beeps and flashing lights. He also had lots of paints and markers, clays and coloured balls and pipe cleaners. Dobby liked to do art, and one wall, the one not plastered with images of Baba Fett and C3PO, was covered with his own work. Isaac knew it was his because it was so similar in style to a half finished painting on an easel near the window.

Isaac was both surprised and not surprised to see that Dobby was good at painting. Maybe brilliant. His paintings, mostly of people and eating for some reason, were strange and distorted, with weird angles and curious lighting, but they had a clarity and a vision. Isaac could see that at once. Dobby had his own thing, his own style. Isaac felt envy, and he felt himself wonder something very, very strange. Was Dobby good at art because he wore a talisman that made him good at art?

He took the square out of his pocket and showed it to Dobby. 'What is it?'

'Square,' Dobby said. 'It's a square, it's a magic square. I made it. It's for you for protection for you.'

'I know. How does it work?'

'I don't know.' Dobby shook his head, while he rocked back and forth very gently. Isaac thought he knew Dobby well enough to know it wasn't agitation, just something he did.

'They work,' he said. 'They do. They just do. They work.'

He went over to his desk and picked up a shoebox and brought it over. He opened it and inside there was nothing but pieces of paper with squares, and not only squares, but triangles and rectangles, circles and pentagons, all divided up with letters, both Roman and Hebrew, and strange symbols. Some were small, like the one he'd given Isaac, with just five or six or seven letters across. Some were figures within figures, circles within triangles within squares. Some were massive – forty or fifty letters in tiny, precise print. He leafed through the box until he found the square he was looking for. He handed it to Isaac.

'Put it in your pocket,' he said. 'Just put it right in there.'

Isaac put it in his pocket. 'What does it do?'

'You can't be cut by sharp things,' Dobby said. 'No sharp things. No sharp. Things. No things. Sharp things.'

'Come on,' Isaac said.

Dobby had a sick, gap-toothed, red-gummed smile. He handed Isaac a needle.

It was sharp. Isaac could see that. It was long and thick and came together in a microfine point, which he pressed to his fingertip. It didn't break the skin. He pressed hard until it hurt, until the skin around the needle turned white and red and purple, but it did not break the skin. Isaac took the square out of his pocket and handed it back to Dobby. He touched the needle to his own skin, and without even having to apply pressure to it a thick drop of blood blossomed around the metal.

Isaac, who never swore, said, 'Wow,' in a low whisper. 'This is real. It's a really, really real thing.'

'It's real,' Dobby said. 'It's real. It's real.'

'But how come no one knows about these things? I mean, you could go on TV. You could be famous. You could, I don't know, make special squares for soldiers so they don't get hurt in war or something, couldn't you?'

Dobby stared at him blankly for a long time. 'No one wants to know,' he said at last. 'They don't want. They don't want it. They don't like it. They don't want magic. It's not okay.'

'Okay, okay. It's not okay. *For them.* It's okay for me, though, right? You gave me that other one. It's okay for me.'

'It's okay for you. For you, yes.'

'What else do you have in there?' Isaac began to feel himself swell with the excitement of possibility. 'Do you have something for like, I don't know, good grades? Or super powers? Strength or invisibility or anything like that?'

'Protection,' Dobby said. 'Protection. And friendship. And combined. Protection and friendship. Together.'

And that was when it struck him. Dobby had not only protected him from Justin, he had made Isaac his friend. He was now drawn to Dobby against his will. But did that matter? Dobby had given him something magical and wonderful. He had been kind and generous when no one else had been willing, so wouldn't Isaac be his friend now anyhow? And if that was the case, then Isaac had to wonder what magic was, anyhow. Was friendship something you could summon with magic, or was it magic itself? Was it a kind of magic so old and so ordinary that no one even saw it for what it was? And if magic followed rules, was dependable and predicable and accessible, like friendship, then why was it even magic at all? Was magic just another name for the science no one understands and for the things no one notices?

Isaac wondered about the other squares in the box, but he didn't ask. He decided he didn't want to seem greedy or rushed. He would find out some other time. Instead, he let Dobby show him his art, and he watched TV with him, and they had lunch together – tuna sandwiches and strawberry milkshakes that his mother made herself. They didn't taste like the kind you got at McDonald's, but they were really good. And Isaac decided he was going to let Dobby sit with him in Justin's seat on the bus come Monday. And it wasn't because of any magic square, either.

On his way out of the house, Dobby's mother stopped Isaac. She held on to his hand in her long fingers, strangely beautiful and yet like Dobby's in their curious length and articulation. She was very, very pretty, and Isaac understood that if he kept coming by he was going to have a crush on her, and yet he saw in all her beauty the seeds of Dobby's deformities. They looked nothing alike, and they were precisely alike.

'Why are you being so nice to him?' she asked. 'You're not – you're not in his program. You're not like him.'

Isaac shook his head. 'He was nice to me. He helped me with something when no one else would.'

She opened her mouth, probably to ask, and then closed it. Maybe she decided it was none of her business. Maybe she decided that a boy like Dobby has so few things to keep to himself that she should let him have this, however trivial.

'Can I ask you something?' he said to her.

She nodded.

'Why do you let him ride the bus?'

'What do you mean?'

'The kids, they're cruel to him. They tease him, they call him names. They throw things at him.'

Her face went hard and rigid. She looked horrified, terrified, embarrassed. 'But,' she said. 'How – I mean. Why didn't he say anything to us?'

Isaac wanted to ask how he could be expected to know, but he wouldn't say that, in part because it was rude, and in part because he did know. He understood it with a sudden and full comprehension that he recognized at once as wisdom, even though it was the first time he'd felt anything like it. And because it was wisdom, he knew not only why, but that he should not say anything. Dobby's mother was horrified, truly horrified, to learn that she had sent her son off to be tormented. She would do something about it now, and that was enough. She didn't need to know the truth, which was that Dobby had not told her not because he was proud or embarrassed or defiant, but because he had expected her to know. He had considered it her business to know, and not knowing was, in itself, a kind of betrayal.

'You'll come back?' she asked him.

'I'll come back,' he told her, and he went home to his own house, to his mother and stepfather, who did not ask him where he had been.

A Great Event

Vikas Swarup

It was a cold winter night on which the Great Writer came to our house. A light snow had fallen in the morning and the headlights on the cars that now passed so regularly through our street on their way to the new housing complex glinted like distant stars lighting up the ice crystals on the tree branches.

There was a nip in the air and a dull, smoky haze had descended to the ground. Most of the animals we saw during the summer were in hibernation. Even the small birds had been chilled into silence, making the mornings rather gloomy and insipid.

A thick layer of snow lay like a fluffy mattress on the gabled roof of our large, and somewhat dilapidated, old house. But inside the drawing room, a crackling fire burned in the hearth, bringing warmth and cheer. The room chimed with the sound of clinking wine glasses and the hushed murmur of an expectant gathering.

On the mantelpiece above the fireplace was an array of framed sepia photographs, mostly of Grandpa. There was one in particular, taken a long time ago, of Grandpa and the Great Writer standing side by side in their military uniforms, their rifles slung over their shoulders, looking intently into the camera with bright, earnest eyes. We had taken special care to wipe this photograph with window cleaner, washing off the thick coat of dust that had made the glass almost opaque. Father had removed this photograph from the mantelpiece and hung it in the foyer, so that everyone who entered the house would see it.

In preparation for the visit, the oversized sofas had been pushed to the corners of the drawing room to make space for people to mingle. Even so, there was hardly any standing room left. The entire town, it seemed, had turned up to meet the Great Writer, and with good reason. He had won every major literary award, bar the Nobel.

The country had grown up reading his poems and his novels. The newspapers were always full of his statements, his past love affairs and conquests. He was visiting our small town for the very first time, mainly to offer his condolences on Grandpa's death, of which he had learned only a few weeks ago. But Father hoped the Great Writer's visit would also help resolve a matter he had been pursuing with the Mayor for the past six months.

Until last year, our house had been the only one on the street, with nothing but dense forest behind it. But a big consortium from the capital had bought up the swathe of land. They cut down all the trees, bulldozed the area to create a level clearing and began constructing high-rise flats. For months we lived with the metallic sounds of construction ringing in our ears. And then, almost overnight, a set of three tall black towers, made of granite and Plexiglas, and equipped with central heating and swimming pools, sprung up. These skyscrapers dwarfed all the surrounding buildings. Their muted gleam seemed to mock the old brick-and-mortar constructions, such as our own house. The consortium had even built an all-asphalt access road to the complex that intersected with the old road right where our house stood, forming a tidy little L-junction where there was earlier only a cul-de-sac.

This new road was yet to be named. A number of suggestions had been made. Some wanted it to be called after a flower, others after a river. One councillor had expressed himself in favour of those modern, meaningless names like 'P Street'. We had been after the Mayor to get the road named after Grandpa, who had died nine months ago. In support of our submission we pointed out his contribution to the Revolution, his service to the Motherland, and his close friendship with National Heroes, in particular with the Great Writer. But the Mayor was refusing to oblige. 'For the street to be named after a person, two criteria have to be fulfilled,' he had told us. 'One, the person must be famous, and two, the person must be dead. Your grandfather is certainly dead, but he is not so famous.' So that is why we needed the Great Writer. To convince the Mayor of Grandpa's eminence.

The Mayor himself was visiting our house for the first time today. A short, portly man with a big moustache, he was fond of singing at social gatherings. Father detested him almost as much as he detested cockroaches, but we acknowledged his position as an important official whose concurrence was necessary for the street to be named after Grandpa.

The Great Writer arrived an hour and a half late in a big, flashy, chauffeur-driven vehicle. As soon as the car screeched into the porch, everyone surged forward to greet him. He was a big hulk of a man and looked younger than his age. He had a thick neck, a protruding jaw, bushy eyebrows, bulging eyes and a shock of unruly hair. He was dressed casually in brown suede trousers and a grey turtleneck pullover over which he wore a tweed jacket. He was accompanied by a tall, middle-aged, striking-looking woman clad in a brown leather skirt and Gucci eyeglasses. We were told she was his Third Wife.

Virtually tripping over Father in his rush to get to the door, the Mayor was the first to greet the Great Writer. 'An exceptional honour, sir, a truly great event,' he fawned as he propelled the Writer inside as though he were the host of the party. The Great Writer paused when he saw the photograph in the foyer. He hugged Father and pressed his hands. 'I am so sorry to learn of your father's death. He was a true comrade. A good man.' We beamed at the Mayor. Now he knew first-hand of the Great Writer's friendship with Grandpa.

Father escorted the Great Writer to the sofa by the fireplace from where he could get a good view of the entire room. As soon as our guest sat down, the boys from the Sunday choir broke into their welcome song, rehearsed over the past five days at St Michael's Church. Selma provided accompaniment on the piano. The Writer listened to the song with a bored expression, and clapped briefly when it was over. The leader of the choir, a tall, gangly boy who stammered whenever he was excited, curtsied before the Writer. 'Sir, is it true that you are g-g-g-going to write a n-n-n-new novel?' he asked, and we sniggered.

By now a large circle had formed around the Writer's sofa. People pushed for a better view. 'No jostling please,' said the Wife in an irritated tone. 'And no stupid questions.' She turned to Father. 'My husband can't bear stupid people. In fact, he can hardly bear people.' Father nodded and signalled to the Waiter, hired especially for the evening.

The Waiter looked smart in his white jacket and black bow tie. He moved around the room with trays in both hands laden with stuffed green olives and small white eggs crowned with red tomato slices.

The Editor of the local paper introduced himself to the Writer. 'I am deeply interested in the creative process. It always amazes me what unsuspected truths the imagination can throw up,' he drawled in his pompous manner.

'The unsuspecting can never grasp the great truths of the universe,' countered the Writer.

'For me writing is truth,' the Editor pressed on. 'To write is to be free. Is it so for you, too?'

'No,' the Writer shook his head. 'Writing is also a form of slavery, the bondage of words. True freedom transcends words.'

'Have you read Márquez's latest?' asked the Editor, turning to what he thought was a more convivial subject. 'I found it a luminous reading experience.'

The Great Writer dismissed this with a wave. 'Humph! Márquez is past his prime. That book is not an experience. It is an embarrassment.'

The Writer had tired of this exchange by now. His eyes shifted to the bar where bottles of wine were lined up like soldiers at a drill. Father had a modest wine cellar. It boasted a few good rosé wines, Madeira from Portugal and Cava from Spain. But Father's most prized possession was a bottle of vintage French Bordeaux, inherited from Grandpa, and unopened for twenty-seven years. He would bring it out once in a while to show it to his friends, but he would never consent to opening it. 'Wouldn't it have spoiled by now?' we would ask each time Father went into the cellar, ostensibly to wipe dust off the bottle, but in truth, for the simple pleasure of holding it in his hands. 'No. Good wine becomes better with age. I will let it mature for another five years and then we will drink it,' he would say.

The Writer tugged at the Waiter's jacket. 'Don't you have anything to drink?' he asked and his fingers darted into one of the trays.

'At home,' he added, pushing a fat olive into his mouth, 'I take Portuguese rum. But when I travel, I only drink French red wine.'

'Get a nice Bordeaux,' ordered the Wife.

'I am sorry, señora, we do not have French wine, but we have some very good local merlots,' the Waiter said diffidently as he balanced the two trays.

'You don't have French wine?' the Wife rolled her eyes at Father.

'Bordeaux. I want Bordeaux,' said the Writer, and banged his fists on the centre table.

There was a moment of perfect silence. All eyes were riveted on Father. The Editor shuffled his feet. The Mayor licked his lips. 'Get the Bordeaux from the cellar,' said Father in a low voice, and we could see the sadness in his eyes.

The owner of the jewellery shop, a frail, old man, with a face lined with deep wrinkles, stepped forward to shake the Writer's hand. 'I am the oldest man in town. I used to be the second oldest, but my rival died last week.' His voice quivered as he proffered a wizened hand. The Writer nodded gravely and looked upwards, as if thanking the heavens.

The Waiter returned with the bottle of Bordeaux in his left hand and a corkscrew in his right. He held out the bottle before the Writer who sniffed at it suspiciously. 'What brand is it? '

'The best. Château Mouton-Rothschild,' replied Father. '1945 vintage.'

'Must have rotted by now,' the Wife scowled.

'Open it,' ordered the Writer, and clapped his big hands.

Father watched in agony as the Waiter drove the corkscrew into the bottle and drew out the cork. There was a slight popping sound, and blood red liquid tumbled into a crystal decanter.

The Writer clutched his glass. He sipped. He gulped. Rivulets of rubescent foam dribbled down his chin on to his pullover. His face became flushed and his eyes shone like big buttons. 'This is good,' he said. 'A modicum of taste, at last.' He grabbed Father's arm and pulled him to the sofa. 'So tell me about your family. What do your children do?'

Father brightened up. 'I have six sons and two daughters. Seven of them,' he waved vaguely in our direction, 'are as remote from literature as… as fire from snow.'

The Writer pondered the analogy for a moment. 'And the eighth?' he asked.

'Ah! That is Raul, my fourth youngest. He has an elegant mind,' Father said, and motioned to Raul who was conversing with Selma near the piano. 'Raul is a budding writer. Not as talented as yourself, of course, but he does show promise.'

The Writer continued to sip his wine. Raul approached the sofa, his face twitching with a nervous tic.

'Raul writes romantic poetry mostly,' Father added, almost apologetically. 'And he has pieces regularly in the local newspaper.'

'Poetry has been comatose in this country since I stopped writing,' said the Great Writer.

'Would you like to see a few samples of Raul's poetry?' continued Father. 'I am sure you will like them.'

The Great Writer grunted.

'Go at once and get your notebook,' Father instructed Raul.

Raul bounded up the stairs and returned quickly with a blue, lined notebook which he placed on the centre table. He pushed back his long wavy hair and stood near the sofa, like a dog expecting a bone. The Great Writer flipped through its pages. His eyes were quiet as he scanned a few lines. Then he threw down the notebook. '*Tonteria!* This is drivel. What kind of romanticism is this? Where is the ardour, the passion?' he taunted Raul, his bushy eyebrows contracting to make folds on his forehead. 'I left poetry in a coma, but people like you, you kill it off forever.'

Raul turned pale. The twitching of his face increased. Selma burst into tears.

The Writer's hard face softened somewhat. He pulled Raul down to the sofa with him. 'Tell me, how old are you?'

'Seventeen,' replied Raul with downcast eyes.

'Just a kid!'

'No!' Raul bristled. 'I write better than anyone in this town. But I lack space and seclusion. Noble ideas require the freedom of solitude, which my five brothers and two sisters don't give me,' he looked reproachfully at us. 'But I know I can become a great writer, like you.' He stared at the Writer with unblinking eyes.

The Writer smiled. 'To become a great writer do you know what is most essential?' he asked.

'Imagination?' offered Raul.

'No. Experience. You need the fullness and value of experience to write great books. Out of experience comes memory and out of memory comes invention.'

We huddled near the Writer, eager to catch every line of this exchange. We were awed by the fearful symmetry of his sentences, the easy cadence of his words, the solidity of his opinions.

'But I have plenty of experience. I have seen death – my mother's and Grandpa's. I have seen joy, and sorrow, and now I have even felt the tremors of love,' said Raul and glanced at Selma who blushed.

'Ha!' the Great Writer laughed. 'You call these petty emotions experience? Where is the Great Event in your life?'

'Great Event?' asked Raul, with a baffled look.

'Yes, a Great Event. An event which marks a divide between the past and the future. An event so cataclysmic, so transformative, it becomes part of the essence of you. And this becomes the well-spring for the manifestation of creative genius.'

'So what was the Great Event in your life?' asked Raul.

'The Revolution, my boy, the Revolution!' exclaimed the Great Writer. 'The flow of your words has to match the flow of the blood in your veins. I wrote revolutionary poetry because I was a revolutionary. Our life was consumed by the Revolution. You youngsters have no memories to draw upon. So it is all unnatural and contrived. You will need a Great Event in your life before you can ever mature as a writer.'

'But the Revolution ended forty years ago,' protested Raul, his fists clenched.

'Then go and start another,' said the Writer. He dismissed Raul, and gulped more red wine.

With a sneer, Raul picked up the notebook and left the drawing room. Father hurried after him anxiously.

The Mayor slid next to the Great Writer on the sofa. 'I'm glad you brought that stuck-up boy down a notch or two,' he said in a low voice, but still within our earshot. 'Last week he punched a magazine editor in the face when he refused to publish his poems. I would have had him arrested but for the fact that his grandfather knew *you*.'

'Really?' the Writer looked surprised. 'That kid looks pretty harm-less to me,' he said and drained his glass.

'You have no idea, sir,' the Mayor whispered conspiratorially. 'Raul is a loony. I have heard he gets these fits. It takes three men to bring him down.'

'Interesting!' remarked the Writer and curved a finger at the Waiter. 'I need a refill.'

The Waiter came running over to us. 'The bottle is finished. Is there more French wine in the cellar?'

We shook our heads.

'Then what to do?' he asked fretfully.

The Editor was making one more attempt to ingratiate himself with the Writer. 'What do you think of our new President? Don't you admire his economic vision?'

'I see no vision,' said the Writer. 'I see only a long, dark abyss.'

'Perhaps the abyss precedes the vision, as night precedes day. We are on the road to Recovery, aren't we?'

'The terminally ill do not recover. They simply die,' observed the Writer dryly.

'So true,' quipped the Jeweller. 'I have cancer. The doctor says I won't recover. I'll die faster than a speeding bullet.'

'An inappropriate turn of phrase,' frowned the Writer. He turned towards his wife. 'Where's the Bordeaux?' he bellowed.

The Wife detached herself from a group of plump ladies and looked around for the Waiter. 'If my husband doesn't get his wine, we will leave this very instant,' she said threateningly to no one in particular.

Father went into a huddle with the Waiter.

Suddenly Raul reappeared, clutching something in his right fist. His hair was dishevelled and he had the same manic look about him as in one of his occasional fits. He advanced towards the sofa on which the Writer sat.

'You said I write nonsense, didn't you?' he said, his glassy eyes glinting like coins in a pond. 'Well, you are wrong. I think and feel like a writer. I know what it is to be human. I remember gestures and shapes. I store words in my mind.' He inched closer to the Great Writer.

The Wife strode forward and tried to grab Raul by the shoulder. With huge force, Raul elbowed her aside. Then he sprung to his feet.

'You may not care less about my poetry, but you should care a great deal for this!' He snapped open his fist to reveal a switchblade. He drew it slowly from its sheath. The orange flames from the fireplace danced on its smooth metal. The Great Writer shrank into the folds of the sofa. The Mayor crept cautiously towards the door. Father was still in conversation with the Waiter in the far corner, oblivious to this scene.

Raul stood immediately above the Great Writer, the knife held tightly in his right hand. 'You may be right about one thing, though. I do need the inspiration of a Great Event in my life,' he said, and slashed at the Writer's neck with the knife.

'Aaargh...' said the Great Writer and clutched his throat. Dark crimson liquid gushed out from between his fingers. He fell forward on the centre table.

'Eeeeeee....!' the Wife let out a piercing scream.

'Police!' the Mayor shrieked.

The Waiter dropped his trays to the floor with a loud clatter.

Father rushed to the sofa. When he saw Raul's handiwork, he crumpled before our eyes.

Raul was still standing there, breathing heavily, his eyes opaque, the blood-stained knife in his grip.

'My Bordeaux's gone bad,' Father mumbled, as he sank to the ground, his head dropping to his chest.

Ten days later, black umbrellas in hand, we stood at the L-junction under a crumbling sky. As the rain came pouring down, the Mayor cut the red cord to unveil the name of the new street. In large, dark blue letters, it spelled the name of the late great writer.

Boys and Dogs

Elizabeth Hay

In the back seat of the car my son asks into the quiet air, 'What's the worst thing you've ever done?'

I turn around to look at the boy who needs a haircut. He's wearing a T-shirt that's far too big for him and he's being baked by the late August sun. 'Well,' I say, 'there was that murder I committed last year.'

He smiles, but just for a second. Then he waits for a serious reply. My glance shifts away. I'm thinking of an interview I edited to make the person look bad, of occasions when I've shaken my children and squeezed their arms as hard as I could, of abusive scalding things I've said to my husband, and of things I've written. But nothing comes forward as the worst. 'I'll have to think about it,' I say.

We're close to Lanark and soon we'll pass through the little town, dipping down to cross a bridge and curving past the most beautiful yellow house set back in the woods. A house we admire, a house my parents would admire. The memory of many drives with them when I was young and they would slow down as we passed a stone house and agree, the two of them, that that was 'a lovely home'. How it used to irritate me, their wistful middle-class hankering, and how understandable it seems to me now.

My husband has no trouble choosing the worst thing he ever did. 'I don't know what came over me. Maybe I'd been picked on so long by my brother that when I saw a chance I couldn't resist. It happened when I went to camp one summer.'

My son watches the back of his father's head as he talks. His dad has a long muscular neck and moderately wide shoulders. His hair is brown, curly. There are pictures of him as a young man when his hair came halfway down his back. Now it's short. You can see the plastic-tipped arms of his glasses curl behind his ears.

'I was eight,' he's saying, 'I couldn't stop picking on a certain kid. All week I was mean to this kid, who just kept asking me to leave him alone. Then, on the last day, I punched him in the mouth and his lip bled.'

'Were you punished?' I want to know.

'I wasn't. I got away with it.' He keeps his eyes on the road and shakes his head in wonder.

My son asks me, 'Have you thought about it?'

I turn around to look at him again. He is my interesting and persistent seven-year-old son. A boy without many friends and I wonder why. 'It seems to me the worst things are my thoughts, not things I've done.'

Then I ask, 'What's the worst thing you've done?'

'I don't know,' he answers, and he looks down at his hands.

Once we get home, I read to him. Usually his sister is here too, they share a room, but she is visiting her grandmother in Boston. He has their room to himself for the first time in his life and he wishes he didn't. I'm reading the story about Odysseus returning home after twenty years and nobody recognizes him except his ancient dog. I stop reading and say, 'That's one of the worst things I've ever done.'

'What?'

'I gave my dog away.'

'Stan?'

'Yes.'

'What happened to him?'

'He was hit by a car.' And even though I've told the story before, I tell it again. That when my first marriage ended we gave Stan away to friends who wanted him – they had asked if they could have him – and he was having a good life with these people out west because they had another dog, and Stan and Shane were company for each other, but then one day, only a couple of years later, Stan got hit by a car. Afterwards, Shane missed him a lot.

'Why did you give him away?'

'I wanted to travel. I went away for a long time.'

After I kiss him goodnight and go back downstairs, he lies awake. He wishes his sister were here. She always sleeps with her face to the door because, she told him once, robbers don't usually come through windows, they come through doors. Even though always sleeping that way makes her ear hurt.

❧

He wakes up thinking about school. These thoughts intensify once school gets underway in September. One morning he hears me downstairs and dresses and comes down too. At the kitchen table he reads the sports, drinks his cocoa, eats a few Cheerios. No, he can't eat anymore. Why not? *Because I feel sick to my stomach, that's why. I hate school.* It turns out he's forgotten to bring home a permission slip, his class is going on a field trip, 'You have to write a note or I won't be able to go, *you have to.*'

I'm positive the trip is scheduled for the following week, there's plenty of time to bring home the permission slip, but it's easier to write the note than to argue with my impassioned son. I write it at my desk upstairs, then bring it down and give it to him while he's eating breakfast. At the door (he is already a few minutes late) I say, 'Do you have the note?'

'Maybe it's in my knapsack.'

He looks in his knapsack, but I know it's more likely to be in the kitchen. I go to look but can't find it. He looks in every pocket of his knapsack.

'You look in the kitchen,' I say.

He runs in rubber boots down the hall into the kitchen, then comes thumping back to look again in his knapsack, and in the pockets of his coat.

I go back to the kitchen and this time find the note, blank side up, under the newspaper on the table. I shove it into his hand. I say, emphasizing each word, 'You annoy me.' Then I pick up his knapsack and sling it over his shoulders. But his face is turned away.

Then, even though I'm still very irritated, I hug him. He squirms out of my arms. He pushes me away. He yells at me as he always does when he's hurt and angry, as quick to accuse as I am, and even more volatile.

Then he's outside and I'm calling after him. Mike. Mike. After I call his name he looks back: I'm on the porch in my old red sweater. Then at the corner, just before crossing the street, he takes me in again with a small fast glance: I'm in the same spot, red sweater, those black pants I wear all the time, arms folded. Then a third time, just before his house passes out of sight, quick. I'm still there, looking after him.

I think about his question. I've been thinking about it ever since he asked it. The question stays with me as much as the sight of him walking down the street in his black rubber boots, his chapped boy-hands jabbing away tears.

The day passes without event. At three-thirty he bursts through the door yelling to me, 'Hi, you long-nosed baby!' We laugh hard and feel great. At the kitchen table he eats two Dream Puffs and drinks half a glass of milk. 'Finish your milk,' I say, and he says, '*No*,' so decisively that we laugh even more. I ask him what it's like outside. He says, 'Rainy, overcast, warm, green. Now in that other part of the world it's dark. How does that happen?'

He likes to boast about how much he's read. He keeps track and tells me. I'm on page twenty-four. I'm on page thirty-two. And at night, when I bend down to kiss him, 'Mommy?'

'Yes?'

'I finished my book.'

'Good for you.'

'Sixty-seven pages,' he says, or, 'eighty-nine pages.'

I get down on my knees beside his bed and rub my face against his. He says, 'You've been eating.'

'Yes,' I laugh, 'apple pie.' Often he says he has a headache and then I rub his forehead.

He needs reading glasses, but the eye doctor says wait six months, your eyes might correct themselves. He hopes not. He knows the glasses he wants. They have green rims and are in a glass case at the doctor's. He also wants braces that glow in the dark, and a retainer. Also he wants roller blades. But more than anything else he wants a bunny rabbit like the one he saw in August when we visited Mark Priest. He's told me several times. I want a baby bunny even more than I want roller blades.

At Mark Priest's he'd held the bunny for a long time after I gave him one of my leather gloves so the little scratchy feet didn't dig into his hand. It settled down into the glove and with his other hand he'd stroked the brown furry head and the brown furry back. In the corner Ned the dog pushed his huge yellow head into the straw nest and stared and licked and stared and licked, fascinated by the bunnies. 'He loves them,' Mark Priest said. Pigeons flew in and out an open window and Ned's tail wagged so hard it knocked the mother rabbit right over.

❧

In those days, when he was six going on seven and seven going on eight, I ignored him much of the time. But often he would not be ignored. He took issue with everything I said. He whacked my bottom. One day he called me into the bathroom to show me the marks on his legs, wrinkled patterns where his jeans had pressed into his skin.

'From your jeans,' I explained.

'Like the mark your watch leaves,' he said.

'Yes.'

'Does it leave the time on your skin too?'

I sat back on my heels and looked at him. He intrigued me and worried me and wearied me, this storm-tossed boy who was too potent to be charming. Either he wouldn't leave you alone, or he retreated into prolonged concentration with Tintin and with Asterix and Obelix.

One day, not long after his question about time, a sparrow flew to the kitchen window and rested on the sill and I studied it for a moment, then asked him about the trouble in school the day before.

He looked at me and maintained stoutly that nothing had happened.

But the night before his teacher had called to say that three boys had him down on the cafeteria floor during lunch and were punching and kicking him.

Mommy. From down the hall.

I wait a moment, my eyes open, I strain to see the time on the bedside clock.

Mommy. Softly.

I go to his room. 'What is it?' Finger on my lips, not to wake his sister.

'I had a bad dream.'

I sit on the edge of his bed and stroke his forehead and hands.

'I was trapped in a car crash.'

'Were you?' I hold his hand. 'What happened?'

'I was trapped in a car crash,' he says again in the same quiet voice. He turns his head to look at me directly. 'I can't sleep.'

'Don't worry,' I say. Then, 'Think about something nice.'

'What?'

'Think about the bunnies at Mark Priest's place. Pretend you're holding one in your hand.'

'Okay. Thank you.'

I go back to bed and lie awake. An hour later he comes down the hall and I keep my eyes closed. He touches me softly. 'Mommy.' His stomach is hurting, he says, and his head is spinning.

I take him to the bathroom. He pees and goes back to bed and so do I. I hear him turning, breathing. After a while, ten minutes, I go in to him and his eyes are closed when he speaks to me. I press my face against the side of his, and his ear is so cold.

He is asleep now.

Asleep still when I go in at six. His ear as cold as a window. Below is the small yard and adjoining alley – unused by cars when we first moved here and grassy as a nineteenth-century lane, but ploughed and chewed up since several neighbours fashioned parking spots out of their back yards.

I gave my dog away in December, 1982. No, March. March of 1983. After C and I managed to sell the house and before I moved into the apartment on Davenport Road. C had moved out first, in December. There were Christmas parties that had to be cancelled, and invitations accepted with the explanation that I would be coming alone. It was a very warm December. I remember reading in the paper about a ten-year-old girl who walked around outside in bare feet. I worked at my desk with the window open and dark warm air pouring in across my papers. In January huge amounts of snow fell, and one day I walked home through the drifts realizing just how alone I was. Stan was there, waiting for me.

He was a mutt, brown and black, a big dog, part collie, part Newfoundland, part German shepherd. And how old? Ah, the treacheries of the heart. I no longer remember how old and try to do the arithmetic as I sit here. I think it was 1976 when we got him as a puppy from a sentimental woman so devoted that she cooked him special stews and called him, not Fluffy, but something akin. And 1983 when we gave him away. And 1985 when he was killed. Eight, maybe nine years old.

He was a bounding, affectionate, softhearted dog. We had a small white Mazda pick-up and Stan would ride on the seat between us if both of us were in the truck, or he would lean heavily into the driver if only one of us was there. A hot date, as a friend quipped. That was when we were up north.

I loved him fiercely and it surprised me, to feel such love. Even though I had grown up with a dog who had been first in my family's heart. I knew about canine devotion, I knew about devotion to a family animal before all else and perhaps because of everything else. That dog, too, our childhood dog, had been left behind.

There were extenuating circumstances. There almost always are.

❧

I find crumbs everywhere, even crumbs of cheese, even crumbs of apple. He works the food with his fingertips, taking tiny bits and inevitably letting many drop. Under his pillow I find many dried-up little balls of snot. He works his lower lip with his upper teeth into something dark-red and chewed-up. He squeezes and works the soft flesh of my arms which he calls fluffy. He says fluffy is his favourite word.

When no one phoned his dad on his birthday, he wrote him a note pretending to be his two uncles, and left it on his pillow.

Happy brthday mrk
haw meny Presinst did
you get hope you have
a nice brthday
laiv Jony Lex

His dad's birthday coincided with Valentine's Day and I remember he came home from school cheerfully enough and had his usual snack of two cookies and a glass of milk, then went into the living room to read his book, and that was when I looked through his knapsack to see if there were any valentines. There weren't any at all. But he didn't seem upset. Supper, piano practice, bath – all passed without incident. Once he was lying in bed, however, he said to me, 'I didn't get any valentines.'

'No?'

'Not even one.'

I looked down at him and felt sorry, impatient, worried, incredibly tired.

'Not even Max,' he said. 'Not even Vince.'

'I guess most boys don't give out valentines. You shouldn't worry. Max and Vince like you a lot.'

'They don't like me at all. They don't even listen to me.'

He was disgusted with them. He was disgusted with me. He was getting even by working himself up and taking his fists to sleep. His sleep, my sleep.

'Not even *one*,' he said.

'Not even this much,' holding his fingers one inch apart.

'Not even *air*.'

ϟ

'This one knows how to spell,' his teacher tells me when I go to see her. Not that she can add anything more to what she said on the phone; she didn't witness the moment when he was being kicked, the lunchroom monitor saw it and reported it because she was concerned. She can only say there haven't been any other incidents to her knowledge and nothing at all like that has ever happened in the classroom. She will certainly keep her eye on him.

'I don't know,' I say. 'He doesn't play with other kids on the street. We've been here over a year and he's never found a way to fit in.'

I can't bring myself to say the rest of it. That every boy on the block plays street hockey, except for Mike. That only yesterday, when he and I walked home from chess club at the community centre, the boys didn't even look up when we walked by. 'You can stay out for a bit and play, if you want to.'

He didn't want to.

Wet snow was falling on our heads. 'What do you call that stuff?' he asked me.

'It's not snow, is it?' I replied, 'and it's not rain either. It's gruel.'

'It's moisture,' he said.

He didn't have any homework but his sister had so much she was in tears. She said she couldn't spell anything. She threw her pencil onto the table when she tried to write rocking chair and realized she couldn't spell it. 'I've been spelling for four years and I still don't know anything.'

That was one worry he didn't have, or so I thought.

The next morning he came downstairs at six-fifteen and pulled out the piece of paper on which he'd started a letter to Mark Priest the day before. But after erasing many times the word 'Dear,' after cursing and cursing, he gave up. He pushed the paper away.

Then he pulled it forward, erased 'Dear' one more time, and began to write.

Then, 'Suck! I suck!'

I was drinking coffee at the end of the table and reading a book. I'd been watching him and he felt me getting mad and he got madder. Finally I told him he could either write the letter quietly or he could go back to bed. But he kept up his anger, pushing the paper around and saying *Suck! Suck! Suck!* until I grabbed the pencil and said, 'Which end do you write with?'

He looked at me.

'This end,' I asked, pointing to the eraser, 'or this end?' pointing to the tip.

He had to laugh. But he didn't want to laugh. He wanted to be mad (how well I know the feeling). He couldn't even write the first word, he couldn't even spell 'Dear.' Why bother talking to Mark Priest about bunnies when he was never going to get one? He knew this for a fact. He would never get a bunny because I didn't want one. He slapped the paper around the table some more until I said, 'Look. I come down here early to have my coffee and read in peace, and in you come ruining everything with your bad temper. If you're going to write the letter,' I said, 'just write the damn thing.'

Then I stomped upstairs.

He got out the Cheerios and poured himself a bowl. He let a few drop on the floor. His mom HATED Cheerios on the floor. 'Happy?' he said out loud.

Then he lost himself in *Asterix in Britain* for a long time.

In the first week of October it snowed. Ottawa often has an early winter and people are so depressed, so hopeful, so desperate that always they're surprised.

At six-fifteen a.m. he pushed open my study door. I turned in my swivel chair and he climbed into my lap. 'Have you washed my pants?' he wanted to know.

'Why?' Sensing trouble.

'Because my toonie is in the pocket.'

I found his pants in the laundry bag in the closet. I handed them to him. He looked for the toonie twice, in each pocket, without success, then threw the pants away in disgust.

I reached to the very bottom of one pocket and pulled out the large two-dollar coin he would swallow a few months later, precipi-tating a five-hour session in the emergency ward that ended when a surgeon fished out the coin with very long tweezers.

Now, with the coin still cold in his hand, he insisted, this son of mine, that I go to the neighbour's right now to borrow *The Hobbit*. The neighbour had offered to lend it to him any time.

'No. It's too early. They'll be asleep. We'll get the book later today.'

He flung off down the hallway and back to his room.

Then, *'Mommy!'*

I closed my eyes. I felt little bubbles of hysteria rising in my chest. How to describe that tone of voice? Peremptory, tyrannical, despotic.

I went to his room. He was lying on his bed. He turned his head to give me a savage, accusing stare. 'Why did you lie to me?'

'Why are you speaking to me this way?'

'You said you got *Little House in the Big Wood* and *you didn't.*'

I looked at him. I thought of his poor sister trying to sleep in the top bunk. I took him by the hand downstairs and into the living room, and put the book into his hand.

A moment later. I was standing over the kitchen sink washing out the coffee pot. He came around the corner. His face was bright red with wrath and his finger was pointing to the offending words on the page. 'Once upon a time.'

'It's not even true!' he shouted.

I never found out what the worst thing was that he'd ever done. Years passed and I asked him if he remembered putting that question to me. What was on your mind? He shook his fifteen-year-old head. He didn't remember. I asked about Vince. Was there some trouble with Vince? He said, 'I remember two things about Vince. He was very nice to me, and he was eight. I could hardly wait to be eight.'

Years later, too, I met again the old friend who took our dog after my first husband and I separated. He said what a great dog he was. And then he told me how Stan died and it was entirely different from what I'd been told at the time. He said that he and his then-wife – his crazy, high-strung wife – went to Hawaii on a holiday and before they left, and without consulting him, crazy Joan had Shane put down because he'd been biting people and acting weird, so Stan was left behind. Shane was gone and Stan was all by himself, wandering around looking for him, and that's when he was hit by a car.

I sat beside him listening to this new version of events – the terrible truth of what happened to Stan – and I didn't say that I'd been told something else. I didn't say anything. I was too busy absorbing the truth and wondering if it was true. Too busy being polite, and stunned, and in pain.

Why didn't I ask? More to the point, couldn't I have helped my son spell 'Dear'? Couldn't I have said quietly, 'Need some help?'

He wanted a dog for the longest time, longer than he wanted a bunny, and finally, despite my family's sad history with dogs, I gave in. We went so far as to make a trip to the country to see a woman who raised and sold black Labs. She had a small farm on a side road, not a farming woman, as such, but somebody who was trying to get by. She took us into the barn and it was dark and the dogs were big, black, and disagreeable. After that my son spoke less avidly about dogs, and one day I remarked to him that since I'd agreed to getting a dog he no longer talked about wanting one. Had he changed his mind? He looked at me thoughtfully and said, 'I still want a dog. But I don't want to make you do something against your will.' His retreat wasn't any simpler than his frontal assaults, but it was a restful change.

Then one morning when it was quiet and I'd come back from a doctor's appointment, when I was reaching into the cupboard for a cup and morning light flooded the kitchen, I saw his life – the daily walk to and from school, the jacket that needed to be washed and would fit him for one more year, the oversized boots bought to last, the woollen tuque that needed to be mended, the endless round of desultory learning, the breaks for recess and lunch, the after-school hunger when he ate all at once an apple, cheese, cookies, cocoa, the

rest of his sandwich, crackers – his fierce memory for lyrics, dialogue, people, facts, his sentimental attachment to me and his dad,
his animosity-filled attachment to his sister, his rapid growth, his
tender goodnights, his energetic good mornings, the sound of pages
turning in his room, his whirligig turnings in the living room, his
jokes, his sudden shynesses. I stood in the kitchen and saw him held
by this place and a part of our small world. He had been alive for
nine years of broken nights and complicated days. He had already
outlived my dog. This same light was pouring through his school-
room window and reaching across the room to the desk at which
he sat, not without nervousness, not without friends, but still on his
own, as was I. For a moment life slowed down and in some deep,
inexplicable way expanded to include him and everything about
him in its large, flowing light.

Kiss and Tell

John Sam Jones

Some of the girls in Seimon's class already seemed much older – and a bit scary. Often they'd huddle into exclusive, whispering broods, and there'd be audible sighs and sometimes shrieks of laughter above their murmuring, and furtive glances at no-one-in-particular. A couple acted like they'd already outgrown their peers; Jane Jones, who'd got breasts that were the Promised Land of boys' dirty talk, almost always had love bites on her neck, and Shân Jenkins boasted about going to the nightclub in Llandudno at the weekends with her boyfriend, who was a management trainee with one of the new, cheap German supermarkets. There was even a rumour that Shân was on the pill.

Seimon had decided it wasn't easy being fourteen. Most of his classmates had started to muscle-up, which made rugby more of a man's game; it made the showers afterwards a real embarrassment too. Naked and puny amongst so many well-developed boy-men, he just wanted to disappear. He knew that puberty kicked in later in some, but why did he have to be the runt, and bear the brunt of so much teasing? Sometimes he imagined himself smaller-than-small so that the others wouldn't notice him – and sometimes they didn't. But then, when the boys he hung around with seemed not to want to see him, he wondered if he'd made himself too insignificant. Being lonely was horrible. Feeling isolated, he doubted himself even more.

At first he'd just daydreamed about Mr Roberts; in Seimon's mind's eye, his favourite teacher would be reading to the class – one of the poems they were studying in a literature project, or perhaps he'd be explaining something about the vagaries of Welsh grammar. Seimon found him fascinating to watch; those hands, with long delicate fingers, always expressive, and that face so animated with passion for his subject and the love of teaching. Then, in one of his early reveries, his teacher smiled at him. It was as if Seimon was the only other person in the classroom and Mr Roberts was only interested in him. The smile encouraged Seimon. Even Mr Roberts' eyes smiled, beckoning, inviting engagement with the poem, the grammatical foible, the infatuation... with language. And Seimon felt special.

Dylan Roberts had gone back into the closet against his better judgement. He could remember the day he'd made that decision; it was late spring and he was driving to the interview for the job as Head of Languages at the new secondary school on the coast. After a sharp burst of rain, from an errant cloud that hung in an otherwise blue sky, a rainbow arched over the growing forest of wind turbines out in Liverpool Bay. Only then did Dylan remember that he'd slapped a rainbow sticker onto the back window of his car after the Cardiff Gay Pride parade. He pulled over before reaching the school to peel it off; he couldn't see himself being out-and-proud in North Wales like he'd been in the capital. He'd got the job, on the strength that he could offer some German and French, and after selling his flat in one of the seedier Cardiff suburbs he'd bought a small house in Rhos-on-Sea, two streets parallel to the promenade.

In a small country, especially one that has recently gained some autonomy from its ruling neighbour, things can change quickly. By 2001 the Welsh Assembly Government was keen to hear from gays and lesbians across Wales – about their experiences of prejudice, their grievances and their aspirations. The new Minister for Education even made a thing about homophobic bullying in schools and in 2005 teachers were offered in-service training on how they could support gay and lesbian students in educational settings. Then Elton John married David Furnish and even the main Welsh language evening news on S4C carried the story.

Elton John was a favourite amongst many of the staff at Dylan's school. The television news coverage and the wedding photos in the newspapers invited unanticipated conversations in the staffroom: Tony Morris, the Head of Maths and three years off retirement, came out as the father of – not one, but two gay sons; Ann Puw, one of the history teachers, talked about her lesbian sister; Jane Edwards, the only newly-qualified teacher at school and not yet twenty-five, shared that she'd grown up in a lesbian household with two mums.

Over the Christmas holidays, Dylan considered these revelations and made a new year's resolution to come out at school. Most of the young women teachers had already guessed, since their attempts to flirt with Dylan had been rebuffed. Only one of his older male colleagues seemed less friendly. The head teacher, a dynamic forty-something in her first headship, praised Dylan for his courage and said he'd be a good role model for the four boys in years ten and eleven who'd come out.

Mr Roberts' coming out was the topic of conversation for a couple of weeks after the Christmas break. Jane Jones thought it was such a waste that someone as handsome and sexy as her Welsh teacher could be gay, and Shân Jenkins, who'd been ditched by the Aldi management trainee at a drunken New Year's Eve party, thought she might try to seduce him. A clutch of the rugby boys cackled a bit, but that was mostly to disguise their own insecurity. In fact, most of Dylan Roberts' students thought it was 'dead cool' that he was gay.

Seimon, though, was surprised… at first, anyway. He knew about gays and lesbians, of course; his parents had even been to a Civil Partnership – one of the very first gay weddings – a college friend of his dad's: Miriam. She was nice, but her partner Kate was built like a wrestler, and a bit like a man – with hairy arms and legs, and always wearing jeans and check shirts. He didn't really know any gay men, except the boys who'd come out at school, but like Graham Norton and Julian Clary on the television, they seemed so girly. He was taken aback when Mr Roberts came out because his teacher was so normal.

Seimon had been slow to discover that touching and rubbing parts of his body – well, that part especially – could feel nice, though he hadn't done it often because he'd overheard some of the rugby boys say that wanking could cause a deformity and even blindness. In the days after hearing that Mr Roberts was gay he wondered if his teacher did it… and whether he did it with other men. Seimon became aroused by these possibilities. For about a week he tried not to think such thoughts, but one night, in the privacy of his room and feeling secure under the duvet, he petted and stroked himself and imagined Mr Roberts doing the same. In some unexplainable way, imagining Mr Roberts masturbating made the possibility of deformity and blindness less credible. After that he did it more often and before too long they were touching one another; even his class-room daydreams became sexual fantasies.

Jane Jones had a reputation for offering boys the chance to explore the Promised Land, if they could afford it; for a pound they could touch her breasts through her school sweatshirt and for two-fifty she allowed their sweaty hands to grope through her bra. Just once she'd let a boy that she liked touch her bare breasts, but that had cost him a fiver. Jane always had money to buy cigarettes and blackcur-rant VKs from the off-licence on the Esplanade, where no one ever asked her age.

'I'd let you touch me up for free,' Jane said to Seimon one day because she felt sorry for him, but she said it loud enough for some of the rugby boys to hear; she wanted to make Griff Thomas jealous. 'Only through my clothes though,' she taunted Seimon with a sug-gestive wink.

Seimon's face turned scarlet. Griff Thomas pushed to the front of the scrum of boy-men and, flicking two fingers at Jane, he sneered: 'Simple sissy Seimon wouldn't know what to do with them. You should see the way he looks at us in the showers.'

'You gay, like Mr Roberts, Seimon?' Jane gibed, loud enough to draw mocking jeers from Griff and his mates. 'Maybe if I give you a feel under my top it'll help you make up your mind.' As she said this she raised her sweatshirt until the pink bead in her navel ring was showing.

Seimon didn't know what to say, or do. That Jane was being so common with him didn't seem to matter too much, but in front of the boys he felt he needed to respond – and at least deny that he looked at them in the showers. But he did look at them in the showers.

Shân Jenkins was one of the Year Nine representatives on the School Council. Her election had surprised a lot of the teachers and some of the students. She took her responsibility as a Year Rep very seriously, almost as if she wanted to spite those that doubted her, and every Thursday lunchtime she'd walk around the school chatting to other students from her year and solicit their views about life in school.

'You're on your own a lot these days, Sei,' she said, finding Seimon sitting by himself at the far end of the field. 'Ever thought of going to the Lunchtime Club?'

'I don't need the lonely kids club when I've got my dreams to keep me company,' he said, because it was hard for him to admit, even to Shân, that he was a bullied loner.

'What sorts of dreams d'you have then?' Shân coaxed, just to be friendly to a lonely kid.

Seimon hesitated, but recalling the gossip about Shân he suddenly felt emboldened. 'I was just imagining being kissed and cuddled by – ' But then he panicked. He couldn't say boyfriend, not even to her. 'My lover,' he mumbled. The word was so alien to him.

'Well, Seimon Gwyn, who's a dark horse?' Shân exclaimed. 'Tell Auntie Shân some more.'

'Nothing to tell,' Sei said, feeling his confidence drain.

'Oh… come on, Sei. Who is he?'

She said he so matter-of-factly… so naturally, that he felt encouraged to tell her.

'It's Dylan,' he said, savouring the sense of importance it gave him, despite the fact that even in his imaginings his teacher was always Mr Roberts.

'Dylan Williams… in Year Eleven?' Shân said with confused curiosity. 'He's not gay; he's going out with Anwen who plays the harp in assembly sometimes.'

'No… Dylan Roberts, Welsh, French and German,' Sei said, more boldly than he'd intended.

'You're kidding, Sei,' she said, remembering the workshop they'd had about sexual abuse on the School Councillor training day – and remembering her own fantasy fling with her teacher after her Aldi management trainee had dumped her. 'Tell me you're just having me on.'

Feeling too important now to backtrack, Seimon embellished his love affair.

✣

On Thursday afternoons, Year Nine had history with Mrs Puw, who was also the School Council link teacher. Shân had begun to like history. Ann Puw offered her classes opportunities to do project work and Shân, with two of her friends, was investigating women's fashion through the twentieth century – and specifically how women's clothes reflected women's roles in society. The three girls had reached the 1970s and though their research into women's lib had been fascinating, Shân couldn't concentrate. She kept looking across the classroom to where Seimon was sitting, and found herself torn between feeling jealous that Sei had got off with Mr Roberts and her responsibility as a School Councillor to report the sexual abuse to Mrs Puw. She kept remembering that the man who'd come to the School Council from the Children's Commissioner's office had emphasized that all children and young people had rights, but with rights there were responsibilities. At the end of the lesson she told Mrs Puw about Seimon and Mr Roberts and felt proud that she'd lived up to her responsibility.

✣

Eleri Clwyd, the head teacher, spoke with a clarity and calmness that belied the nauseating clench of her stomach. Dylan was suddenly choking on the room's stuffiness and the abhorrence of the allegation against him. His union representative, a woman in her fifties with too much make-up and dark-rooted platinum hair that made her look tarty, reached across to touch his shoulder. She offered a faint smile of reassurance.

'You'll be suspended without prejudice pending further investigations,' Eleri Clwyd said.

Dylan's complexion turned the colour of cheap household candles and his mouth seemed to fill with dry, gritty sand. There were questions he wanted to ask, but his usual fluency with language and lucidity of thought were shunted into a siding... and in his mind's eye there was only Seimon Gwyn, smiling.

The Castle Morton Jerry

Nicholas Shakespeare

We called it the Castle Morton Jerry, though I never knew why. Ever since a child I remembered that band of cold thick fog suspended above the river opposite our cove, sometimes all morning until the sun burned it off. When the jerry rolled in like that, you couldn't see anything. Walking home, you'd reach out your hand and you'd feel a hard object and you'd have to decode what it was, whether it was a gum tree or a fence post or the leathery, nearly round face of Old Stan who jerked awake as he did on that day.

'Hey!'

'Sorry, mate,' when I saw that I'd blundered onto his deck. And when he'd seen who it was and relaxed, at least enough to stop hollering at me for poking him out of his sleep, I said: 'This jerry – I really do loathe it, you know.'

Old Stan must still have been half asleep because he stared at me almost like he was seeing himself at my age, fourteen, and then he said in a careful voice, 'You shouldn't hate it, boy. That's the same thing as hating what you come out of.'

'Come out of this horrid fog? Sorry, Stan, I don't follow you.'

He looked at me in a thoughtful way. 'Granny Gordon never told you about the jerry?'

'Reckon only thing Granny Gordon told me was not to pick my nose.'

'She didn't hum you this song?' and his cracked voice warbled through the mist, thinning it a little:

'*So I hauled her into bed and I covered up her head, just to keep her from the foggy, foggy dew.*'

'Granny Gordon wasn't the humming type,' I said. 'And I don't recall her telling me no stories.'

'Well, maybe she had enough on her hands bringing you up to

want to go spading about in the past. But if it wasn't for the jerry you wouldn't have a nose to pick, none of us would,' and that's when Old Stan told me about the *Castle Morton* and the story his grandfather Ralph who ran the ferry service at Two Mile Creek told him.

❧

'You grew up knowing Huonville, but before it became "Hoonville" it was Victoria and before that it had no name that I'm aware of. You've got to remember how remote Tasmania was then, before it was woodchip heaven. Believe you me, boy, this place was *remote*. It wasn't even called Tasmania, it was Van Diemen's Land. And this valley was one of the remoter valleys in Van Diemen's Land. Why, there wouldn't have been more than three bluestone houses and eleven men in a hundred square miles of thick bush. Mr Gordon – your great-granddad – and his four convict workers; Mr Hacking and his four workers, and my granddad Ralph. All single men of notorious and immoral character, as the Governor in Hobart liked to put it. And in the whole district just one solitary female – Granny Lawrence, a noisy, irritable woman who was lame in one leg and had a fleshy mole on the side of her chin, and a scar on the tip of her crooked nose and over her right eyebrow, and whose rare grin opened on a row of missing teeth. Oh, and sheep. You sure your own gran never told you anything about this?'

'I already said.'

'Personally speaking, I never believed the stories about Mr Gordon's riding boots and Granny Lawrence's soreness at finding traces of a ewe's back leg in one of them. All I do know, the situation was pretty desperate for a lusty and profligate man. And don't imagine matters were easier in Hobart. It was common knowledge how Mr Gordon once rode on his horse for three days through the bush in order to dance at a ball – at the Bellevue, I believe – where he was much disappointed to discover that the settlers and officers all had to waltz with each other. You must realize that even in Hobart there were thirty men to every woman. Who knows what desperation would have done to Mr Gordon and the ten other fellas down here if it hadn't been for the Castle Morton Jerry.

'Well, like I tell you, things being so desperate on the island at that time, the Governor got in touch with Mrs Elizabeth Fry in London and a committee was formed to send a transport ship to Hobart filled with 'desirable, free and single women'. This was the *Castle Morton*, built in Nova Scotia, 472 tons of copper-sheathed white oak and black birch. On board were two hundred young women, some of them the most beautiful and elegant ever to come to Van Diemen's Land. Plus a chaplain, a naval surgeon and a matron to keep those women clean and orderly on the four-month voyage to "Hobart Town on the Derwent" – where they were to enjoy free board and a roof over their heads and a lot else beside. Only trouble is, after four months at sea, the *Castle Morton* got disoriented in a southerly coming up the channel. Instead of sailing into the Derwent, where she was first sighted, she sailed without realising it into the mouth of the Huon nearby. You listening now?'

'Yeh, I'm listening.'

'You'll be listening real good, I reckon, when you hear what my granddad told me about that altogether memorable day. Ralph watched it all happen. He was settled on the sandspit here when mid-afternoon came through the cold front from hell. A storm blew up and he observed a ship in distress. He didn't know there were two hundred eligible women on board, including some convicts from the London Female Penitentiary. All he saw was this sailing vessel off Bruny Island dragging her anchors and in danger of being wrecked. The southerly carried the ship past the entrance. Ralph could see she was in great danger. The rapidity of the tide made him fear that she might be forced on the west side of the sandspit and he hoisted a bedsheet on a pole, but couldn't keep it up in the violent wind. So he ran to Mr Gordon's farm and requested two of his men to go with him and make a fire on Bluff Point and another on Norman Cove to guide the ship in.

'The smoke of one fire was seen on board. A stay sail was hoisted and the ship bore westward, clearing the sandspit with the help of the steering fires.

'Ralph alerted the crew to the dangers of another sandbar and directed them to sheltered water. He shouted "Starboard!" and they wore round. "Port!" and they did so. He told them: "Let go your anchor!" They did so. And then the gale died down as suddenly as it blew up.

'It was coming on dark when Ralph launched his whale-boat and rowed out with the help of Mr Gordon's two men.

'The Master who pulled Ralph on board was Mr Henniker. He was sufficiently wary to keep his passengers down below and out of sight until he had ascertained where he had anchored, plus the identity of his young saviour. Beside Mr Henniker stood the Chaplain who had fallen down a hatchway in the gale and dislocated his shoulder. Beside the Chaplain stood the Surgeon and Matron. All four officials stood in a row and stared by the light of Mr Henniker's lantern at Ralph and the two disreputable-looking figures who had clambered with him on deck, systematic thieves and liars both of them, and both with faces blackened from the smoke of the bonfires they had lit and dressed in trousers and jackets stitched from the skankiest-smelling kangaroo skin.

'Ralph overcame his natural shyness to take control. He told the Master that if he kept on the east shore on the mud flat he would be sheltered from any further gale.

'The Master thanked him. Then he said: "I have 198 women on board bound for Hobart who have suffered much sea-sickness." And explained that he was most anxious to disembark them after so many months at sea and constant drenching by storms and heat. He looked again uneasily at Ralph's two companions and then at Ralph. "This is Hobart, right?"

'"Yes, yes," said Ralph, a quick-witted fella. "This is Hobart all right."

'"I was expecting," the Master said, "I was expecting something bigger." He had seen through his telescope two clearings and a bark hut. None of his crew had been before to Van Diemen's Land. He had imagined a bend on the river surrounded by cleared banks covered in buildings.

'"No, you have arrived in Hobart," said Ralph, "most certainly. This is what we like to call the... the outskirts."

'"The outskirts," the Matron said glumly.

'"We were expecting a Landing Committee," threw in the Chaplain, wincing.

"'I will go this moment and fetch them," promised Ralph, and said that he would be back with the Landing Committee at first light.

'Well, as soon as Ralph rowed ashore he ran helter-skelter all the way to Mr Gordon's house. As it happened, Mr Gordon knew about this Girl Boat and its cargo of Reformers. It was because of the *Castle Morton* that Ralph found Mr Gordon saddling up, preparing for another long ride through the scrub to Hobart. Even so, his spirits were considerably reduced at the idea of having to compete with 3,000 single men at the wharf. And not only 3,000 men. Also waiting in Hobart were the Ladies Committee composed of all the respectable matrons of the colony and excited to inform the passengers of the *Castle Morton* that their Committee had enabled each and every one of the 198 to be engaged in service and provided for respectfully. There were in addition at the dockside a small squad of police waiting to march the women under guard up Macquarie Street to the government hotel, the Bellevue, which had been appointed to house the newcomers. I tell you, lad, the arrival of this ship was a large and significant event, and it caused quite a stir. Once word got out that the *Castle Morton* had been spotted at the mouth of the Derwent more crowds turned out than for the execution of Matthew Brady. Mr Gordon didn't stand a chance. Nor did Mr Hacking, nor did young Ralph, nor any of the other eight assigned men in the valley. And that's when the jerry comes down the river to assist.

'In the night the southerly eased off into a light offshore wind. Early next morning a current of cold air tracked down from the mountains through the gulleys and marshes and fed into the river. It hit the warmer water in a tube of dense rolling mist, a big cloud of it that spilled out into the channel and locked the ship in a chill moist fog.

'On the *Castle Morton* they woke up to a virtual whiteout. Couldn't see a thing. They knew it was a beautiful day, bright and sunny outside. But inside the jerry, the Master couldn't see the Matron shivering across the quarter-deck, leave aside the sourness of her expression. He certainly couldn't see that they weren't in Hobart on the Derwent.

'At eight o'clock that morning Ralph rowed out Mr Gordon and

Mr Hacking, both dressed in their neat Sunday best, to the ship. Noise travels over still water. They could hear the coughs below deck as the women put on the new set of clothes that the Matron had issued, the demure uniform to include, of all things, a veil.

'Mr Gordon introduced himself to the Master. He had been at Harrow public school before he became a forger and spoke well, at least well enough to put the Master at his ease.

"'I regret that this mist has kept away the Ladies Committee. They have sent me as their representative. You may tell me with complete confidence anything you would have told them."

"'Then I will tell you, Mr Gordon, that never have women been more commodiously accommodated as on this passage. You may be assured that much attention was paid to guard them against evil. From the moment they boarded in Woolwich, I urged upon them the most decorous and orderly conduct and a strict obedience to the regulations which the Chaplain and Matron thought needful to adopt. And this morning I impressed on them, I dare say for the thousandth time, how the Governor will take a truly paternal care of them on their arrival in Hobart town."

"'As you say, they will now be in excellent hands," said Mr Gordon in his Harrow voice.

'The other officials were keen to follow the Master's lead and trumpet their own contributions. The Surgeon-superintendent was a long-nosed martinet called Guthrie. He said: "I was asked by Lord Goderich to land them as uncontaminated as they were sent on board. This I have done. No spirituous liquors were allowed, no visitors."

'The Matron, who had mustered the women every morning to check their personal health and cleanliness, said: "I think they all have high hopes of marriage to wealthy settlers. Most have already been assigned as general servants. One or two are very bad, but a considerable portion of them are respectable and deserving characters."

'Then it was the turn of the Chaplain: "I have told them the measure they have adopted in leaving their native land to go into a foreign country is a matter of vital consequence and under the Divine Blessing it may prove of the greatest benefit, but otherwise the very reverse. By their good conduct or the contrary they will form their own characters."

"'Well, let's get on with it," said Mr Gordon, enthusiastic to speed along the process of disembarkation. He urged the Master in the strongest and most persuasive terms to remain with his crew on board, and promised to make it his topmost priority to arrange with the port authorities to have the *Castle Morton* fully provisioned with fresh water, mutton and oysters as soon as the mist dissolved.

'Relieved to be shot of his charges, the Master ordered the women to be led up on deck and watched them step into Ralph's whale-boat in groups of ten at a time. They sat with their faces obscured in their veils, their hands resting on their bags, and Mr Gordon and Mr Hacking were most careful to say nothing as Ralph ferried the first party ashore, where a cart and three men waited to escort the women to Hobart, that is to say "Nettlepot", as Mr Gordon, who came from Cumbria, had baptized his three-roomed establishment.

'Once on shore, Mr Gordon and Mr Hacking were replaced in the whale-boat by two willing rowers who laboured under the strictest instructions to remain in a state of cemetery silence until they had landed safely every single female. Only on the last journey did it prove impossible for the rowers to contain themselves. Ralph told me how the jerry had barely swallowed the *Castle Morton* behind them when his two crewmen began touching up the women and trafficking to obtain their services at the lowest penny. If the women couldn't see them, they knew where their hands were!

'The jerry lasted until late morning before the sun broke it down and it disappeared, and Master Henniker looked around and saw through his telescope that he was anchored in the middle of nowhere.

'I won't go into the disgraceful scenes that were enacted under Mr Gordon's roof. Let us simply say that the women who came ashore that morning swiftly became acquainted with our habits. But they turned out well, some of them particularly so. They'd have been wasted on respectable landowners, your great-grandmother most of all.

'Her name was Harriet Fay. She was the daughter of a Baptist minister from Richmond, a respectable servant and useful, delicate woman whose mistress regretted parting with her and who had been engaged by a gentleman as a governess to his brother's children in Hobart.

'As I say, I don't know what happened over the next days and weeks at Nettlepot or at Miles Cottage, which was Mr Hacking's place, or here at Two Mile Creek where Ralph had taken Mary Malvern, a pert and artful young pencil-maker with a round face who'd been transported on suspicion of stealing fur and fourteen yards of bombazine. I do know that surprisingly many women chose to remain in the valley after the mistake was discovered, and these included Harriet Fay and Mary Malvern. Harriet's conduct especially was said to disappoint all expectation formed of her in London. When it was known that she was living with some men in the country in an improper way, a delegation was sent by boat, a sort of rescue mission to sail her back to Hobart, but she declined the advice of the Committee, saying: "I'd rather be hanged than leave here." And after living myself in this same cove for eighty-two years I reckon I know how she felt.

'So don't go knocking the jerry, lad. Without it, you'd be piss in the wind. And now help me up. And when you've done that you can look behind you. All the time I've been talking, it's been turning into a fine day.'

Bunker's Lane

Melvin Burgess

The whistle. The door bangs and Toms sticks his ugly head in each doorway and blows again.

'Up you get, you ugly little bastards! Up, up, up, you horrible little toads.'

Every morning, just like the army. It was the only training he'd ever had. When a boy at the end of one of the dorms burst into tears – he'd been awoken from a lovely dream into a world of pain – Toms glared at him in a mixture of incomprehension and disgust. You never cried in the army.

'You pathetic little shit! Get up and stop snivelling,' he roared. It made him want to hit the little wimp. Weakness didn't get you anywhere. When Toms had been in the army, weakness might very well have cost him and his mates their lives. Now, it just cost you a beating from Toms. There was no war left but here was Toms, still having one, all on his own.

Nick, Davey and Oliver met in the corridor along the dorms, which ran the length of the building and connected the two houses. Nick noticed at once how pale Oliver was. He hadn't slept a wink all night. He got close up to him in the press for the loos.

'How'd it go?' he asked.

Oliver nodded. He jerked his head and led Nick back into his dorm. He waited until everyone was out, then put his hand under the mattress and pulled out three packets of twenty Bensons.

Nick was so surprised he almost yelped. He grabbed them and wrapped them up in his towel.

'Bloody hell, Oliver! How'd you manage that?'

'I know where he keeps them.'

'Jesus. Bloody hell.' Nick shook his head and grinned. He'd never really believed Oliver could do it. But the smile faded on his face as he looked at Oliver. He'd never seen anyone look so scared.

'It's OK,' he said quietly, looking round to make sure they were alone. 'You've done it. You're a hero, Oliver.'

'We have to go now.'

'Why now?'

'He'll know it was me. Creal'll know.'

Nick licked his lips. He hadn't thought of that.

'And there's this.' Oliver thrust another package at him – an envelope.

'What's in it?'

Oliver gave him a look so appalled that Nick thought better than to ask again. He brushed his hand over the younger boy's hair, nodded and gave him the thumbs up. He stuffed the envelope down his pyjamas and went on to the loo. In a cubicle, behind the locked door – the only place in Meadow Hill where you could get on your own – he had a look to see what was inside.

He couldn't believe what he found inside. Oliver had stolen photos of Mr Creal with naked boys.

'No. No, no, no. Oh, no. Oh shit. Oh, Oliver. What have you done?'

It was simply terrifying. His throat went dry, his hands were trembling. He'd been locked away and raped for just threatening to tell. What would they do to him if they knew he had this stuff?

Suddenly he was furious. This wasn't part of the plan. This was the unspeakable. Now he had the whole filthy experience re-branded into his memory like a curse, because of these stinking images and it was all that little shit's fault.

They'd bloody kill him. Really – maybe they would actually kill him if they found this stuff on him. They'd go that far, wouldn't they, rather than spend the rest of their lives in jail.

Still trembling, Nick began ripping up the pictures and flinging the remains in between his legs into the pan. He tried to tear the lot up, but there were too many. He got through four or five before he came to his senses and sat there, panting.

Why had the little rat done this to him? But of course, he already knew the answer. It was revenge. It was standing up for yourself. Oliver was trying to reclaim his life.

For a second, Nick had a glimpse of the kind of courage Oliver had shown. To do this! To own these pictures was to own what had happened – to remember it, to keep it with you, to make it a part of you. It was something Nick was utterly unable to do for himself.

Oliver was braver than anyone he'd ever known.

Nick shook his head. Amazing! How hard had it been for Oliver, stealing these from under Creal's own nose? He'd slept with them under his pillow all night. No wonder he handed them over as soon as he could.

The little blond slip of a boy had shown them all the way.

Nick flipped through the pictures again. It wasn't just Mr Creal – there were other men here as well. He recognized one of the men who had raped him in the Secure Unit. Got ya! You bastard. See how they liked being locked up and raped – because sure as hell that's what would happen to them when they went to jail. Nick had heard stories of what happened to nonces in the nick. He just couldn't wait for it to happen to lovable old Uncle Tony Creal.

He stuffed the photos down his pyjamas, took a breath and left the loo. He wasn't even going to tell Davey about this. It wouldn't be fair on him. It wasn't fair on him either. Just to know the pictures existed was more of a weight than he wanted to carry. But he was going to anyway.

They were going down Bunker's Lane. They had to. If they failed now, God knows.

Davey was waiting for him outside the toilet, pretending to wash his face. As soon as Nick came out, he joined him and they walked together back to the dorm.

'We're on,' said Nick.

'He got 'em?'

'Three packs.'

Davey looked at him in disbelief. Nick patted his towel and nodded.

'Three packs? The little git.'

'It's this morning,' said Nick.

'Now?'

'Creal will know he took 'em.'

Davey pulled a face, and shook his head.

'What's up with you?'

'It's a set-up, innit?'

'No!'

They were back in the dorm by now. Nick managed to stash the cigs under his mattress while they started to make their beds, carrying on their conversation in snatches and whispers. 'Little Oliver nicks something off dear old Tony? I don't think so. Soon as we set off they'll be on us. It's just an excuse to get us.'

'They don't need an excuse.'

'It's a set-up,' insisted Davey. 'It's the wrong day an' all. Why so quick? Why can't we wait for Friday like we planned?'

'I told you, Creal will know he nicked 'em.'

Davey snorted in disgust. 'It's too bloody quick, mate. You'd be mad to run on the back of his say so.'

Nick paused. It wasn't the fact that Oliver had stolen the fags that had him convinced – it was the fact that he'd stolen the pictures. But now it was time to make up the beds and there was no way he could attract attention by sneaking Davey back to the loos to show him those.

'Trust me, mate,' he said, looking Davey hard in the eye.

Davey shook his head. 'It's not you I'm worried about, mate.'

Nick felt a surge of anger. This was the last thing he needed. 'You coming or not?'

'Am I bollocks.'

'Then we'll go without you, mate.'

Davey shot him a glare of sheer hatred and looked away.

'Tell you what,' hissed Nick. 'You can stay here on your arse wanking off old men if you feel like it. I'm out of here.'

Davey didn't reply.

'Shall I tell Andrews to leave you an' all? Or what?'

The whistle blew for inspection. Davey turned away.

'Tell him what you want, I don't care.' He went to line up by the snooker table for Toms, with Nick following angrily behind.

❧

The morning rush was always the same – get to the toilet, get your bed made, wait for inspection. Most of the boys didn't bother with a wash. Then downstairs, set out the tables, serve breakfast, clear up, then straight away off to school. The only chance he had to bribe the prefects was while the breakfast things were being put away.

Sixty ciggies. It wasn't bad. They stood as good a chance as anyone ever did.

He snuck up to the prefects one at time and pushed a packet into their hands. Andrews looked sharply at him.

Nick nodded. 'Twenty to leave me, Oliver and Davey,' he said.

'Three of you? And bloody Oliver? I'll want more than this, Toms'll never believe he can get away.'

Nick shook his head. 'That's all there is.'

'I could report you anyway,' hissed Andrews. 'I want more.'

'It's all there is. Report me and I'll tell how you got 'em,' said Nick. He shrugged. Andrews shrugged. He'd known what Nick was going to say before he asked. But it was always worth a try.

'OK?' said Nick.

'Right.' He looked Nick in the face for the first time and nodded. 'Including Oliver.'

Andrews paused, then nodded again. 'Him, too.'

Nick walked off to deal with Julian and then with the third prefect, Taylor, from Oliver's side of the house. A while later, he saw the three of them together in a huddle. He would have given the world to know what exactly they were saying.

❧

What made Bunker's Lane so desperate was the chase. They literally hunted you down, like wolves after the deer; and like all predators they were always fiercer, crueller and harder than you were. But there were tricks. One was to do it in herds, like the deer. At least some of you would get away. With any luck, when the other boys saw three of them set off, they'd set off too and give them more of a chance.

And if you were small and you couldn't run, like Oliver – then you had to use a bribe. Use a bribe and hope for the best…

It was almost half a mile to freedom – half a mile of mud-sliding, chest-heaving, lung-bursting running. If you could go fast enough to convince the prefects that they weren't going to catch you, they might just give it up. It was the one thing the runners had on their side – they cared. They cared desperately or they wouldn't be running. The prefects had just their pride to lose and perhaps a beating if they didn't put up a good show. It wasn't the same.

Davey took his place next to Nick and gave him a scowl. 'I told 'em to leave you, too,' hissed Nick, but Davey looked away. Nick was furious. It could never work, not without Davey. And who was going to get caught with those pictures tucked down the back of his pants? And what would happen to him then?

They lined up outside in the yard. Oliver looked as if he was about to die of fear. Nick tried to give him an encouraging smile, but it felt like a sneer on his face.

The crocodile began to move. Davey was watching him. Nick looked away. It was too late to stop now.

Calm down, thought Nick to himself. Keep your mind clear. He looked across at Oliver, who had gone literally green, it was a wonder no one noticed. Nick managed a wink. Oliver just stared, slack-jawed, like a fool.

They paused briefly as another line of kids from the other side of the building joined them, then carried on. Closer. Twenty yards. Ten.

Then they were there.

'Go, go, go!' yelled Nick. The whole crocodile jumped as three figures leapt out of the line like dogs at a racetrack, skidding on the wet grass, rushing towards the hedge that hid the mouth of Bunker's Lane.

'No way!' yelled Davey, as he hurtled like a rocket past Nick. No way was he getting left behind. Nick's spirits soared.

Yes! A shout went up – 'Oi!' The call to hunt. Out of the corners of his eyes he saw the prefects come to life, bodies flung forward, straining towards them. It meant nothing, they had to chase hard so long as they were in sight of the staff. Once they were behind the bushes they'd see if they were taking the bribes. Nick glanced quickly round. The bastards were going full pelt. And Oliver was already falling back! Please, God, let him make it to the bushes!

He hit the leaves and twigs in an act of faith, he couldn't see through. They lashed at his eyes and face and then he was out the other side into Bunker's Lane. The ground broken, the cobbles slippy and he had to slow down. A few yards away Davey hit the ground with his arse and bounced back up with a grimace of pain. But where was Oliver? Christ!

Then the bushes parted and there he was.

'Off the path, Oliver, get off the path,' gasped Nick over his shoulder. If he stayed on the Lane the prefects would have to pass him to chase the rest of them – it was asking too much. He waved his hand to show the way. Oliver gasped and skidded off behind the bushes. Behind him he could hear the prefects, Andrews and Julian, shouting and cursing – shouting too loudly perhaps, to convince the staff. Nick prayed they'd slow down or even stop once they were through the trees, but they were still coming on strong. He skidded – looking back over his shoulder like that was making him lose his balance. He hit the ground, splashing into a puddle, jumped up and ran off again, full pelt.

They were gaining! He'd lost vital seconds helping Oliver. He knew the prefects would have to get at least one of them. It couldn't be Oliver, it couldn't be Oliver! It couldn't be him, either, not with what he had in his back pocket.

And it couldn't be Davey because Davey was his mate. But Davey was miles ahead already. Nick could see his white face glancing back at him.

'Come on!' he yelled. Nick redoubled his efforts – but the footsteps he expected to hear behind him weren't coming. He risked another look back – they were falling back! The prefects were falling back, the bribe was working. He was as good as free.

It just occurred to Nick that he hadn't seen Andrews the last time he looked when he heard a shout –

'Oi!' It was Andrews. He was off the path – after Oliver, the bastard! Nick swerved, jumped over a fallen log and ran into the trees and stopped, gulping for breath, trying to listen. He could hear the sounds of running.

'I've got you…!' sang Andrews.

'Leave him, Andrews,' screamed Nick.

'Nick, you twat!' yelled Davey ahead, not breaking his stride.

Nothing was going to make him stop running, but Nick held back. The other prefects had turned off the trail to go for Oliver too, now. He could hear them somewhere behind him, cracking a joke.

Nick doubled back. He heard the chase – heard the thump and the wind knocked out of the smaller boy's throat. He rushed back and burst out of the trees almost on top of them. Andrews was heaving Oliver off the ground by his hair.

'Please! Please!' yelled Oliver, his face a mask of panic. Nick took a step forward towards them.

Andrews watched him closely. 'Oi, over here!' he yelled. There was an answering cry. Reinforcements. Nick paused, unsure of what to do – unsure of what he could do. But already he could hear Julian and Taylor coming through the trees.

'You're dead,' Andrews told him quietly; and he nodded his head, meaning, get out quick, run!

'Let him go,' demanded Nick. Andrews smiled slightly and shook his head. Nick glanced longingly at the way to freedom.

'Don't leave me, please, don't leave me,' begged Oliver, in a voice of pure panic.

Andrews slapped him hard. 'Shut up,' he commanded.

The other prefects thundered up and Nick's legs made up his mind for him.

'I got the package, Oliver – I'll be back. Tomorrow!' he swore. He had a flash of Oliver's white-green face; then he fled.

But now, of course, Julian and Taylor were between him and freedom. He'd thrown away his chance as far as they were concerned, and they were really after him now. He could hear two of them coming up fast. There was no way. There really was no way. They were bigger, faster and stronger than him. He was stuffed. Already they were right behind him.

Nick redoubled his speed – and then suddenly crouched down in the mud and leaves. Julian couldn't brake in time and tripped head-long over his back and went flying into a tangle of brambles, with a scream of pain.

The other prefect was right behind him, but Nick jumped up and seized a branch in his hand without even thinking about it. A good big stout stick a couple of metres long. As Taylor came running up, he swung it. He could see from the older boy's face that he really wasn't expecting Nick to actually do this. He froze and stood there a picture of surprise, watching the end of the stick whistle towards him. He turned his face away at the last minute so he never got it across the front of his face, but across the side. It made a sickening crack and down he went like a dummy.

Julian was back on his feet by this time. He was a big lad, but he paused when Nick waggled the stick at him. On the ground, Taylor was rolling from side to side, clutching his face and groaning. There was blood all over his hands and face.

'What have you done?' yelled Julian.

'I'll 'ave you too,' hissed Nick. Julian got down to look at Taylor, who was bleeding thickly from his scalp and ear.

'You're mad,' Julian told Nick.

Nick backed off and shook the stick at Julian. 'You want some, you fucker?' he asked. 'You want some? I'll break your neck.'

Julian just goggled at him. Nick was breaking all the rules. Men hit big boys and big boys hit smaller boys. But smaller boys never beat up big boys with a stick.

'You're mad,' said Julian again; but he stayed where he was. Behind him, Andrews appeared, holding on to Oliver. He stood watching impassively among the rhododendrons. Nick stuck the stick under his arm, and half walked, half ran towards Bunker's Lane. A second later, when he looked back and saw Julian helping Taylor to his feet, he knew he was free.

He broke into a trot. He reached a wall higher than his head and had to jump up to peer over it. There was a road, hedges and a row of semi-detached houses looking back at him. He clambered over the wall, looked around him – and there was Davey, jumping out from the cover of some overhanging bushes. He ran to him. They stood there together looking at each other and shaking their heads and grinning.

'I'm lovin' it! I'm lovin' it!'

'Yeah…'

'Ran like a tornado, mate.'

'Leaving like a bleedin' jet plane, wannit?'

'Oliver?' asked Davey, pulling a face.

'Bastards got him. But I got…' Nick patted his back pocket. It was only then that he found that the photos had fallen out of his pocket as he ran, every single one of them. They were scattered all through the woods up and down Bunker's Lane for anyone to see.

'The pictures…'

'What pictures?'

Nick shook his head. He didn't even want to think about it. It was too late. And Oliver was going to have to face the music alone.

Jacks

Jane DeLynn

The room is quiet and sunny, in the middle of the day her mother and father are taking a nap. She has to go to the bathroom but she's been told never to enter their room without knocking. She did this once when she had a nightmare but it took them a long time to answer and they seemed annoyed. Now she never knocks, but tries to go back to sleep until they wake up. She does this now, on the polished parquet floor of her bedroom. The sun warms her body, tiny particles of dust float in the air. They must always be there, glowing in the sunlight, how come she hardly ever notices them?

When she wakes up the sun is no longer on her body and she is cold. Her parents are still in the bedroom. She makes playing noises to wake them, then calls for them, though not very loudly. She doesn't use their real names, but names used only by her. 'Mommy' and 'Daddy'. But they don't hear her, they're still asleep. Or maybe they hear her and don't want to get up. She doesn't blame them. Children are not all that interesting to adults. Her relatives ask her questions but their eyes wander when she answers.

She can probably go to the bathroom by herself, they've been teaching her how to pull down her panties and climb up on the toilet seat and wipe herself off. But she usually tells them first, and they watch to make sure she's doing it right. This is number two, which is brown and messy. She doesn't think she's done this alone. What if she gets some on her hands when she's wiping herself? What if she makes a mistake and goes in her pants on the way to the bathroom? After holding it in as long as she can, she pulls down her panties and lays a shiny brown turd on the floor of her bedroom. A bit of steam rises from it, like when Millie the maid irons her blouse.

Her father comes home very happy. Surprise! They have a new car! The first car they've ever owned! They go downstairs to look at it. Most people still don't have cars so you can park wherever you want for as long as you want, you don't have to change sides so the streets can be cleaned. There's a car there, but it's not in the new style where the trunk part is flat like the front. Instead, the roof curves all the way down to the rear fender. And the car is a darkish green, not one of those cheerful new colours. Can their car have been stolen even though Jimmy, the doorman, is standing right in front of their building? But no, her father unlocks the door and shows her mother the front and back seat and the glove compartment. Her mother smiles, she's going to learn to drive. Even Jimmy says something nice about the car. Only she is upset. Her father lied, it's not a new car.

'No, but it's new for us,' says her father.

She doesn't like cereal, she doesn't like eggs, milk is even worse, especially when it's warm and smelly like in those little cartons they give you at school. She doesn't like liver or any vegetables except frozen pees. Deli meat is okay but you can't have that for dinner. She likes mushy foods like potatoes and apple sauce but not ice cream because it's cold. The only meat she likes is lamb, especially when it's chopped up in tiny pieces with ketchup on top. Mostly she cuts the food up in little pieces and pushes it around on her plate. Or she puts some on her fork and brings it to her mouth, then puts it down without touching it when her parents aren't looking. She takes huge gulps of milk and then runs into the kitchen to spit it out in the sink. She chews so slowly her parents give up and start clearing the table for dessert. Then she puts the rest of the food in her pyjama pocket, to throw out later in the garbage.

One day her mother catches her. She starts covering the food she throws away with napkins, but her mother is suspicious and pokes through the garbage after dinner.

She tries the kitchen window. It's not on the street but an airshaft, no one will ever know. But one day the superintendent comes to the back door. Twelve floors down beneath their window lies a pile of rotting food. The food is attracting rats, which are very dangerous.

They bite people and give them rabies. Does she really want to give the super rabies? her mother asks.

Next comes the toilet. All food ends up there eventually, it usually just spends time in the stomach first. Flushing is sometimes a problem. Bits of hamburger may float on top, too light to get sucked down. Beets are so heavy they drop to the bottom and stay there. Often she has to flush a bunch of times. Digested food goes down much easier.

The flushing makes her parents suspicious. So she stops using her bathroom, which is also the guest bathroom, and switches to the toilet in the tiny bathroom off the maid's room. No one but Millie, who comes twice a week to clean the house and take care of her, ever uses it, so she can leave the food there until her parents are watching TV or reading the newspaper, or even the next morning. But sometimes she forgets, and one day when Millie goes into the bathroom to change into her uniform, she discovers the unflushed food. Although Millie promises not to tell her mother, that night she receives a long lecture about the starving children in China.

On the wall of the bathroom is a secret passageway called a 'hamper' into which her parents throw dirty clothes and sheets and towels. It must be like the postal system in Paris her uncle told her about, where mail travels in vacuum tubes from one post office to another. Only laundry tubes must be much bigger, because laundry is bigger than mail. But clean laundry doesn't pop out of the hamper, it's delivered in neat bundles of light blue paper by the boy from the Chinese laundry. So maybe the New York Laundry System isn't a vacuum after all, but more like a playground slide, where if you get stuck in the middle a kid from above bangs into you and pushes you down. So clothing from the upper floors pushes clothing from the lower floors over to Broadway where the Chinese laundry is. In this jumble of dirty underwear and shirts and pillowcases how will anyone be able to tell where the food comes from? Even if they figure it out, the Chinese talk terrible English so they won't be able to tell her mother.

Then a terrible smell starts emanating from the hamper....

❧

Three French men with oily black moustaches and wearing berets are outside the door. They've forced Jimmy, the elevator man, to give them the keys to their apartment so they can kidnap her. She can hear them at the door, fumbling with the lock.

It's just a dream. In school that day the teacher read them a story, and the story was set in a country called France, about a bunch of fishermen. Nothing scary actually happened in the story, but something about the moustaches and striped shirts and pants with wide legs frightened her. She doesn't know anyone who looks like that, and instead of a home they live on a boat.

But maybe it's not a dream, just because there are French sailors in a story she heard at school doesn't mean there aren't French sailors outside her door. They're very quiet so as not to wake anyone. She strains to hear them, but the sound of her own heartbeat gets in the way. Meanwhile she keeps falling asleep, then she forces herself awake. She thinks of calling her father for help, but he'll just open the door to show her no one is there and the sailors will rush in and kill them. Or they'll hide in the fire stairs, to fool them into thinking everything is all right, and come back later when they're asleep. Even if her father rings the elevator for Jimmy and Jimmy says everything is all right, that won't mean everything is all right. They've threatened to kill Jimmy if he says anything, so of course he can't. The only thing to do is stay awake and hope her father helps her when they break in, instead of hiding in the bedroom with her mother. They might kill him, but he always tells her he loves her more than anything in the world.

She's watching *Howdy Doody* on TV. The TV is only a few months old. When it came it looked just like a piece of furniture with a grey piece of glass in the front of it and she wasn't very excited. But now she loves Howdy Doody and Clarabell and Buffalo Bob. Her parents wrote for tickets but so far they've never gotten any, even though every day on the show there are kids not just from New York but all over the country. The screen isn't very large so she lies on the floor close to it to make the picture look bigger, despite the danger from radiation. Her mother keeps her company, but sits further away on a big chair with cushions. Howdy Doody says something to Buffalo Bob that the kids in the peanut gallery find uproarious, but she doesn't understand it at all. She turns to ask her mother. But her mother has her head back and her mouth open, she's asleep. How can her mother fall asleep during *Howdy Doody*, the best show in the entire world?

Her mother explains to her that adults don't find *Howdy Doody* very interesting. Not only that, but in the not-so-distant future she'll outgrow it herself, long before she's an adult. She says that's impossible, she'll watch *Howdy Doody* forever. But it's true, next year the show is not so interesting. But she continues to watch it, partly because she doesn't like to admit her mother is right, and partly because not liking *Howdy Doody* makes her feel guilty. Not just about Howdy Doody and Clarabell and Buffalo Bob – but all the other people and things she might stop loving someday.

She makes a mistake and tells her parents she's nauseous. The last time she was nauseous, her father made her get over his knee and pounded her on her back until she vomited. This made her feel better, so now he wants to do this again. But it didn't make her feel better, because it's the vomiting she's scared of even more than being nauseous. What's so terrible about vomiting? For one thing, there's the smell, which itself is enough to make anybody vomit, partly there's the look of it, lumpy like oatmeal but with an even more disgusting pinkish brown colour, partly there's the taste it leaves in her mouth, which even toothpaste and gargle can't get rid of, and there's a burning feeling, like someone put out a cigarette down her throat. Even worse is what's going on in her body, as if her stomach isn't hers but belongs to some wild animal she has no control over. It's not she but this animal who decides if she's going to vomit, and even when she knows it's coming she doesn't know exactly when, so if she breathes at the wrong time she can choke and die. This is not just a story, a boy at school knows several people this happened to.

Her father says he won't try to make her vomit, he just wants her to lie down over his knee. She doesn't know why this should make her feel better, but he's made a promise so she has to trust him. But when she lies down he pounds her on the back until she vomits. He says isn't she glad she feels better? She's furious at him for breaking his word.

❧

Johanna, who lives in a big white house on the same block as her grandmother, is the only friend she has in New Rochelle. She would see Johanna playing outside her house with her little brother, and her father would tell her to go over and say hello. But she was too shy to do this, and Johanna's dog frightens her. One day her father drags her by the hand to meet her family and after this they sometimes play. She is not sure whether Johanna likes her or just plays with her because her mother tells her to. Once she rang the bell and her mother said Johanna was busy, but she sees her a little later in the upstairs window playing with some friends. After this she never rings Johanna's bell, but hangs around outside or drives up and down the street on her bike hoping to run into her.

Today they are doing an experiment. Johanna says that when you cut a worm in half it doesn't die but each half becomes a new worm. This doesn't make sense, because which half would be the real worm? How would the other worm get its brain? Do they ever remember they were once one worm and get confused? They dig for worms, and when they find them they squish them in half with sticks. Sometimes the worm just lies there, but sometimes the parts crawl off in different directions. All of a sudden Johanna says she doesn't really like her, she only plays with her when none of her regular friends are around. 'I don't like you either,' she says, and throws a handful of dirt at Johanna. Johanna throws some back. She throws another handful, but this time the dirt gets in Johanna's eye. She screams she's blind and runs off. She should find her and bring her home, but she's scared to face Johanna's parents. She spends the rest of the day sitting by the window, waiting for the police to come and arrest her.

❧

She's in her baby bed. It's not exactly a crib, but there are sides so she won't fall out. Every night her father comes to tuck her in, and every night after he tucks her in he opens the window, because the cold night air is good for her. And every night she asks him to shut the window, because she wakes up freezing in the morning. And every night, after he tells her how good the cold air is and she tells him how she hates being cold, she gets him to shut the window. And every night, after he shuts the window, she makes him promise not to open it after she's fallen asleep. And every night he makes this promise. But every morning she wakes up freezing, with the window wide open.

It's Christmas, they're driving in the car to pick up Millie. Millie isn't usually with them on Christmas, but this year her grandmother is having a big party. She loves Millie, even doing chores with her is fun, not like her mother. She likes to watch her tuck the sheets in, tight like in the hotel she once stayed at. She likes the way Millie pours wax so it spreads like a puddle you can see your reflection in. But ironing's the best, the sizzle as the iron turns the water into a white cloud of steam with that clean laundry smell. Millie talks to her about her sisters and her nieces and nephews, even the men she goes out with. No one else talks about life this way to her, no one talks to her about real things at all. She can tell things to Millie she can't tell her mother.

Millie lives in Harlem. Harlem is supposed to be bad, but it doesn't seem all that different from her own neighbourhood. Except in her neighbourhood white people live in the big apartment buildings and Puerto Ricans live in the brownstones, whereas in Harlem negroes live in all the buildings. Her father hates the Puerto Ricans because they sit outside on the stoop listening to the radio and drinking beer out of paper bags, instead of getting jobs they live on welfare. Even negroes are better. But she likes the Puerto Ricans, the music is cheerful and the people are friendly and she even likes not understanding the language.

Millie looks strange out of her uniform. She's all dressed up in high heels and a fancy dress and a hat with mesh halfway down the front and a bit of fur wrapped around her shoulders. Her family insists on meeting them, shaking everyone's hand in turn. They want everyone to come upstairs and have a drink or a piece of cake, but her parents insist they are already late. The car is full so she has to sit on Millie's lap. Millie keeps kissing her and telling her she loves her and although normally she would like this today Millie has a strange smell she doesn't like. She's also talking loudly in a way that's hard to understand and that she can tell annoys her mother. Millie turns the radio up very loud and when her father asks her to turn it down she turns it down only a little then she turns it up all the way again and they start fighting. Then Millie slumps forward with her head against the dashboard and gives a little snore. Her father says he's going to take her home and turns the car around. Millie says it's Christmas, what's wrong with a little fun? By the time they get to her grandmother's she'll be fine. She gets angry, then she sulks, then she apologizes, finally she cries, black stuff running down from her eyes. Her hair is a mess and her mother has to give her a handkerchief to blow her nose. Millie hasn't brought her keys so they have to stop and find a phone so she can make sure someone is home. This makes her mother even angrier, because Millie's always told her she has no phone. The people they met before are waiting downstairs, but they're no longer so friendly. Millie begs her mother not to fire her, she desperately needs the money. Her mother says she'll call Millie the next week but she knows she won't. She's mad at Millie for the strange smell and the way Millie is acting but she's even angrier at her parents for making a fuss about it.

Saturday afternoon her father asks her if she wants to go the movies. 'But we've already been to one,' she says.

She has a blue parrakeet named 'Happy'. Happy cannot have been very happy, because she rarely plays with him and never cleans his cage. Nonetheless, unlike most small birds, Happy lives for years. Then one summer she comes home from camp, and Happy is gone. They were cleaning the cage, her father said, and Happy escaped, they didn't write her at camp because they didn't want to upset her. She doesn't believe them. Either they took Happy to the ASPCA because they were tired of him or they left the cage open on purpose so he would escape. Her parents swear they're telling the truth. 'Perhaps it's just as well,' her mother says. 'He may have found another family he'll be happier with. It's not like you cared all that much about him.' This is true, but she cries bitterly even more because of this.

❧

Saturday afternoons in the fifth and sixth grade she meets her friends in front of the local movie theatre. There's always a double feature, plus newsreels and cartoons. They don't check ahead of time to see which movies are playing or when the 'A' feature starts, they walk in in the middle of one movie, watch the end of it and all of the second, then leave in the middle of the first when it gets back to the part where they came in.

One day, in the middle of *Some Like It Hot*, she realizes she laughs at the jokes a little bit after her friends do. Not much later, just a fraction of a second. But this bothers her. Either she has no sense of humour and only laughs because other people laugh first, or she has a sense of humour, but her brain is slower than everybody else's. She's always gotten the best marks in class, but maybe it's not because she's smartest, but only because she tries the hardest. Maybe she's secretly stupid, and has been fooling everyone all along.

Most important is that no one find this out. When she watches a movie she repeats the actors' words in her head, then sees the words printed out like in a book, then she reads the words. But all this takes time, so she decides to try to understand the dialogue as it's being said. The lag disappears, then it goes the other way, soon she's laughing before her friends do. This is good, even though this kind of watching takes more effort and is not as much fun. And there's a different kind of lag, as if her body knows to laugh a little before her mind does. And she still doesn't know whether she laughs because she thinks something is funny or because it's the kind of thing other people think funny. Usually she guesses right, but sometimes she finds herself laughing all alone in the big theatre. The memory of this torments her for days.

❧

She sits on the polished parquet wood floor of her bedroom, her legs spread out at approximately a forty-five-degree angle to her torso. She throws a small rubber ball in the air, lets it bounce, then picks up a six-pointed metal star in her hand and catches the ball. There are ten of these six-pointed stars, and she forces herself to pick them up one by one without dropping any until she has all ten in her hand, then she goes on to do the same in groups of two and three and so on. Sometimes, if she makes a mistake, she forces herself to go back to the beginning and start all over again. Sometimes she uses her left hand instead of her right. Sometimes she lets the ball bounce twice and sometimes she doesn't allow it to bounce at all, or she bounces it against the wall instead of throwing it in the air. After a while she stops playing with the jacks, but continues to bounce the ball against the wall. She likes the sound the ball makes, she tries to hit it the same way each time so the pattern stays the same

Her mother walks in the room. 'It's a beautiful day,' she says. 'Why aren't you downstairs playing with your friends?' Back then it was safe to play on the sidewalks, the doormen made sure they didn't cross the street or get in strange men's cars. She tells her mother she is having fun playing by herself. Her mother asks if she had a fight with her friends. She says no, she's just in the mood to be alone. Her mother looks at her in this way she has. She tells her that childhood is wasted on the young, and that someday when it's too late she'll realize this was the happiest time of her life.

When her mother leaves the room she starts playing jacks again, though her heart's no longer in it. She's always known there was something wrong with her, now her mother knows too. And she's not happy either, even though this is the happiest time of her life. Which means she'll never be happy. Unless her idea of happiness is wrong, and it's not as great a thing as she thinks it should be. This is possible, many things are not as great as she thinks they should be. So maybe she's happy and just doesn't know it, not that that does her all that much good. In any case, to prove to herself and her mother and father and anyone else who might be watching that childhood isn't wasted on her, she goes downstairs to play with her friends.

Opera In My Head

Meg Rosoff

There's an opera in my head. It's a perpetual opera that plays night and day. At the moment, the villain is singing a low E flat, rough and purring like an antichrist, and traffic rumbles along in the background in menacing polyphony waiting to dissolve in the scream of a car alarm. I conduct ever so slightly with the fingers of my left hand, horns enter... now! The timpani tut tut tut of a passer-by and the far-off wailing wowwow of an ambulance rushing away in the key of D major provide the harmony.

Is this normal? Would you call it normal to experience the world this way? How would I (or you) even know? Filter my experience through a hundred thousand other brains and what would they hear? I know from experience that what makes me laugh is just as likely to make you cry.

Not that it matters. Normal or not, the truth is that other people hear noise, I hear music.

My parents don't hear anything at all. My adoptive parents. I don't know who my biological father is, or my mother either, which is strange. How must it feel for a baby to rock for nine months, heavy with symbiosis, until one day it is pushed out into a shrill white world, and there, at the end of the road, be given away to strangers? I don't know how it felt to me. My eyes were barely open, my brain blank with fear, my heart too tiny and earnest to grasp this turn of events.

I have a picture of her in my head. Not a real picture, of course. In my head she is tall, like me. But her hair is dark, and her eyes too, so that even in my imagination there is a gulf between us, a chasm that leaves me unexplained and inexplicable.

I listen to the city's hum as I cross the road, insert my ticket (flick-flick) into the machine and step onto the escalator, down into the ground to get out of the rain. Like the ants, or perhaps Orpheus. The melodies flow in my veins.

I can hear a lovely exhaling deep vibration down here in the underground, like a tuba playing its lowest notes, and I wonder whether it's the sound made by the centre of the earth, a distant song floating up through the tunnels of the Northern line.

Over the years, I've been tempted to conduct a world-wide search of violinists or horn players or opera singers. Surely one of them would recognize me, I'm easy to pick out of a crowd. Somewhere, someone would claim my nearly white hair, my pale, pale skin, my pale blue eyes. People never fail to ask if I'm adopted, unless they have perfect manners.

As we thunder through the tunnels, in the background I can hear a high E shrieking, not a pretty note, but satisfying. Wikki-takkah wikki-takkah wikki-takkah wikki-takkah. The train pulls into the station, two notes – a major descending fourth – precede the closing of the doors. I'm conducting in 2:2 now, swingy and danceable. I wish I could get the world to play with me, follow my beat, instead of always having to fall into the powerful sway of its atonal syncopation. Sometimes it makes my head hurt to listen.

I should be a cellist. I've been told that quite spontaneously by people who know even less than I do about my past. I have the look, they say, by which I guess they mean strange, mermaidy, otherworldly. It seems a shame to waste looks like mine on someone who doesn't play the cello, or possibly the harp. But my father is tone deaf and my mother distracted, and I never demanded a violin, or a harp, or a horn. Of course we have a piano, like all nice families, and though it's out of tune I can play it perfectly well. All I have to do is place my fingers lightly on the keys and they know where to go. If I stop thinking and let my hands do what they will, I can play anything I've ever heard. This makes people uncomfortable because it is not natural. Except, of course, for me.

I used to think anyone could do it, that everyone was the same. When I was a child, people would wind up music boxes or toys to tinkle out graceless little tunes when the world was already humming with thirty or forty melodies. What other people called silence shouted at me and for years I wore a thick felt hat, even in summer, to filter the noise. My teachers told me to take it off, and I did. I've never looked for trouble until now.

I almost never leave the house. It worries my family, but I'm happy in my room, reading books and lying very still, listening to the sweetly muffled world. Sometimes I choose my own sound, but just as often I listen to the music in the walls.

Noise is leaking out of the headphones worn by the man on my left. I can identify the noise from the bass line. Listen hard and you'll hear it too – the rhythm so even and metallic it has to be robot noise. When a person plays you can feel his face in the sound, the furrow of a brow, the concentration in the jaw; the melody mutters and stutters like a heartbeat, it has its own life. That song is dead. If I had a switch that would shut him down, I would. Eight stops to go.

Everyone I know exists in a particular key. My sister Alice, for instance. No matter how she dresses or acts or works at school or at ballet or with me or her friends, everything about Alice settles in the key of F major. One flat. It suits her. Not too complicated, not too interesting, but not C major either. Not without redeeming characteristics. She wasn't adopted. It's one of those well-known phenomena: just when the desperate couple finally gets delivery of their adopted child (me), the woman falls pregnant. We're eight months apart in age, Irish twins, a few thousand years apart in everything else. We mostly ignore each other. She wants to be an actress or a pop star, like her best friend, and her second best friend, and her third best friend. I would like to know who I am before I decide what to be.

My father is A major: strong and bright with no dark undertones, nothing hidden or suspicious, no melody that doubles back when you aren't looking. When I was little, he used to take me (not Alice) to the café near the football stadium on Saturday mornings and order me a full English breakfast with bacon not sausage while he read the paper and drank coffee. English breakfast is still my favourite food, even when the eggs are too greasy or the bread is fried. It can get me through a whole day, so I don't feel hungry again until the next morning, when I want to have it all over again.

He doesn't understand how my brain works, though I've tried to explain, but this doesn't interfere with the love I feel for him. He loves cars. I have no idea what he feels when he looks at a new car, though I can hear the music of it, the soft, slightly rough flicker of an engine that hasn't been driven-in yet. He goes on about the smell of a new car but my other senses are not what they should be. Yet I can hear the long shining curve of untouched metal, hear it as a glissando, ascending, sparkling, slightly staccato, violins. If it's a black or a dark grey car he fancies, we slide into a minor key after a few bars. I don't know why, that's just how it happens. New cars play Schumann. Old cars play Charlie Mingus.

Over the years, my family and my teachers have worried about me. One doctor wrote: 'The patient assigns unusual significance or meaning to normal events and holds fixed (false) beliefs. She hears internal sounds and experiences other sensations not connected to an obvious source.' I know he wrote this because he sent a copy of the letter to my parents.

But what did he mean about not connected to an obvious source? How much more obvious can it be? The handicap is not mine, it belongs to him and everyone like him. They are the ones who are disconnected. Their voices rise in a chorus, a hundred strong, all singing from a similar but not identical piece of music. A hundred voices, all off-key. And because they're tone deaf, they call me a freak.

I clutch my precious piece of paper. There is no photograph clipped neatly to one corner, as I always imagined there would be. A name, an address, a date, a time. And that's all. Yet even from these bare words, sounds flow, the sound of a voice, sweet and dark and far away. The key is C-sharp major, seven sharps that speak, singsong: (F)orget the (C)ouple who (D)elivered the (G)irl from (A)wful (E)arly (B)etrayal.

Three more stops.

I love my family for choosing me when they didn't have to, for not throwing back the peculiar creature they discovered (too late) they'd fostered, for standing by me, stalwart, unquestioning, despite how many questions they must have. I love how much they try to understand, despite seventeen years without real progress.

Last stop. The doors swoosh open and my fellow passengers and I hear an announcement, recorded, Mind the Gap: E, A, C-sharp. E,

A, C-sharp. E, A, C-sharp. You'd have to be deaf not to hear it. The voice over the tannoy says something nobody can understand, but I'm humming the words as I step into the lift.

The cold air is a relief. I open my coat to it and walk through streets chaotic with symphony, a Charles Ives scene with bands of players marching at me from all directions. Schoolboys, housewives, men in suits, bicycle couriers, children, babies, old ladies. Mothers and fathers. The noise is exuberant, glorious, crashing with life. My fingers twitch and my feet feel for the beat, my breath trails swirls of cold January smoke, and then, once I've found the rhythm for myself (a complex, changeable beat), I try as usual to shape the world's dance, tell each part when to come in with the purposeful sweep of a baton that isn't there.

I check the address once more. This is the building and the number and the street. I wonder what makes a person act after years of inaction. I wonder at her decision to leave me. Didn't she pine, didn't she regret the emptiness where a child was supposed to be? Perhaps she filled up her sad sad soul and her lonely hours with music and danced away from me a little more each year, waltzing stately and calm, or whirling wildly like a dervish.

I buzz the door (A-flat), wait to hear the click, turn my feet into a metronome and count the stairs out in tidy measures, 1-2-3-4, 1-2-3-4. I am not afraid exactly, but I can feel each hair prickling erect on my skin.

And then I stop, because what I hear is so exactly what I want to hear: a storm, driving unruly; a roomful of singing voices. The voices are wild and desperate, beautiful as swan song.

All this I can hear drifting down the wide, elegant old staircase as I make my way slowly to the top.

When I get there, the door is ajar, and I lean against it, not certain that the time is right for me to go in. The storm has begun to abate and the guests throw themselves to the ground, relieved to be alive. Through the open door I can see a woman, though not her face. She is miles away, or so it seems at first, this woman. An enormous shining black wall hides her from me, all of her except her two feet, feet that could belong to anyone. The woman is making the great inanimate beast sing a song as familiar to me as the sound of my

own breath. The music alternately whispers and thunders, passion-
ate, powerful, frightened. She knows I have arrived but is not yet
ready to see me, so she greets me like this, in the language we both
understand though she doesn't yet know that I do. I circle round to
her profile and in the movement of her hands I can hear her voice.
It fills me with love and fury. For once there is no room for music
in my head, the music is all around me, all the instruments playing
together, sweeping me up in their embrace, murmuring, caressing,
shouting, full of explanations and excuses, loaded with lost history
and drowned words, more expressive than a touch or a glance or a
shared past.

She is pale like me, and we are together for only the second time
in both of our lives, her blood pounding thick and glorious in my
veins. She is playing Beethoven. As I advance across the room to her,
every fibre of my being sings sings sings.

The TW, part Q

Markus Zusak

I

He was thirteen and seemed to live on raisin toast and Tic-Tacs. When he walked to school, the two tastes merged in his mouth and his right pocket rattled with spearmint.

His appearance: blond and dishevelled.

His eyes: doubtful.

His name: Rory Winter.

And he wanted to be a writer.

The problem was that he never received any decent results for any story he ever wrote. He had the imagination of an airless football. That's what his old man, Teddy Winter, had said. Teddy Winter always used football metaphors. Teddy lived on meat pies and beer cans. But he was friendly enough. The criticism was actually delivered as a compliment, like it was the best thing for his son to follow in the feet of his older brothers. 'Working with your hands, mate.' That's what he'd said. 'You haven't worked unless you've got your hands dirty.' Teddy's palms and fingers, wrists and arms were the colour of a 2B pencil. He was coloured-in, by work, by coal, and a pretty dark hole.

But this is Rory's story, and his brother's, not Teddy's, so let's get back to the thirteen-year-old, and the strange events that were about to unfold.

II

At the age of thirteen years, ten months and six days, Rory Winter was writing his fifty-sixth story.

It wasn't very good.

Truth be told, it was bloody terrible.

It was about a boy who had some sort of cyst in his head and at any given moment, for any given reason, he could explode. He actually wanted it to be a full-length novel, and the boy (named Dieter Jerrico) would find love, adventure at sea, time-travel (for the cyst also gave him strange, fantasy-novel powers), and eventually, death.

But he exploded on page three.

That was the end of that.

III

Rory folded the pieces of paper into quarters and slid them under his bed, along with the other fifty-five stories, one rusting matchbox car, eight pieces of assorted Lego, and one stolen picture of a dazzling woman from one of his mum's trashy tabloid magazines. 'There,' he said, not exactly in triumph. He'd written novels before: a four-page thriller, a two-page romance, and his greatest disaster – a six-word horror story in which he couldn't make it past the first sentence. *The murderer arrived at six o'clock.*

What Rory didn't know was that he already had an audience.

He had his first reader – and that reader was the biggest bastard of them all.

IV

Enter Johnny Winter, Rory's sixteen-year-old brother.

Johnny Winter was a grunter. He grunted to say hello. He grunted to say goodbye. There was a grunt for 'You idiot', a grunt for 'Not bad'. There was even a grunt for 'That's pretty funny'. It was a bit like the over-quoted idea that Eskimos have numerous words for snow. Rory's brother had a thousand grunts, each signifying something a normal person would actually say. He just couldn't be bothered. 980 of the grunts were derogatory. Fifteen were conversational, and a precious few were compliments.

He had already left school, an apprentice plumber.

He never really said much, even when he was younger, but now, stranded somewhere between boy and man, he barely said anything at all. The situation needed to be desperate for him to truly open his mouth. Teddy and Adelle Winter were frustrated by his lack of communication. His two other brothers thought he was a complete bastard. Rory *knew* he was a complete bastard. The proof was in the constant drubbings, hidings and batterings he meted out in the Winter backyard, whether it was football, rugby, boxing, cricket, everything. And he cheated too.

Still, what Rory didn't know was that this teenage thug with next-to-zero speech was his greatest fan.

When Rory wasn't around, Johnny Winter would wave an arm under his brother's bed, searching out the stray papers, cursing when he found some Lego, smiling at the beauty queen his brother had also secreted amongst the words and dust.

His favourite story was the one called *The Leatherneck*. It was sheer crap, of course, and even if Johnny Winter was well aware of this fact, that didn't mean he couldn't admire the effort. He thought it was hilarious in its stupidity, especially the part when the protagonist, Henry Devoe, threw the grenade at the wall and it bounced straight back and landed in his trusty sidekick's open palm. As they tossed the grenade back and forth, Johnny Winter laughed and laughed at his brother's moronic ideas. His plumber's hands shook, his muddy eyes positively shone, and he laughed like Boo bloody Radley in the gold bedroom light.

V

The fact was that Johnny Winter hated plumbing. No, hate was too weak. He despised it. He regretted following his father's ideology of dirty hands and football. When it came to his younger brother, he had one noble idea.

Maybe, he thought, just maybe this kid can be a writer, like he dreams. He'd just have to improve. A lot.

VI

One thing to note about Johnny Winter is that he wasn't an idiot. Bastard, yes. Idiot, no. I mentioned earlier that he pummelled Rory mercilessly in the backyard, but his torture techniques extended beyond mere battery. He was capable of psychological pressure as well. For example, one afternoon, when they were conducting the after-school ritual of eating toast and watching *Get Smart*, Rory made a monumental error. He left his two toasts in the lounge room and went back to the kitchen to find something to drink.

Now, anyone with an older brother knows this was a mistake; you don't leave food unsupervised.

And what did Johnny Winter do?

Did he hide the toast?

Did he shove them both in his mouth, waiting for the moment to grunt something that translated to 'Don't ask me where your toasts have gone'?

No.

He took each piece of the square bread, folded it in half, took a massive bite out of the middle, then unfolded it again and put it back on the plate.

Of course, Rory could still eat them, in spite of the enormous holes that had magically appeared dead centre in each toast. But he felt ridiculous. He knew he'd been beaten. Most importantly, however, he knew what the toasts signified – that Johnny Winter was in charge, and also that he had imagination.

Which leads us now to the necessary point.

The fact that he was in charge meant that he was calm enough to be capable of anything. The fact that he had imagination meant that he could love Rory's stories and simultaneously understand how bad they were – and how to fix them.

So he came up with a plan.

VII

The plan involved a birthday, a beach, a dark bedroom, and a typewriter the colour of a peach.

On June 27, Rory Winter turned fourteen.

There was a small assortment of presents next to his bed in the morning:

A block of Cadbury's Fruit and Nut with a twenty-dollar note inside.

A lump of surfboard wax – like a creamy white hockey puck.

An advertising poster for the film, *Rocky III*.

And a typewriter.

All of the other presents were self-explanatory. Each had a card attached – the chocolate and money from his parents, the poster and wax from his two other brothers.

To Rory,
Happy Birthday.
Nathan.

And so on.

The typewriter, though, was the odd one.

There was no card, but the fact that all other family members had been accounted for, well, that only left Johnny.

With his feet on the cold floor, Rory rubbed at his morning-hair and swallowed the awful night-breath in his mouth. He looked at the typewriter and over at his brother's bed. He touched the black lid with his toe before putting his hands under it and bringing it to his lap.

Only when he opened the case did two important things happen.

1. He realized that this typewriter didn't have any keys.
2. Johnny Winter, who was facing the other way, apparently sleeping with force against the right wall of the bedroom, said, 'Happy Birthday, Dipshit'.

Trying to ignore the fact that his brother knew about his stories, and therefore probably the beauty queen under his bed, Rory looked closer now at the typewriter.

It was from the 70s.

It wasn't one that you plug in.

And as I mentioned earlier, it was ripe-peach red, and there were small stubs where the letters should have been. They stuck up like sanded twigs of metal. Amputees.

With great perplexity, Rory touched a few of those stubs, and that's when the laughter emerged from somewhere inside Johnny Winter's sheets.

VII

What good is a typewriter without any keys?

That was the question in everyone's mouth in the Winter household that afternoon.

'He's a bloody lunatic!' their father said. He even pointed a 2B finger in Johnny's direction. 'That's like giving someone a…' He struggled. '…a car without a steering wheel!' He reached for something familiar. 'Or a football boot without laces!' That was better. A football simile.

'Well,' said Johnny, the bastard coming out of him. A grunt turned into a sentence. 'It's still better than a block of chocolate and twenty bucks, isn't it?'

Spoons fell.

An ear was pulled.

An 'As long as you live under this roof' speech was made.

The big miss was that no one looked at Rory Winter downing his raisin toast at the table.

The keyless typewriter was in his lap, and he was smiling.

He'd just have to go out and find the missing pieces. Easy.

VIII

Or at least, that was what he thought.

After school he walked through town, Tic-Tac in mouth, from the newsagent to the second-hand shop, from the second-hand shop to the printers, from the printers to the Two-Dollar shop (he was getting desperate), and from the Two-Dollar shop home. There were no typewriter keys anywhere.

When he made it to the kitchen, he found the *Yellow Pages* and made some calls. No luck in the neighbouring towns either. All that was left was raisin toast and *Get Smart*, and watching Johnny eat and grunt some laughter when Maxwell Smart screwed up one of his gadgets and squirted the Chief with water.

IX

A week passed, and Johnny finally felt the need to do something regarding the typewriter again. It was past midnight, and the two brothers were both in bed.

'You awake?' Johnny didn't move his head. He spoke up at the ceiling.

'Yep.'

Darkness.

'Your stories are fucking pathetic.'

Rory was shocked, but he knew this was it. A quick swallow and an answer. 'I know.'

'But I know what to do.'

'What the hell are you talking about?'

He still didn't move, but Johnny Winter's voice suddenly changed. He stared straight up at the ceiling but he cracked a little now. 'Bloody hell, Rory, you don't know a God damned thing, do you?'

'No, I don't.'

Now the moon came out from the clouds. Their window was yellow.

'Just… Jesus,' said Johnny. He was up on an elbow now. 'Tell me something, Rory. Tell me about the best thing that ever happened to you. Or the worst thing. Or the most frightening thing. Or even the most boring. And don't forget any details or I'll kill you.'

'What?'

This time he didn't answer. Johnny leapt from bed and had his hands around Rory's throat. It actually took a few seconds for Rory to feel the weight of his brother's strength. He's strangling me! he realized. He's killing me!

But he wasn't, not really.

He was only shaking him.

X

Slowly, Johnny let go and stepped easily back towards his own bed and dropped in, quiet as air, before covering himself. He even faced the other way. 'Now,' he said, 'let's try that again.'

Panting, Rory answered. 'You're crazy.'

'Talk. Your best day ever. Or your worst. Or –'

'Okay!'

Rory Winter spoke at the yellow window with tears on his dark cheeks. This is what he said:

XI

'It was three years ago and we were at Cronulla Beach with our shitty, third or fourth-hand surfboards. Football season wasn't on so we could go to the beach without Dad being on our backs about training and all that. My board was a twin fin, remember? No one rides twin fins… But anyway, both our boards were waxed good and hard. They had wax like buttons… like buttons of hard skin. Once a person stood up on one of those boards, there was no slipping. The problem was getting up in the first place… until the day I'm talking about.

That day I'd been in the water for an hour. It was an after-school surf – traditionally shorter than a regular one – and you were already out of the water, you big sook, standing with a towel across your shivering shoulders, and your board shorts sucked to your legs.

Anyway, one moment I was sitting on my board and the next, over a small lump of swell, I saw a perfect wave standing up in front of me. Somehow, I turned. I paddled. Without thinking I was picked up and I was catching my first fully-fledged wave ever. I was riding across it, shocked, amazed, half crazy, half making sure I didn't bugger it up and find a way to fall off.

The wave was noisy.

That's what I remember.

The board at my feet, it was bloody flying. I could have sunk my hand into the wave still rising beside me.

You know what the strangest thing was, though?

It was something in the corner of my eye. I could barely see it, barely hear it, but it was there… It was you.

The towel had been dropped at your heels and you were cheering at me from the shore. Your arms were held up, shaking the air like you just shook my throat, you bastard. And your mouth – it was wide open, grinning. I could see your teeth…

And then, twenty minutes later, once I'd got out and we walked up the beach, we got in the car.

You were in front. I was in the back.

That was the unwritten rule.

You'd even told me as we were about to get in.

It was Grunt Number 486: *I'm in the front, you're in the back, Dipshit.*

As we were driving home, Mum said, 'That was some wave, Rory,' and I remember smiling then with the salt drying on my face, and I heard you grunt in the front, but I could tell you were smiling too.

The end.'

XII

When Rory stopped speaking, there was no reaction from the other side of the room. Not a word, not a grunt. Barely even any breath. Rory simply looked at the yellow window now, and a few minutes later, when the clouds came back and there was complete darkness again, he rubbed the tears from his face and wiped them on his pillow. He felt at his throat.

When he slept, he dreamed of water and waves and a beach ball moon. He could feel sand beneath his feet. Even when he sensed someone standing over him and woke with a shock, there was no one there.

XIII

In the morning, he stumbled out of bed towards the bathroom, feeling a circular, engraved sort of pain on his cheek. Had he slept in a funny position? Did he have cancer? (Always straight to the dramatic first thing in the morning.)

He went to the toilet, feeling at the strange mark on his cheek.

He walked to the sink.

He looked in the mirror.

And had to look again.

'No,' he said, but it was true.

Rory Winter walked slowly back to the bedroom and searched his bed, and it didn't take long before he found it next to the pillow. As his brother slept with vehemence against the wall, Rory held it in his hands – the same letter that was burned into his cheek… It was the same key he'd slept on between near-strangulation and the alarm clock.

Q.

After a few minutes of sitting on his bed, he pulled the typewriter from underneath and placed the Q key into the correct position – position number one on the keyboard. Only twenty-five to go, God love him.

We could argue till the cows come home, but I actually think

Rory Winter was kind of lucky. Not many writers learn their lessons through near-strangulation, and it would be an odd story to tell if he was ever published and asked about the exact turning point for his writing.

'The turning point?' he could say. 'That's easy...' He could shrug a little, too, if he wanted, before talking about the moon on the window.

Brothers strangle out of love.

May Malone

David Almond

The story was that May Malone had a monster in her house. She kept it in chains. If you went round to the back of the house and put your ear to the wall you'd hear it groaning. You'd hear it howling at night if you listened hard. There were stories about May and a priest from Blyth. There was a baby, it was said, but the baby was horrible because it was born from such a sin. Even weirder tales were whispered. The devil himself had come to May and it was the son of Satan living in her house. She's been with horses, with dogs, with goats. Anyway, whatever it was you'd risk your body, your sanity and probably your soul if you got too close.

Norman Trench was ten or eleven at the time. He lived in the new flats in Felling Square. May's house was at the bottom end of Crimea Terrace, not far from the muddy green where the lads played football.

Norman's mam tightened her lips when he asked her about it.

'Them daft tales! Take no notice. What's done is done. Just keep away and leave her be.'

To look at May Malone, you'd never think she had a monster. She was getting on, but she wore tight skirts, she dyed her hair, and she wore high heels that clicked and clacked on the pavements as she hurried along. She was lapsed. Everyone knew the tale of how she'd stood up and cursed the priest in church itself, then stormed out, and never went again. You could see people's faces closing down as she hurried by. She rarely spoke to anybody and you could see that nobody wanted to speak to her. Except for some of the blokes, who sighed, and followed her passing from the sides of their eyes.

Norman was a miserable kind of kid. Yes, he had some reasons – a brother that'd died, a dad that'd gone wrong with the drink. But everybody's got something to put up with. He just took everything too seriously. People used to go, 'Cheer up, lad. It might never bliddy happen.' And once or twice he yelled back. 'It's happened already, so bugger off!' He thought about death and dying all the time. He thought about the devil and Hell. He told the priest in confession about it once and the priest said, 'Ah, we all have great crosses to bear, my son.' He peered through the grille, trying to get a good look at Norman. 'Desolation of the heart can be a sign of God's call,' he said. 'Do you ever feel you might have a vocation, lad?'

His mam had been through everything he'd been through, of course, and worse. But she had a cheerful heart. 'Let's have a smile,' she'd say, and he'd curl his lips up and try to please her, but that just made things worse. 'Oh, son,' she'd say. 'Don't grow up so sad. God's good, the world is beautiful and heaven waits for us.' Made no difference. Norman believed in none of that. He was shutting down. He couldn't stop himself, even when the lads started moaning.

'Why can't you just enjoy yourself, man? You're like a wet bliddy Monday morning.'

And they started to turn their backs on him, like he was May Malone, or running away from him and howling, like he was her monster.

It was October when Norman went to May's for the first time. It was turning cold. The nights were cutting in. He waited till dark then he went down to the end of the terrace and into the back lane. He scrambled over the wall into her back yard. He went to the house wall and pressed his ear to it. Nothing. Maybe a radio somewhere far away. The distant voices of the lads echoing on the green. He concentrated. All he heard was his heart, then the noises of imaginary monsters inside himself. He tiptoed to the kitchen window and cupped his hands, peered in and nearly yelled with fright. But it was just his own staring eyes that goggled out at him. Nothing else.

Next time he went, though, he was sure there was a bit of grunting, a bit of squeaking. May came into the kitchen and made a pot of tea and put some biscuits on a plate. She looked out. Norman pressed right against the back yard wall. Then she leaned up and pulled the curtains shut. Norman climbed back out again and stood in the dark at the end of the terrace. He lit the cigarette he'd bought at Wiffen's shop that he'd said was for his mam. A river bell rang. A door clicked open and shut on Crimea Terrace and footsteps hurried up towards town. He drew deeply on the cigarette. He coughed. He stood looking down through the night towards the river. All this is getting me closer to hell, he thought.

'Where you been?' his mam said when he got back in.

'Football,' he said. 'With the lads.'

'Good. That might cheer you up, eh?'

He kept going back. Maybe he had it in his head that he'd be able to go to the lads and say, 'It's true. There is a monster. Come and see,' and that that'd sort everything out. But there was nothing, and soon the lads were taking no notice of him at all. It was like they didn't even see him, like he wasn't there. Probably they'd even forgotten all about the monster.

Then he stepped out of Wiffen's one afternoon and May Malone was right in front of him. She had a green coat on. Her eyes were green. Her fingernails were bright red.

'So,' she said. 'Would you like to see my monster?'

Norman gulped and blinked.

'Well?'

She didn't smile. She wasn't cross. Her voice was crisp and clear.

'Yes, please,' he said.

'You won't want to be seen walking with me. Follow me down in five minutes or so. Come to the front door.'

And she clacked away.

He smoked his fag as he walked down Crimea Terrace. He was trying to seem nonchalant.

The door was ajar.

'Don't just stand there,' she said from inside.

He sidled through. She was waiting in a narrow corridor. She put her hand across her mouth and widened her eyes.

'Oh no!' she said. 'You're inside May Malone's house! Lightning will strike at any moment!'

Everything was neat and clean, just like her. There was a door open to a living room. He saw a couple of armchairs, a couple of ashtrays. There was a decanter with what looked like whisky in it, and a couple of glasses. There was a painting of a Chinese lady on the hall wall. A red light was shining from upstairs.

She smiled. 'Come and see.'

She took him towards the back of the house

'You won't tell anybody, of course,' she said. 'I decide who knows.'

She opened a door.

'This is my boy, Alexander.'

It was a small room. Light was coming in from a skylight in the ceiling. There was a narrow bed against the wall. A boy was sitting on a little blue sofa. His head was slumped onto his shoulder.

May knelt beside him and put her arm around him.

'Alexander,' she whispered. 'Here's a new visitor for you.'

She turned his head to Norman. One of his eyes wasn't there at all. The other was just a little crease in his face. The eye gleamed, like it was far away.

'His name is…' she whispered.

'Norman,' said Norman.

'Norman. Come closer, Norman.'

She looked at him.

'You're not going to hesitate *now*, are you?'

He knelt down beside them. She turned Alexander's head so that his eye was towards his visitor. She lifted his hand and rested it on Norman's face. Alexander grunted. He squeaked.

'Yes,' murmured May Malone. 'Yes, I know.'

She smiled.

'Alexander says you are very beautiful,' she said.

Norman couldn't help staring into the tiny distant eye.

'He says you are like an angel. And isn't *he* beautiful, too?' said May. '*Isn't* he?'

'Yes,' said Norman at last.

'Say hello. Go on. He can hear you, even though it might seem he can't.'

'Hello,' whispered Norman. 'Hello, Alexander.'

Alexander squeaked.

'See?' said May. 'He answers you. He is a boy, just like you. He is getting older, just like you are. He needs a friend. He needs to play.'

She sat on the edge of the bed. She smoothed her skirt over her knees and smiled at the two boys.

Alexander suddenly turned his face upwards. There was a pigeon on the skylight. His mouth pursed and he cooed.

'Yes!' said May. 'A bird! And look at the clouds, Alexander.' He raised his hands and opened them over his head. 'See? He knows that the world is beautiful, Norman.'

Alexander trembled. Norman could feel the excitement rushing through the boy as the bird fluttered its wings above.

'Now,' said May. 'I would like you to take him out, Norman.'

Norman looked at the door and got ready to run. She smiled.

'Just into the yard at first,' she said. 'What could be difficult about that?'

Norman couldn't answer. Alexander's hand moved onto his and held it gently.

'Who's his father?' Norman dared to say.

'Ha! You *are* a nosey bugger, aren't you? Are you a churchgoer?'

'Yes.'

'I thought so. Those black-gowned priests. They blasted me. Don't let them blast you, Norman, with their Thou shalt nots.' She touched her boy's head. 'They said this angel is a devil. Never mind his father. Will you take him out?'

They helped Alexander from the sofa. May Malone opened the

door. Norman held Alexander's arm and guided him out into the place where he'd only ever hidden in the dark. It was late afternoon. The sun was descending in the west. There were great streaks of red and gold across the sky. A storm of starlings swept over them from north to south. The city rumbled, the river bell rang, the lad's voices echoed from the green. Norman imagined walking towards them with May Malone's monster at his side. He imagined May Malone watching them all from a bench nearby. Alexander reached upward, upward and he moaned with joy. He held Norman and cooed into his ear. May Malone watched from the doorway.

'See? It's easy enough, isn't it?' she said.

They soon went back inside. They took Alexander to his room. He lay on the bed.

'Tired out,' said May.

She sat by him for a time.

'He is as he is because he is as he is. No other reason. And he is quite as capable of joy as any of us. More so, in fact.'

She leaned towards Norman.

'You, for instance,' she said, 'must stop being so sad. You know that, don't you?'

'Yes, Miss Malone. '

'Just open your eyes. The world is a strange and gorgeous and astonishing place.'

She looked at her watch.

'Now,' she said. 'You will come back again, won't you?'

'Yes, Miss Malone.'

'And you won't tell anybody, will you? Not until we're ready.'

'No, Miss Malone.'

'Good.'

She kissed his cheek. He said goodbye to Alexander. She led him to the door.

Norman walked up Crimea Terrace below the astonishing sky. He kept touching his cheek where May Malone's lipstick was, where the memory of her lips was. He kept remembering Alexander's tremble of excitement. A man was hurrying down, with the rim of his trilby tilted over his eyes.

'Hello,' said Norman.

The man flinched, looked at Norman in astonishment, then gave a broad grin.

'Aye, aye, lad,' he said, and he winked.

Norman kept going. All the sadness was lifting away from him as he went uphill, like he was opening up, like everything was starting to be cleaned, like he was starting to see the world for the first time.

Father and Son

Alberto Manguel

> Augustine, bishop and doctor. b. in Numidia, 354; d. at Hippo, 430. Augustine was the son of a pagan father, but his mother, St. Monica (cf.) was a Christian, and as such he was brought up, though baptism was yet to come. At sixteen he was sent to Carthage to finish his education, and here he was soon living with a young woman, to whom he was devoted for fourteen years; they had a son, Adeodatus, whom his father always cherished. After being attracted to the teachings of Manichaeism, he obeyed his mother's dying wishes, abandoned his wife and son, and went to find a job as a teacher in Rome. Adeodatus died shortly afterwards.
>
> Donald Attwater, *A Dictionary of Saints*

Once again, the boy dreamt of his father. The room he slept in, two floors below ground, remained cool into the morning, but as often happened when he had these dreams, he woke up bathed in sweat, calling out his father's name. The servant (the nurse never seemed to hear anything during the night) came running, as he always did, bringing water and a towel, certain that the boy was suffering from his usual fevers, like those that afflicted the people of the marshes. He had mentioned this diagnosis to the boy's mother, and yesterday she had called in the doctor who, after running his hands all over the boy's stomach and legs, prescribed a herbal concoction which the patient poured out when no one was looking. 'Is he dying, doctor? Is he dying?' was all the woman could think of asking.

Dying, the boy reflected, was women's business in this house. From his friends he heard of the death of males: soldier uncles commemorated by a rusty sword, hunter brothers crushed under a cornered boar, athlete cousins immortalized in songs paid for by grieving parents. But here, in this house, the men didn't die, they were merely absent and, the boy thought, dying requires a presence. The women were always preparing themselves for agony: shuffling, sighing when they spoke, hugging their bodies in the morning air and mumbling prayers on their beds at night. They coughed, shivered, bustled around as if trying to escape something the boy failed to see. His mother, his aunt, the nurse, the maids suffered wordlessly in every corner of the house. And his fearful grandmother, of course. His grandmother, as she was dying, had refused to complain or ask for anything, wouldn't say whether she was afraid or cold when the room filled with shadows and the shutters would not keep out the night wind, and the fire shrivelled down to a few last embers that glared at her from the hearth. She held a small bronze cross in her hands, like the ones they now sold in Carthage, in spite of her son's disapproval, and she lay there waiting (a trapped rabbit, the boy thought), a tremor rippling the sheet from time to time as if something were crawling under the linen across her ancient body.

The father's absence had made the few images that the boy possessed of him clear and bright, etched in fire, conjured up unexpectedly, in the midst of all kinds of different memories. For instance, whenever he thought of his grandmother, he would see his father standing by her bed, holding her hand and not moving, every line of his features clear and his eyes (remarkable eyes, everyone said) so distinct that he could make out the peacock shades of the irises. For someone so constantly absent, the impression left by the moments of his presence were remarkable. The boy could almost count them, the times he remembered him in the house, the times he had watched his father as he strolled in the garden, or as he sat abstracted at his table, glimpsed through the door of the study.

There was one occasion he often thought about. The boy was sitting with his father at the table. Lunch was as usual: fish, cheese, bread, fruit and wine mixed with water. But now that his father's shadow lay across the food, everything on the garden table seemed different, a ceremonial setting made out of the daily elements transformed by the gaunt, elegant presence who moved his grey hands over the dishes, feeding himself and never saying a word. The boy had watched the hands help themselves to a piece of fish, a hunk of cheese, lay them side by side on the plate, then break off a piece of bread, dip it in the oil, blot it in the salt and carry it to the mouth. The thin lips had closed, the black-rimmed jaw had moved, the eyes had remained fixed on a certain point in space that seemed to concentrate all thought, shutting off the world.

Next to the table, dozens of bloated figs had fallen among the grass and lay there, rotting. Red-eyed flies, large and elongated, buzzed around the dead fruit and, from time to time, rose up and circled the table. The boy had watched his father's eyes move heavily, following the flight of one of the flies as it darted from the fish to the cheese and back again, as it took off once more, hurried like a tightrope walker round the rim of the bread basket, lifted itself into the air for one last moment and descended slowly onto the tabletop. The boy had watched his father's right hand rise slowly as in a benediction, hover over the fly that seemed to wait, quivering, for what was hopelessly to come, and then fall with a crash. The fly was on its back, its thistled legs moving frantically. Up rose the hand and down it came again. Now the fly lay dead, the iridescent eyes still gleaming. The hand had brushed it off the table and had wiped the palm on a napkin. The eyes had moved back to stare at the same distant point. The ceremony was over.

Had his father ever been young, he wondered? A middle-aged man, he looked, up to the day the boy last saw him, as if behind the taut skin the eyes belonged to a much older face, something nearer to the skeleton that lay beneath. The boy had seen the starving children that sometimes came into town with the caravans from the south, and there was something in their emptiness that seemed dug out by a long, painful passing of time; it was this emptiness that he had seen in his father. But he must have been young then.

'The first time I saw your father,' Romanian, the old scholar, had said, 'he was about your age. Same bony frame as you, all eyes and hands.' Romanian had told him, many times, of his joy at finding a youngster whose intelligence had not been dulled by superstition, whose questions opened doors instead of shutting them, and whose spirit of contradiction was always welcome because it aimed forward, never back, never into the smug all-knowing silence of the common adolescent. *Egregium forma iuvenem*, Romanian remembered him, *et fulgentibus armis*, a youth of wonderful beauty and resplendent weapons. But his face sad and his eyes downcast, Augustine had completed the verse. *Sed frons laeta parum et deiecto lumina voltu.* Augustine had later said that he'd felt this ghostly image as a lesson held up to him, or a warning.

Augustine had arrived in Romanian's house with other students, led by their tutor for a day's outing. Romanian accepted such visits as his manorial duty, to show the puppies a few obvious treasures, give them a glass of milk and honey cakes, send them off with the sly feeling that they had escaped class.

The tutor had marched his brood through the garden and, more out of habit than interest, had pointed out the clean partitions of the early January blossoms, white cyclamen to the left, pink and lilac cyclamen to the right, light and dark. He had told them to observe that the tall wild Phoenician rose trees were planted in intertwined groups of three and that the pool of water lilies had seven sides. He had explained the story of the death of a deer-headed Achteon, illustrated in a large mosaic that covered the courtyard floor. He had reminded them that the orchard behind the garden was forbidden to them and that they were to take off their sandals before entering the house. Romanian had greeted them at the doorway.

Romanian had led them through the house stopping at the customary remarkable pieces and the boys stared at the painted statues, admired the scenes of combat and pillage, smirked at the mature Danaës and Ledos, grinned at the pubescent Iphigenias and Prosperines. When he told them the story of Mani laid out in an intricate pattern of mosaic, they gaped at the manacled and shackled figure of the old bearded man, rising into a single golden cloud representing heaven. 'A burning torch was used to ascertain his death,' the scholar told the boys. 'Then the body was cut into pieces, like that of Dionysius, and the severed head was nailed above the gates of Bet-Lapat.' One of them had asked what had happened to Mani after his ascension. 'He sits with the Father and Son,' Romanian had answered, 'and is one with them in the spirit.' Years later, Romanian told the story to the boy who was now dying, but by then it was a secret.

Augustine continued to visit the old scholar in his house. One afternoon, Romanian had pulled out a big black parchment notebook that contained information about every one of Mani's writings: how much he had paid for it, where he had got it, when it could be published, whether it could be seen. 'It's all yours,' he had said to Augustine. 'All these books I have here, they're yours. I'm past the age of enthusiasm, and tired, and I want to spend the last years of my life doing other things.' And he had given them to Augustine.

Augustine had taken the books and had studied them carefully. Later, before deciding to abandon both his woman and his son, an act which he never believed was a betrayal, Augustine had burned them all. The woman had looked at him in fear, since Romanian was dead by then, and she believed in the sanctity of gifts. 'He and I will talk about it when we meet again,' Augustine had replied to her unspoken question.

Many times, the boy had heard speak of the kingdom of the dead. The servants, of course, and his mother, his grandmother, his tutor, each described a different landscape inhabited by those who had left the casing of their body and gone to a place outside mortal time. They were all dreadful, and he imagined them as separate regions of one vast realm inhabited by all manner of foreigners, wave after wave washed on those shores from which no one returned. Of all the people he knew, only his grandmother, strict and unsmiling, had seemed to long for that place where she would see The Risen One, and in that hope she had closed her eyes and waited, wordless, all the long night into morning. His father had shaken him violently when he had started to cry, telling him that he offended her ghost who so lovingly had sought release. So he had stood there, blinking in the darkened room, while his father led friends and servants in a song of praise, and the priest waved his hands over the body, sprinkling water from a bowl.

The boy preferred, in his own mind, other regions of the distant kingdom. He wanted the place to be a response to his fears, a mirror image of the world he knew, and not a better, exalted place in comparison to which he was meant to despise all the things he loved here, upon this shore: his afternoons in the courtyard, his excursions in the mountains, the dusty summers and the foggy winters, the games with his friends and the conversations under the fir tree in the garden, the collection of strange stones that he kept on his shelf, the first time he had read the adventures of Aeneas, the taste of water, the taste of dates, his mother's voice.

So he imagined himself as now, drifting down a river of thick waters and dark clouds, towards a cold, empty place in which strangers with haggard faces wandered about blindly, unable to remember the names of those they had loved. Here were those who in their lifetime had hated their brethren, or struck their father, or entangled their servants in fraudulent dealings, those who brooded alone, tight-fisted over their riches, like so many of whom Romanian spoke of, down in the City, and also those lovers of whom he had read in books, and traitors awaiting punishment, all in a fear that was perhaps more terrible than the punishment itself. Such a place he was willing to imagine, because then the sheets felt perfectly cool in the warmth of the evening, and the smell of cooking that drifted through the door made him almost hungry, and he could sink contentedly into the thought of the great fields beyond the walls, and the small shivering trees along the road, and the clouds.

Once he had heard his grandmother tell his father: 'The only faith you hold is that of Virgil,' and he had felt that he too held that faith. Secretly therefore, without moving his lips, while the priest was performing the ritual movements, the boy had intoned the verses over his grandmother's dead body.

Inclusi poenam exspectant. The class had memorized the lines and learned the rules of versification, and studied the grammar and the history which the tutor (who was Greek) explained to them in a supercilious tone. But the tutor's monotone voice and the repeated chorus of the other students had hammered out the lines and flattened the rich music, so that the boy had felt there was nothing left to enjoy in those emptied syllables and mechanical stresses. He had known that he must return to the poem all on his own, and he had done so, on one of his long walks, saying the verses out loud, shouting them at the attentive asses who behind wooden enclosures guarded the livestock from the attack of desert cats.

It was on one of those walks that he had witnessed his second death. He hadn't been sure of what they would say at home when they found out that he had not gone to class. He hadn't thought about it. He had let the day take over in his mind, and the sun and the open country, and he had walked on and away, leaving the road, looking down at the clods of earth and the stubs of straw, trying to keep his balance but stumbling from time to time and grazing his hands and knees on the stones, till he was out of breath and could no longer tell where he found himself. Once, he'd startled a turtle dove nestling on the ground and it had risen flapping its wings in front of him, the same colour as the earth, and had disappeared over the hump of a cave.

At first he'd thought it was a pile of dirt, a mound like the ones the land heaved up here and there across the desert. But on the far side the mound gaped open, too large for a foxes' burrow. He looked inside. Three Numidians, two men and a woman, stood bowed in the gloom of the cave, around a small fire. One of the men, small and wizened like an old child, was waving a branch over the flames. The other, much taller, held a slack bundle in his arms. The woman stood motionless behind them. The tall man laid the bundle on the ground and, as one end became unravelled, the boy saw the face of an adolescent, the dark cheeks streaked with white lines. While the magus continued to wave the branch, uttering shrill bird-like cries to which the woman responded with a single repeated word, the tall man bent over the shrouded body, took the head with both hands and stared at the closed eyes. The boy had heard the servants talk about the funeral ceremonies of the Numidians. Now he recognized the mourning ribbons around the father's waist, one for every year of his son's lost life, and the stripes of paint on the dead face which the mother would have traced before the ceremony. Did his father ever look upon him like that, with such intensity, as he lay asleep in his room? Would he look upon him like that when he, the son, lay dead, if he died still young, like this other boy? That was what he had thought then.

The magus had taken a long piece of wood and handed it to the tall man. Without a word, he'd raised the wood and had brought it down on the joints of the body, three times, knees, elbows, neck, cracking the bones through the cloth. The mother had cried out. Very tenderly, the magus had then gathered the body in his arms, set it down on the fire and, as the flames spluttered under the weight and rose and caught the wrappings, he'd arranged the body on its side, curled into a ball, as if to allow it to return in the position in which it had come.

World of mirrors, the boy had thought without words, reflecting the shape of limbs, waves of grass, knuckles of stone, the natural world an imitation of his body, stretching out, unfolding, multiplying. Into this he would grow when dying, here was the shape and colour he would become, strong as the hard earth, brittle as the twigs, compact and yet sifting as sand.

I may change, he had thought, I may lend another tone or pitch to the sounds within me, but the instrument itself will be the same, fashioned like his, his double. And I can't escape, every departure is like this one, every transformation like the one he suffered. Not even in my misery can I be only myself, every time I cry I repeat his cry and every time I fall, the place into which I fall turns out to be astonishingly familiar.

The boy drifted in and out of a soft dark space where his mind stopped touching, seeing, smelling. In and out from light to darkness and back, till he could not tell one from the other. Out into his room, his bed, his body, in again to a place where they had no existence. And in the brief moments during which the world was solid again, he wished to see his father's face as it leaned over him, the keen eyes, the penciled beard, the long strong cold fingers reaching out to where he was, or almost was, or had just been, before he drifted away once again, letting go, the shore fading for one last time.

The Girl Who Ate Death for Breakfast

Eva Hoffman

She's sitting in her hard, uncomfortable chair only because she must, and she's banging her metal spoon on the edge of the table. The metal is thin, and the sound it makes is tinny and not as powerful as she'd like.

'Please,' her mother says, turning towards her from the counter, where she's chopping some vegetables. 'Stop that, and eat. Finish your breakfast.'

The girl stops the banging, and stares at the porridge bowl instead. She stirs the spoon in it lackadaisically, but she won't put it in her mouth. She won't. It'll make her sick.

Her mother looks at her sharply and comes to sit next to her at the table.

'Don't you like it?' she asks. 'Or are you just being stubborn? Doesn't it taste good?'

She shakes her head no.

'No what?' the mother asks. 'No it doesn't taste good?'

The girl shakes her head again.

'Come on,' the mother says, and she dips the spoon in the porridge and brings it up to the girl's mouth. 'Just be good. I won't have you starving, things are bad enough. Just try, it won't do you any harm.'

The girl tightens her lips in protest, but then she sees something in her mother's eyes – something pleading, or angry – that makes her feel even worse than the porridge, and she opens her mouth and lets the mother feed her.

'See?' the mother says, bringing another spoonful to her mouth. 'That wasn't so bad.'

The girl knew the mother would say that, because she always does. But it is bad, it is horrible, and she only continues to eat so that the look in the mother's eyes won't come back. Something has gotten mixed up in the porridge, and she feels nauseous as it goes down into her throat. She hopes she won't be sick. Then she remembers the dead pigeon she saw yesterday, and she knows that's what she's tasting in the sticky, bland substance. The bird was splattered on the ground, all grey and feathery and broken, and nobody was paying any attention to it. A boy half-slipped on it, and wiped his shoe against the rough path.

She feels she might vomit, and swallows hard, and shakes her head to make her mother stop from forcing the spoon into her mouth.

'Okay,' the mother says. 'We'll stop for a while. Then you'll finish. There's just a little bit left.'

The girl looks up to see whether it's okay to ask a question.

'What is it?' the mother asks.

'When is Puki coming home?' the girl asks in a small voice, and immediately wishes she hadn't, because the mother's eyes fill with that look again, except it's even worse than before. She shouldn't say another thing, but she wants to know, she wants to force her mother to say when Puki is coming back. So she looks right into the mother's eyes, even though she can hardly stand it, they're so dark and sad. She feels as though they're a liquid force which might swallow her up. Puki is somewhere in them, she knows, and also the answer to where he is, what he is like. She hardly remembers him, but she knows that everything would change if he came back. It would be wonderful to have a grown-up brother, even better than a father, because she could play with him, and he would take her everywhere. Anyway, she knows she will never have a father; even the word is disappearing from where it used to live.

'I told you already,' the mother says desperately, angrily. 'Puki isn't coming home. Don't you understand?'

'But you said he might,' the girl says timidly. 'That he might come back sometime.'

'I thought so at first...' the mother says, and looks desperate again. 'Oh please. Don't make me repeat it. It's bad enough, don't you understand? Just finish your breakfast. Please.'

She eats a spoonful, because she so wants to make that look go away. But when the porridge goes down her throat, it tastes like that look, so that she almost gags.

'Now what's happening, why are you like this, what am I going to do...' the mother says in a hopeless voice, but at that moment, there's a knock on the door, and the mother changes her face quickly, so that it is sort of stiff like a mask, and she gets up to open the door. Mrs L. comes in, as she does every few days. Her hair is curly and bouncy this time, but she moves in a heavy, slow way.

Mrs L. looks around gravely, inspecting the sparsely furnished room, with its rickety table and bare walls, and the girl can tell that she's remembering the house the way it was before the fire; with really nice furniture and a rug with many colours and shapes which changed when you stared at them. She knows that Mrs L. is thinking the house is sad now, drab and empty.

'How are you doing?' Mrs L. asks, and her mother sighs and shrugs, and Mrs L. nods slowly, as if she understood exactly what her mother means.

'Did you hear...' Mrs L. says, and her mother asks, 'You mean they're going to open them...?' and Mrs L. nods again, and neither woman speaks for a while. Then her mother suddenly bursts out, 'No, I can't take it anymore! I don't want to find anything... I won't go. What good will it do, anyway... No good at all!!' She's almost shouting now, and then her face sort of collapses. 'It's too late, too late for everything,' she says. 'They should have thought of it... before. Now I just want to be left alone... with whatever is left.'

She looks at the girl as she says that, and Mrs L. raises her eyebrows meaningfully, and the mother says, 'Please, can you go out and play for a while? Outside? Just don't leave the garden, you know that, don't you?'

She nods and slips off the chair with relief, and runs out of the house, and tries to feel glad, but she can't, really. She's feeling lonely. The women want to talk without her, about what they will find, what they might find... In the graves, she knows that, they'll be opening the graves. She's heard enough, in the village. She wonders whether the people who come out of the graves after they're opened are alive, or only half alive, so that maybe you have to prop them up at first, and feed them lots of strong broth. Or are they dead and have to be brought to life again. She wonders whether they ever get to be completely alive, or whether they're like those ghosts in the stories, or the ones she's heard about in the village, haunting their living relatives... Why didn't her mother want to go and look...? She might find something. The word 'father' almost comes to her mind, but she pushes it away.

Well, maybe she'll find something too, something that will surprise the grown-ups... She runs the length of the garden, to the back fence, and looks through where one of the slats is missing. She sees something flickering through the thicker woods out there, shadows and a movement, yes, it's a person, it must be a person, a man... Not her father, because she saw him... She was very small then, but she remembers, the shots, the enormous men bursting into the house, her father standing against the wall... Oh. No. No!

Puki. The figure flickering in the woods is Puki, it must be, she must run after him. She squeezes through the opening in the fence, and pauses, not knowing what to do next. A bird sings something lovely. She hears some woody sounds, sees shadows moving along the ground and through the trees, yes, a figure, a man, he's moving through the woods, quickly... She knows her mother thinks Puki is dead, even though she's never said so. But she knows he isn't, she just knows it, he's only been away because of the bad men, hiding in the woods, waiting for the right moment to return... Will she recognize him...? Yes, of course she will, and he'll scoop her up in his arms and will call her his little sister... Aahhh... Her heart beats fast, but she starts walking into the woods. She must be brave, must tell him it's okay to come back. Everyone will admire her so much, and her mother will be so happy... She's the one who will make it all better! She winds her way through the thickening trees, and suddenly it's darker, and she doesn't know where she is, and there, again... No! No! It's the enormous men, moving towards her, closing in on her. It's them, the evil ones, she's seen what they did, she saw her father flattened out like that pigeon, except he was so big, and the blood spurting out of the head was dark, and the body did a strange movement, up and down... That's what she most remembers, she saw it just before her mother turned her away, clamped her to herself in a tight, angry embrace so that she felt like she was choking...

Now she can feel her heart beating very hard, the figures are coming closer, no, no, she cannot breathe! She's seen them in the village, the same ones…

She throws herself on the ground in a passion of fear. Oh, she doesn't want to be dead, but she knows she can be flattened out in a minute, like that pigeon, she's almost that small, that crumbly…

The next thing she knows is that her mother is calling her name, in that scary scared desperate voice she has. The voice penetrates the girl like some sharp painful insertion into her chest, so that she's instantly alert and afraid in a different way. Then her mother lifts her up, with a sort of anger, and holds her too close to herself, so that the girl can hear the beating of her heart.

'What happened?' she asks, her face flushed and with some sweat on it. 'Why did you leave the garden when I told you not to?'

Her voice comes out very small. 'I was looking for Puki,' she says. 'I think I saw him…'

Now her mother gets really angry, and sets her down on the ground, and stoops down towards her, her face redder than before.

'Let me tell you once and for all,' she says sternly. 'Puki is dead. He won't come back. He's dead. Do you understand? I can't keep telling you over and over again. I just can't.' Then she starts crying, and the girl's heart twists in this awful way which she recognizes, because it has happened before. It hurts, not quite like when she bruised her knee, but even worse, because she doesn't know how she will ever get this pain out of her chest, out of her… It may stay there forever.

'Oh my child,' the mother says, ceasing to cry, just sniffling a little. 'I can't explain it all to you, not yet… You're too small, too small. But please, don't do anything like this again… If anything happened to you…'

The mother doesn't finish the sentence, but the girl nods and takes the mother's hand. When they walk into the house, the mother decides she needs a nap. She doesn't feel sleepy at all, but she obeys without protest. She closes her eyes, but is afraid to fall asleep, because she feels as though something bad could happen any minute. She opens her eyes sneakily, and sees that the mother is holding her head in her hands, in that terrible way that tightens the twist in her own heart. She closes her eyes again, this time not to see what her mother is doing. Who will protect them, who will protect her mother…? She has to do it, but she doesn't know how, she isn't strong enough… Through her doziness, she sees the figures flickering through the woods, elusive and evil… She comes to, and feels the porridge come up in her gullet, bland and nauseating. Death. That's what she's eaten with the porridge, and now it's in her, she can feel it. Then the fear and the bland death and the twisting hurt on her heart get all mixed up, and all of a sudden she can't help herself any longer, and she's crying, the tears pouring out and out, as if they were endless. Then her mother is there, picking her up on the bed and hugging her.

'What is it?' she asks. 'What is the matter?'

'It's the men…' the girl sobs out.

'Oh darling,' the mother says, 'those men weren't real… And the real ones won't come back, I promise. They don't have their guns anymore, they can't hurt us. Do you understand?'

She nods, uncertainly, but the crying doesn't stop.

'What is it now?' the mother asks.

'It's the porridge,' she says, helplessly.

'The porridge?' the mother asks, mystified.

'There was something bad in it…'

'What? What was it? It was good porridge, I tasted it.'

The girl hides her face in her mother's dress. 'I don't want to die,' she says.

Now her mother is holding her face in her hands, and then kissing her. 'Oh my darling,' she says, 'you won't. No, no, no. It's over, I promise you, it's over… You'll go to school in a few weeks, won't that be nice? Won't it? You'll play with other kids, you'll like that, won't you?'

'And you'll be here when I come home…'

'Always,' the mother says, in a strong voice. Then she adds: 'And if you don't like it that much, you don't have to eat porridge for breakfast.'

'Really?' the girl asks, suddenly cheered up. 'I don't?'

'You don't,' the mother says. 'You can have nice fresh eggs. From Mrs L's. hens, you would like that, wouldn't you? Now go to sleep, all right?'

The girl nods and holds her mother's hand, as she dozes off. She sees that her mother is gently smiling. Everything will be different from now on, she thinks. Even though the twist around the heart is still hurting. She'll go to school, and have those nice-smelling notebooks, and learn things. And someday she will find Puki. Because nobody ever saw... Because she loves him so much... So she could find him. Then her mother will be really happy. Everything will be all right.

Biographical Notes

David Almond is the author of *Skellig, Kit's Wilderness, Clay* and many other novels, stories and plays. His work is translated into thirty languages, and he has won a string of major awards, including the Carnegie Medal, two Whitbreads, two Smarties Prizes and The Michael L. Printz Award (USA). His latest books are *My Dad's a Birdman* and *The Savage*. An opera of *Skellig* will be premiered at The Sage Gateshead in November 2008. He lives with his family in Northumberland, England.

Margaret Atwood is the author of more than forty books of fiction, poetry, and critical essays. Her most recent publications are *Moral Disorder*, a collection of interconnected short stories, and *The Door*, a collection of poetry (both 2007). Her novel, *Oryx and Crake,* was short-listed for the Man Booker Prize and the Giller Prize in Canada. Her other books include the 2000 Booker Prize-winning, *The Blind Assassin, Alias Grace*, which won the Giller Prize in Canada and the Premio Mondello in Italy, *The Robber Bride, Cat's Eye, The Handmaid's Tale, The Penelopiad,* and *The Tent*. She lives in Toronto with writer Graeme Gibson.

André Brink has been writing full-time since retiring from the University of Cape Town. His novels have been translated into thirty-three languages. The latest, *The Blue Door*, which will be part of a trilogy, was published in 2007. He is at present finishing a memoir, *A Fork in the Road*, expected in early 2009.

Dorothy Bryant has published twelve novels, and one of them (*Confessions of Madame Psyche*, 1987) won the American Book Award. The first of her seven plays, *Dear Master*, 1991, won the Bay Area Book Critics Circle Award. She is a native San Franciscan, daughter of immigrants from Northern Italy. Her latest novel *The Berkeley*

Pit, 2007, blends elements of her family history and her lifelong residence in the San Francisco Bay Area.

Melvin Burgess was born in London in 1954 and was brought up in Sussex and Surrey. He started writing in his twenties and wrote on and off for fifteen years before having his first book, *The Cry of the Wolf*, accepted for publication by Andersen Press in 1990. *Junk* won the *Guardian* Children's Fiction Prize and the Carnegie Medal, and four other novels of his have been shortlisted for the Carnegie Medal: *An Angel for May*, *The Cry of the Wolf*, *The Baby and Fly Pie* and *The Ghost Behind the Wall*. He writes full time and lives in Manchester. Visit his website at: http://web.onetel.com/~melvinburgess/

Jane DeLynn is the author of the novels *Leash, Don Juan in the Village, Real Estate, In Thrall, Some Do* and the collection *Bad Sex Is Good*. Her essays and stories have been published in a number of magazines and anthologies, most recently in *Vital Signs: Essential AIDS Fiction* and *Turn Back Before Baghdad: Original Frontline Dispatches of the Gulf War by British & American Correspondents*. Her work has been translated into German, French, Norwegian, Spanish, and Japanese.

Junot Díaz was born in Santo Domingo, Dominican Republic. His fiction has appeared in *The New Yorker*, *The Paris Review*, and *The Best American Short Stories*. His latest book, *The Brief Wondrous Life of Oscar Wao*, was a *New York Times* bestseller, as was his debut book, *Drown*, which also received a PEN/Malamud Award. He lives in New York City and is a professor of writing at MIT.

Nadine Gordimer was awarded the Nobel Prize for Literature in 1991. She is the author of fourteen novels and several short story collections. Her latest collection, *Beethoven Was One-Sixteenth Black*, was published in November 2007. Educated in South Africa, she has been made an honorary fellow at Harvard, Yale and Leuven (among other universities), and she was awarded an Honorary Degree from Oxford University in 1994. She lives in Johannesburg.

Elizabeth Hay writes short fiction and novels. Her most recent book is *Late Nights on Air,* which won the Scotiabank Giller Award in 2007. She lives in Ottowa, Canada.

Eva Hoffman grew up in Cracow, Poland, before emigrating to Canada and then the United States. After receiving her Ph.D. in English and American literature from Harvard University, she worked as senior editor at *The New York Times.* She is the author of *Lost in Translation, Exit Into History, Shtetl, The Secret* and *After Such Knowledge.* She has also lectured internationally on issues of exile, memory, Polish-Jewish history, politics and culture. She has taught literature and creative writing at various universities, including the University of East Anglia, MIT and Columbia. Her literary awards include the Guggenheim Fellowship, the Whiting Award for Writing and an award from the American Academy of Arts and Letters. In 2007, she was appointed Fellow of the Royal Society of Literature. She currently lives in London, and works as visiting professor at Hunter College, CUNY.

John Sam Jones studied creative writing at Chester. His collection of short stories, *Welsh Boys Too,* was an Honour Book winner in the American Library Association Stonewall Book Awards 2002. *Fishboys of Vernazza* was short-listed for Welsh Book of the Year. His first novel, *With Angels and Furies,* was published in 2005. His second, *Crawling Through Thorns,* has recently been published by Parthian.

He has worked in education and public health for more than thirty years, and he lives with his civil partner in a 300-year-old farmhouse in the Rhinog Mountains in north Wales.

Etgar Keret, a Tel Aviv native, has published four books of short stories, one novella, three graphic books and a children's book. His works have been translated into twenty languages. *Wristcutters, A Love Story* – a feature film based on his novella and starring Tom Waits – was featured at the Sundance Film Festival (2006). His movie, *Skin Deep,* won first prize at several international film festivals and was awarded the Israeli Oscar. In 2007, Keret along with his wife and co-director, Shira Gefen, won the important Camera d'Or prize at the Cannes Film Festival for their first movie *Meduzot (Jellyfish)*.

David Liss is the author of five novels, most recently *The Whiskey Rebels*. His previous books include *A Conspiracy of Paper*, winner of the Edgar Award for Best First Novel, *The Coffee Trader*, *A Spectacle of Corruption* and *The Ethical Assassin*. His novels have been national bestsellers and have been translated into more than a dozen languages. He lives in San Antonio with his wife and two children, and can be reached via his website, www.davidliss.com.

Alberto Manguel was born in Buenos Aires in 1948 and became a Canadian citizen in 1985. He has lived in Israel, Argentina, Italy and England, and now makes his home in France. He is the author of four novels, including *News From a Foreign Country Came* (McKitterick Prize, UK and Writers' Union of Canada Award for Fiction) and *Stevenson Under the Palm Trees*, as well as several works of non-fiction including (with Gianni Guadalupi) *The Dictionary of Imaginary Places*, *A History of Reading* (Prix Médicis essai, France), *Into the Looking-Glass Wood* (Prix France-Culture, France), *Reading Pictures* (selected by Simon Schama as best art book of the year and short-listed for the Governor General's Award in Canada), *With Borges* (Prix Poitou-Charentes, France,) *A Reading Diary*, *The City of Words:the 2007 Massey Lectures*, *The Iliad and the Odyssey: A Biography* and *The Library at Night*.

Uri Orlev was born in Warsaw, Poland, in 1931 and spent the early years of World War II in the Warsaw Ghetto. After being smuggled out of the ghetto and hidden by Polish families, Orlev and his younger brother were sent to Bergen-Belsen. They were freed two years later and emigrated to pre-state Israel. Orlev has published twenty-nine books for children and youth, as well as fiction for adults. His books have been translated into thirty-eight languages. He has won more than forty literary awards both in Israel and abroad. His most recent prizes include: the Hans Christian Andersen Author Award (1996), the Yad Vashem Bruno Brandt Award (1997), the Ze'ev Prize for

Lifetime Achievement (2002), the Andersen Award (Italy, 2003), the Premio Cento (Italy, 2003), the Best Audio Book for Youth (Germany, 2006) and the Bialik Prize (2006).

Judith Ravenscroft, who lives in London, has won several awards for her short stories.

Meg Rosoff was born in Boston and lived in New York City before moving to England in 1989. She worked in publishing, politics, public relations and advertising until 2004, when she published her first novel, *How I Live Now,* followed by *Just In Case* and *What I Was.* Her novels have won the Guardian fiction prize, the Michael L. Printz award, and the Carnegie Medal. Meg lives in London, with her husband and daughter.

Raša Sekulović is a translator and editor who specializes in contemporary English literature from all over the world. He has translated poetry and fiction by numerous renowned authors, including Salman Rushdie, I.B. Singer, Hanif Kureishi, Margaret Atwood, Julian Barnes and Ian McEwan, and he is the editor and founder of the literary magazine *Shakespeare & Co.* He is a prominent child rights activist who has long campaigned for an end to all forms of violence against children and for the global promotion of non-violent communication. He lives in Bangkok.

Nicholas Shakespeare was born in Worcester, England in 1957 and grew up in the Far East and South America. He is the author of five novels including *The Vision of Elena Silves* (Somerset Maugham Prize), *The High Flyer* (for which he was chosen as one of Granta's Best Young English novelists in 1993) and *The Dancer Upstairs* (chosen by the American Libraries Association as the best novel of 1997), which was filmed by John Malkovich. He divides his time between England and Tasmania.

Ali Smith was born in Inverness in 1962 and lives in Cambridge. She is the author of *Free Love, Like, Hotel World, Other Stories and Other Stories, The Whole Story and Other Stories, The Accidental* and *Girl*

Meets Boy. Her story collection *The First Person and Other Stories* will be published in October 2008.

Vikas Swarup is an Indian diplomat who is currently serving as India's Deputy High Commissioner to South Africa. His first novel, *Q&A,* is being made into a film and translated into thirty-three languages. His second novel *Six Suspects* was published in July 2008.

Karina Magdalena Szczurek was born in Poland in 1977. She grew up in Austria and the United States. She currently lives in Cape Town with her husband, André Brink, and their three cats, Glinka, Mozart and Salieri. Recently, she completed her Ph.D. on Nadine Gordimer's post-apartheid writing. She has consequently decided to free her own short stories from the proverbial drawer.

Adam Thorpe was born in Paris in 1956. He is the author of fourteen books of both poetry and fiction; his novels include *Ulverton, No Telling* and *The Rules of Perspective.* His work has been translated into many languages. His latest novel is *The Standing Pool* (Jonathan Cape, 2008).

Katherine Vaz, a Briggs-Copeland Fellow in Fiction at Harvard and a 2006–7 Fellow of the Radcliffe Institute, is the author of two novels, *Saudade* (St Martin's) and *Mariana,* which was published in six languages and selected by the Library of Congress as one of the Top 30 International Books of 1998. Her collection *Fado & Other Stories* won the 1997 Drue Heinz Literature Prize, and *Our Lady of the Artichokes* won the 2007 Prairie Schooner Book Prize (University of Nebraska Press, Fall, 2008).

Patricia Volk is the author of the novels *White Light* and *To My Dearest Friends,* two collections of short stories, *All It Takes* and *The Yellow Banana*, and the memoir *Stuffed*, which is being made into a movie. Ms Volk has published stories, book reviews, and essays in dozens of magazines, including *The New York Times, New York, The New Yorker, The Atlantic, Playboy, GQ,* and *O.* She was a weekly columnist for *New York Newsday* and lives in New York.

Richard Zimler is the author of seven novels, including *The Last Kabbalist of Lisbon,* one of the four works that make up the author's Sephardic Cycle, a bestselling series of interlinked historical novels. The other books in the series are *Hunting Midnight, Guardian of the Dawn* and *The Seventh Gate.* He lives in Porto, Portugal, and can be reached via his website: www.zimler.com.

Markus Zusak was born in 1975 and is the author of five books, including the international bestseller, *The Book Thief.* He lives in Sydney with his wife and daughter.